THE SHADOW:

The Mask of Mephisto
&
Murder by Magic

THE SHADOW NOVELS
by *Walter B. Gibson*

THE HAND
VOODOO TRAIL
THE RACKET KING
MURDER FOR SALE
THE GOLDEN VULTURE
DEATH JEWELS
THE GREEN HOODS
CRIME OVER BOSTON
THE DEAD WHO LIVED
VANISHED TREASURE
THE VOICE
CHICAGO CRIME
SHADOW OVER ALCATRAZ
SILVER SKULL
CRIME RIDES THE SEA
REALM OF DOOM
THE LONE TIGER
THE VINDICATOR
DEATH SHIP
BATTLE OF GREED
THE THREE BROTHERS
SMUGGLERS OF DEATH
CITY OF SHADOWS
DEATH FROM NOWHERE
ISLE OF GOLD
WIZARD OF CRIME
THE CRIME RAY
THE GOLDEN MASTER
CASTLE OF CRIME
THE MASKED LADY
SHIPS OF DOOM
CITY OF GHOSTS
SHIWAN KHAN RETURNS
HOUSE OF SHADOWS
DEATH'S PREMIUM
THE HOODED CIRCLE
THE GETAWAY RING
VOICE OF DEATH
INVINCIBLE SHIWAN KHAN
THE VEILED PROPHET
THE SPY RING
DEATH IN THE STARS
MASTERS OF DEATH
THE SCENT OF DEATH
"Q"
GEMS OF DOOM
CRIME AT SEVEN OAKS
THE FIFTH FACE
CRIME COUNTY

THE WASP
CRIME OVER MIAMI
XITLI, GOD OF FIRE
THE SHADOW, THE HAWK
  AND THE SKULL
FORGOTTEN GOLD
THE WASP RETURNS
THE CHINESE PRIMROSE
MANSION OF CRIME
THE TIME MASTER
HOUSE ON THE LEDGE
LEAGUE OF DEATH
CRIME UNDER COVER
THE THUNDER KING
THE STAR OF DELHI
THE BLUR
THE SHADOW MEETS THE
  MASK
THE DEVIL MASTER
GARDEN OF DEATH
DICTATOR OF CRIME
THE BLACKMAIL KING
TEMPLE OF CRIME
MURDER MANSION
CRIME'S STRONGHOLD
ALIBI TRAIL
THE BOOK OF DEATH
DEATH DIAMONDS
VENGEANCE BAY
FORMULA FOR CRIME
ROOM OF DOOM
THE JADE DRAGON
THE SOUTHDALE MYSTERY
TWINS OF CRIME
THE DEVIL'S FEUD
FIVE IVORY BOXES
DEATH ABOUT TOWN
LEGACY OF DEATH
JUDGE LAWLESS
THE VAMPIRE MURDERS
CLUE FOR CLUE
TRAIL OF VENGEANCE
THE MURDERING GHOST
THE HYDRA
THE MONEY MASTER
THE MUSEUM MURDERS
DEATH'S MASQUERADE
THE DEVIL MONSTERS
WIZARD OF CRIME

THE BLACK DRAGON
THE ROBOT MASTER
MURDER LAKE
MESSENGER OF DEATH
HOUSE OF GHOSTS
KING OF THE BLACK
  MARKET
THE MUGGERS
MURDER BY MOONLIGHT
THE CRYSTAL SKULL
SYNDICATE OF DEATH
THE TOLL OF DEATH
CRIME CARAVAN
THE FREAK SHOW
  MURDERS
VOODOO DEATH
TOWN OF HATE
DEATH IN THE CRYSTAL
THE CHEST OF CHU CHAN
FOUNTAIN OF DEATH
NO TIME FOR MURDER
GUARDIAN OF DEATH
MERRY MRS. MACBETH
FIVE KEYS TO CRIME
DEATH HAS GRAY EYES
TEARDROPS OF BUDDHA
THREE STAMPS OF DEATH
THE MASK OF MEPHISTO
MURDER BY MAGIC
THE TAIWAN JOSS
A QUARTER OF EIGHT
THE WHITE SKULLS
THE STARS PROMISE
  DEATH
THE BANSHEE MURDERS
CRIME OUT OF MIND
THE MOTHER GOOSE
  MURDERS
CRIME OVER CASCO
THE CURSE OF THOTH
ALIBI TRAIL
MALMORDO
JADE DRAGON
DEAD MAN'S CHEST
THE MAGIGALS MURDER
THE BLACK CIRCLE
THE WHISPERING EYES
RETURN OF THE SHADOW

THE SHADOW

The Mask of Mephisto
&
Murder by Magic

As originally told by
WALTER GIBSON
(Alias "Maxwell Grant")

PUBLISHED FOR THE CRIME CLUB BY

DOUBLEDAY & COMPANY, INC.

GARDEN CITY, NEW YORK

1975

All of the characters in this book
are fictitious, and any resemblance
to actual persons, living or dead,
is purely coincidental.

Library of Congress Cataloging in Publication Data

Gibson, Walter Brown, 1897–
    The Shadow.
    CONTENTS: The mask of Mephisto.–Murder by magic.
    I. Gibson, Walter Brown, 1897–   Murder by magic.
1975. II. Title.
PZ3.G3594Sh [PS3513.I2823]   813'.5'2
ISBN 0-385-03712-0
Library of Congress Catalog Card Number 74-18800

CONTENTS

INTRODUCTION
by Walter B. Gibson

It was early in 1931 when I became acquainted with The Shadow and adopted the pen-name of Maxwell Grant in order to write four novel-length stories recounting his adventures. These were to appear in a quarterly periodical titled *The Shadow—A Detective Magazine.* When the first two issues sold out, the publishers, Street & Smith, decided to make it a monthly magazine, so instead of an intermittent year's work, I found myself embarked on a steady project. Acting as The Shadow's raconteur proved so much to my liking that I moved steadily ahead of schedule, and it was good that I did, for sales increased so rapidly that by the end of a year, I was offered an unprecedented contract to deliver twenty-four 60,000-word stories in the next twelve months, to put the magazine on a twice-a-month schedule.

I met my quota within ten months, putting the magazine so far ahead that there was never any question about keeping up the new pace. By then, I had developed The Shadow from a somewhat nebulous figure into a substantial character with a crew of competent agents, who helped him solve and strike down crime, but he still remained much of a mystery to friend as well as foe. During his early exploits, he appeared in various guises and disguises, depending on the particular quests in which he was engaged. Mostly, he doubled for a much traveled millionaire named Lamont Cranston, using that identity while the real Cranston was away in some distant region.

In action, The Shadow loomed as a cloaked figure, materializing from out of the night, rescuing helpless victims and striking terror into the hearts of evildoers. However, he reserved such theatrics for occasions when they formed a logical climax to a well-developed sequence of events. Between times, The Shadow proved himself a master of deduction as well as disguise. While his major missions were to stamp out mobs or smash spy rings, he often tabled such routines in order to find a missing heir, uncover buried treasure, banish a ghost from a haunted house, or oust a dictator from a mythical republic.

There was no limitation to the story themes as long as they came within the standards of credibility—which proved easy, since The Shadow was such an incredible character in his own right that almost anything he encountered was accepted by his ardent followers.

Although the success of The Shadow caused a flood of new "character" magazines to appear on the newsstands, ranging from outright imitations to new departures, with forays into fields of adventure and science fiction as well as crime, the only such magazine to go twice-a-month and maintain that schedule was *The Shadow*. Many modern students of the "thriller" era have totally overlooked that fact; and now that the question has been raised, they may be quite surprised to learn that the answer was known before *The Shadow Magazine* embarked on its stepped-up schedule.

Widespread surveys taken while the magazine was appearing monthly showed that a large majority of newsstands sold nearly all their copies within the first two weeks of issue. While other character magazines might show an early flurry, their sales were either spread evenly over the entire period or gained their impetus about the middle of the month and sometimes not until the third or even the fourth week.

From the writing standpoint, this made it advisable to adhere more closely to the Cranston guise and to emphasize the parts played by The Shadow's well-established agents, since regular readers evidently liked them. Also, it meant "keeping ahead" of those regulars, with new surprises, double twists in "whodunit" plots, and most exacting of all, a succession of villains who necessarily grew mightier and more monstrous as The Shadow disposed of their predecessors.

Some stories themselves were titled after such formidable antagonists as The Black Master, Gray Fist, The Cobra, The Condor, The Python, The Crime Master, and The Mask. Some became so formidable that they were allowed to escape The Shadow's vengeance long enough to return in a future story in order to meet their deserved doom. These included The Voodoo Master, The Hand, The

Wasp, and The Golden Master, who figured in four novels with suspenseful intervals between each reappearance.

This continued happily until April 1943, which marked the magazine's twelfth anniversary. Then, with the curtailment of paper during wartime, it went back to a monthly schedule. Some four years later, it went bi-monthly, then quarterly and finally was suspended with the Summer 1949 issue, titled "The Whispering Eyes."

With its demise, The Shadow Magazine was consigned to an undeserved limbo. A history of Street & Smith, written in 1965, stated that 178 book-length novels were written by Maxwell Grant. That figure has been cited in articles ever since, as though it was something phenomenal. What is really phenomenal is that I actually wrote 282 Shadow novels during the life of the magazine, a mere 104 more than the total given. Whoever checked the bound files must have noted that it went monthly during the first few volumes and was still going monthly during the last few volumes, so there was no need to check dozens of volumes in between.

The first radio program featuring Lamont Cranston as The Shadow went on the air late in 1936, and was adapted from my novels, of which more than 100 had already appeared in print. Other characters from the magazine were also used, and Lamont Cranston acquired a girl friend named Margo Lane, whom I included in The Shadow Comics, which began in 1940 with continuities that I based on The Shadow novels. When The Shadow Magazine went monthly, Margo appeared quite often in the novels, including the two that have been chosen for this volume.

By then, the period of the super-villains was past, dwarfed by the holocaust of World War II. In Murder by Magic and The Mask of Mephisto, you will find The Shadow matching wits with crafty murderers who have done their utmost to lead you—and The Shadow!—along false trails.

PART ONE

THE MASK OF MEPHISTO

I.

It was Mardi Gras night and New Orleans was lush with light, mellow with music, bizarre with costumery. Everybody cared except Ken Langdon.

Reluctantly Ken was forced to admit that he wasn't entirely sad. Mardi Gras Day presented the last and biggest in a long procession of days filled with noise and revelry.

Tomorrow—or specifically at midnight tonight—Carnival would be over and quiet would again be in order. Ken's headaches would be ended and Wingless Victory would be finished.

Wingless Victory was the statue that Ken was molding in his upstairs studio in the patio off Dumaine Street, if anybody cared to know. The trouble was that the people who cared didn't know. As a result, Ken was four months behind on his rent, which was bad business in the French Quarter where everybody else was only three. But this was Carnival time and Ken's landlord, whoever he was, had probably gone amasking with the rest of New Orleans.

Revelry was drifting up through the arched entry to the patio and filtering its way into the room that Ken called a studio. Into that medley shrilled a familiar sound that Ken recognized, the ring of the telephone bell in the downstairs renting office.

Usually Ken paused breathless at that sound, hoping that some patron was summoning him to accept a fabulous offer for Wingless Victory when completed. Those phone calls always proved to be for someone else, but tonight Ken wasn't taking chances.

Ken hurried out through the door and scurried down the outdoor steps to the courtyard which he crossed at a speed the neighborhood rats would have envied. Breathless, Ken unhooked the telephone.

The voice came thickly:

"Mr. Kenneth Langdon? Could I speak to him?"

"This is Langdon." Ken couldn't believe that it had happened. "What can I do for you?"

"Would you like to make some money?"

"Why, yes. Of course the statue isn't finished—"

"One hundred dollars?"

Ken tried to answer but couldn't find words. The toil of six months was heavy on his hands and this insult was too much. What Ken might have said would have been plenty if the voice hadn't intervened:

"One hundred dollars for one hour's work."

It was foolish, but so was Mardi Gras with its weeks of revelry, pageantry and idiocy. Ken gulped aloud that he would listen and the voice proceeded, its phrases still thick but disjointed.

"The costume," it said. "In the box—in your studio—wear it, you understand?"

How Ken would wear a costume that didn't exist was something of a question, but he didn't argue it. He just said, "Yes."

"Follow the schedule," the voice continued. "You will find it with the box. You understand?"

This was clearing the situation somewhat.

"Half payment in advance," the thick voice promised, "and the remainder later. If you agree, dial this number."

The voice gave a number, the receiver clicked and the call was over, leaving Ken wondering if it were all a joke. However, Ken decided to dial the number that the voice had given him.

The number didn't answer in the three times Ken tried it, so he decided to go back up to the studio and lay some more clay on Wingless Victory.

The usual lights in the courtyard were missing. But between the glow from the little office and Ken's upstairs studio, the archway was reasonably visible.

As he started back Ken could have sworn that there was something in that archway, a solid something that slid away hastily as he approached. By the time Ken reached the arch and looked through, there was nothing to see except Dumaine Street and the passing show of masqueraders who were turning Frenchtown into anything but a haven for harassed sculptors like Ken Langdon.

Still wondering who had sneaked out through the arch, Ken reached his studio and climbed the ladder that brought him on a line with Wingless Victory's chin. On the top step of the ladder was a package neatly tied and thoroughly delivered just as somebody on the telephone had promised it would be.

Ken opened the package.

It was hard to swallow Mardi Gras, tough to admit that the Carnival could breed artistic merit. But Ken's eye was stirred by the contents of that large, square package.

The costume proper was a mass of crimson sheen, a cape as gorgeous in texture as it was ample in proportions. The black ruffle around the neck was obviously intended for a contrast and Ken saw why when he studied the remaining contents. Out from the box peered a devil's head so realistic in its ruddy features that Ken wished he could do as good a facial with Wingless Victory.

A Mask of Mephisto and a masterpiece!

From the costume fluttered an envelope which Ken plucked promptly from the floor. Within it was a sheet of paper with a typewritten schedule telling the places where he was to be at given times. And that wasn't all; the envelope also contained fifty percent of Ken's wages in the form of a hundred dollar bill torn in half.

This Mephisto proposition was devilishly clever.

The sponsor had certainly invested his whole hundred, but Ken would be an equal loser unless he followed the trail to its completion, an equal loser both of the trail and the hundred dollar bill.

Ken caped himself in the crimson robe, picked up the Mephisto head and set it down over his own. Peering down through the ample nostrils of the nose, he read the time sheet and found that he was due to be parading along Canal Street in exactly ten minutes. He set forth, wearing what the well-dressed Satan should wear.

Frenchtown struck Ken as a strange world on this last night of Carnival. The narrow streets with their overhanging balconies and lattice ironwork were the same, but the people looked different. True, they were in costume, but that hardly accounted for their odd behavior, for the way they stopped and stared.

Ken Langdon was stopping these maskers in their tracks!

If His Mephistophelean Majesty had popped up in person from the antiquated paving of the French Quarter, he couldn't have riveted the passers-by in any better style.

But why?

Somewhere along Royal Street, the answer filtered through. It wasn't the horror of his costume that impressed them; it was the magnificence.

Whoever had squandered too much on this Satanic outfit had done it well. Never had a more resplendent Mephistopheles stalked the by-ways of New Orleans during Mardi Gras. As the murmurs of appreciation reached Ken, he began to feel a pride, even though the costume wasn't his own idea.

Ken found himself liking Mardi Gras until he reached Iberville Street. There something happened that wasn't listed on his schedule sheet. The admiring eyes that trailed the magnificent Mephisto opened wider as they saw a rival for the title of the Carnival's outstanding masker.

They came face to face, Mephisto and The Shadow!

Cloaked in black, his features lost beneath the downturned brim of a slouch hat, the masquerader who confronted Ken immediately stole the show. Until a moment before, this black-clad personage had been inconspicuous in the general parade, but in contrast to the flaming crimson of Mephisto's regalia, The Shadow's somber garb literally leaped into prominence.

It was as if some impossible challenger had risen to meet an equally fabulous foe, and the prominence that The Shadow gained so suddenly gave a startling realism to the Mephisto who confronted him.

Then, as the eager crowd jostled forward to witness what seemed an actual crisis, the masqueraders were separated by the swirl. Through design more than chance, The Shadow blotted himself into the patchy darkness where the street lights were few, while Mephisto, with all his gorgeous shimmer, was forgotten by the eyes that stared after the cloaked figure that disappeared so suddenly.

And Ken Langdon, swirled along toward Canal Street, was looking back, wondering what had become of the cloaked Nemesis who had disturbed the triumphal parade. Again, however, Ken's majestic trappings were attracting attention from new observers who hadn't seen The Shadow's brief eclipse of the brilliant Satanic grandeur.

This singular encounter was a mere incident amid the masked revelers who were celebrating the end of Carnival's reign, but it had all the semblance of an omen, The Shadow's crossing of Mephisto's path!

II.

Around a corner where no one would have expected him to reappear, the masker who wore the black cloak and hat stepped suddenly from a doorway. With a few short strides he reached a masked girl who was wearing a short-skirted Columbine costume and literally plucked her from the crowd.

Next they were sweeping through the door of a little cafe where a sleepy waiter was eyeing a stretch of empty tables. Taking a table in a subdued corner, the man in black removed his hat and dropped back his cloak, while Miss Columbine discarded her domino mask.

The girl spoke first with a slight laugh of relief.

"I knew this would happen," she said. "You just can't do it, Lamont."

"Do what, Margo?"

The man's query had an even tone that went with his calm face. Both were habits with Lamont Cranston. Being used to them, Margo Lane suspected that Cranston knew exactly what was in her mind, but she didn't say so. Instead:

"You can't put on a black coat and hat and expect people not to notice it," Margo declared. "That is not if you let them see you, not even during Mardi Gras."

"You're positive?"

"Absolutely positive."

"Then why talk in negatives?" queried Cranston with a slight smile. "That's all you've been using, Margo, and all that backs your argument was my chance meeting with that chap in the Mephisto outfit."

Margo had to admit that Cranston was right. Among all the quaint characters represented by the merrymakers, The Shadow had been the least noticed until the Red Devil had popped up to meet him. Still, Margo was wondering why Cranston had chosen his Shadow costume and that brought up the question of why he had come to New Orleans at all.

"I was perfectly happy at Miami Beach," sighed Margo, ruefully, "until I received your wire telling me to fly to New Orleans for Mardi Gras Day. I suppose you've been here all along, enjoying the preliminary features of the Carnival?"

Cranston shook his head.

"No, Margo. I just arrived from New York today."

"Just to see the parades?" queried Margo. "Well, I suppose they're worth it. The Rex parade was wonderful and I really can't wait to see the night parade of Comus."

"Except that you aren't going to see it, Margo."

A flash of indignation sparked Margo's dark eyes; then smiling it away, the girl treated the subject as a jest.

"So I won't see Miss Muffet and her tuffet," declared Margo, "Jack and his bean-stalk, or the rest of them. The floats are all supposed to represent Mother Goose stories, you know. I just delight in Mother Goose."

"You'd better read up on it then. You won't find Jack's bean-stalk in among those yarns."

"Anyway, I wouldn't miss the parade for a thousand dollars!"

"Not for a hundred thousand, Margo?"

There was something so steady in Cranston's tone that Margo knew he meant it. In reply to Margo's questioning eyes, Cranston passed a small, thin-paper certificate across the table. The official look of the paper impressed Margo and as she read its title, she exclaimed:

"Why, it's a ticket for the Louisiana Lottery!"

"A winning ticket, Margo. Worth a hundred thousand if it draws the grand and only prize."

"But I thought the Louisiana Lottery was banned!"

"So was horse racing," reminded Cranston, "and recently. Certain ways had to be designed for people to stake money, and the Louisiana Lottery was one of them. It always had a solid reputation in gaming circles. Therefore its revival won immediate confidence."

"But how does the lottery pay off—and where?"

Cranston answered that with a question of his own.

"Did you ever hear of the Krewe of the Mystic Knights of Hades?"

Margo shook her head, then said brightly:

"It sounds like one of these New Orleans Carnival associations."

"It is," stated Cranston, "but the Knights of Hades are strictly secret and do not parade. They hold a Ball of Death in what they term the Devil's Den and all the guests are strangers."

"Why strangers?"

"Because New Orleans is full of them, all fighting to get invitations from the dozen or more organizations that are unable to fill all requests."

"But how is anyone invited to the Ball of Death?"

"By lot." Cranston emphasized the words. "Names are picked from hotel registers or other sources and the invitations sent."

"And what goes on at the Ball of Death?"

"Some curious ceremony with a Wheel of Fate in which the winner is called the loser and is banished from the Realm Below, with some slight gift so he won't feel too unhappy. Only this year, the gift may be different."

The point dawned slowly on Margo. Then:

"You mean that the Krewe of Hades is the front for the Louisiana Lottery!"

As Cranston nodded, he tossed an engraved card across the table.

"Your surmise is correct, Margo, and there is the proof."

Reading the card Margo saw that it was an invitation to the Grand Ball of Death, to be held in the Devil's Den, otherwise known as the Hoodoo House, under auspices of the Scribe, the Seneschal and the Messenger, the official representatives of his Satanic Majesty, Mephistopheles the Faust.

Margo frowned. "There's no name on the invitation."

"Nor on the lottery ticket," reminded Cranston. "One simply went to the holder of the other."

"But how did you get them, Lamont?"

"I bought the ticket for a thousand dollars. It cost a dollar originally but it turned out to be one of the lucky fifty that qualify for the grand drawing of one hundred thousand dollars. It has a potential value of two thousand dollars and its owner was willing to settle for half."

"And he gave you the invitation card too?"

"That's right, Margo. Just as I am giving both to you."

Really startling, this offer which explained in part why Cranston had summoned Margo to New Orleans; yet the girl couldn't quite understand why she was needed to serve as proxy.

"It wouldn't hurt if either of us drew the lucky number, Lamont—"

"But it might if someone else did," interposed Cranston, "and the chances are fifty to one that someone else will. I wouldn't care to be immobilized as a guest at the Ball of Death."

"Why not? It sounds interesting."

"Then you can have it, Margo. I want to see what happens to the prize-winner when he leaves the Devil's Den."

The possible complications sprang to Margo's mind.

"You mean somebody might try to grab the prize money!"

"There are rumors, Margo," said Cranston, with a smile, "that somebody does intend to acquire that bundle of cash. Also it has been stated, in fact stipulated, that the sponsors of the lottery will guarantee complete protection to the winner. However—"

"However you're not sure which will happen?"

"On the contrary I am sure. I intend to see that the winner does not become a victim and that the prize money does not disappear. Whatever personal effort may be required should prove worth it."

Knowing Cranston's penchant for adventure, Margo could quite understand. Too, it was now plain why he had chosen the panoply of The Shadow instead of some gayer costume for the particular part that he was to play in the affairs of Mardi Gras.

Time was evidently short, for Cranston immediately suggested that they start from the cafe and as they reached the streets where lights seemed brighter than ever in the much-thickened dusk, Margo realized that it must be almost seven o'clock, the hour when the grand parade of Comus started and the hour also, that the Knights of Hades, disdainful of the parade that was regarded as the big event of Mardi Gras, had set for their reception in the Devil's Den.

It was then that an afterthought struck Margo.

"The Masked Mephisto!" she exclaimed. "The man in the gorgeous costume that everybody noticed until you came along! Could he be the Satanic Majesty of the Krewe of Hades?"

"He probably was," returned Cranston. "As head of the Knights of Hades, King Satan makes the rounds of other functions to pay his respects—or disrespects. Since it wasn't time to meet him officially, it was better to avoid him."

Those were the last words that Margo heard from Cranston, for he had become his other self, The Shadow. On the gloomy street that they had reached it seemed that slender Columbine was walking all alone, for the shrouded figure that stalked beside her was like a shade of night itself.

Yet despite The Shadow's presence, Margo Lane shuddered. Somehow her recollection of the crimson-clad Mephisto with his leering, insidious mask, was a fearful thing that boded further ill!

III.

At an alleyway a few blocks deeper in the French Quarter, Margo Lane paused suddenly as a gloved hand clutched her arm. At that moment Margo was forgetful of her qualms for she was interested in what little of the Comus parade she might expect to see.

Down the street was a float mounted on a flat car some twenty feet by eight, with four bedecked mules hitched patiently in front of it. The float had a crew of several men, all in fancy costumes, but Margo was more interested in the grotesque decorations that topped the cart. The theme was Humpty Dumpty, represented by an enormous egg supporting a squatty dummy figure, the combination rising to a height of eighteen feet.

Then, as the gloved hand turned her toward the alley, Margo heard The Shadow's whispered parting:

"Hoodoo House. Have your invitation ready."

Wishing she'd never come to New Orleans, Margo tripped along the cobbled paving of the alley, hoping only that The Shadow's eyes were watching her venture into what seemed oblivion. As she reached the door of the grim stone house that blocked the alley, it opened, gushing a mass of welcome light. Handing her invitation card to the costumed attendant, Margo Lane entered the Devil's Den.

Other guests were coming to that same alley. The Shadow saw them as he glided further along the street, to the darker vantage of a deep doorway. Satisfied that all was proceeding normally where the Ball of Death was concerned, The Shadow turned his attention elsewhere.

What interested The Shadow was the single float which by now should be on its way to join the Comus parade which was forming at St. Charles Avenue and Calliope Street. Just why Humpty Dumpty should be so far out of line was something that called for investigation.

The same applied to the two slinking figures that were working their way along the front of an opposite building. They were men in dark clothes, barely visible in the last vestiges of twilight. Sensing their menace, The Shadow drew a brace of automatics from beneath his cloak and began to glide across the narrow street.

The skulkers acted before The Shadow reached them. Switching from their sneaky tactics, they bore with one accord upon the mummers who were standing around the float. To a man the entire float crew found themselves with guns planted in the middle of their backs.

As docile as the harnessed mules, the costumed men allowed themselves to be marched across the street and into a deserted building that adjoined the little alley.

The Shadow followed, ready to intervene in case the situation showed violence, but the gaudy prisoners were thoroughly subdued. They allowed themselves to be bound in a room where their captors locked them, while The Shadow watched from the darkness of the outer doorway. Then the captors stripped off their baggy outergarments and emerged in trappings quite as fancy as those worn by the prisoners.

One crew was simply replacing the other and The Shadow could well understand why. His whispered laugh denoted that understanding as he moved out to the street, there to await the next developments.

Those developments were under way in the Devil's Den, where Margo Lane was finding that the Knights of Hades were far more convivial hosts than their sinister title indicated.

The Den consisted of a large, square room, with a platform accommodating an orchestra beneath a quaint old stairway that turned at a landing and angled its way to the floor above. The orchestra was playing an old and merry tune called "The Devil's Ball" while the presiding officials greeted the numerous guests.

These officials wore badges which identified them. One was the Scribe, who had a set of whiskers that would have suited Father Time. Another was the Messenger, clad in a skeleton outfit with a skull painted on its hood. The third was the Seneschal who wore a military uniform of the zouave type with red trousers and blue coat.

Attending the masked Seneschal were four guards attired in similar but less imposing uniforms, their whole regalia being a simple blue. They were busy serving drinks in mugs that were fashioned like miniature skulls. Since none of the other guests had qualms, Margo accepted one of the mugs and looked around at her fellow-visitors.

Nearly all the delegates were men and through their various masks they were admiring Margo's Columbine costume with its short skirt and sleeveless jacket. The costume was the sort that would have made Margo's legs appear too long if they hadn't been so shapely, and they were commanding generous attention until the music stopped.

Then came a sonorous announcement from the bearded Scribe that brought all eyes about.

"I, Scribe, salute you!" With folded arms the speaker surveyed the group. "I cannot say that I welcome you, because soon one of our members will be gone, back to the drab life that dwells outside this Nether Region."

Unfolding his arms, the Scribe gestured to the Seneschal who in turn commanded the guards to unveil a bulky object that was standing in the corner. Its covering lifted, the object proved to be a lottery wheel which was brought to the center of the room.

"It is your turn, Messenger." The Scribe bowed to the man who wore the skeleton costume. "Your sad duty will be to banish some unfortunate who will no longer share our happy misery."

The Messenger took over while the guests waited breathless. They watched his skeleton hand sift the wadded papers that rested within the lower rim of the broad wheel. The situation grew more tense when the Seneschal approached, bringing a sealed box that looked like a jewel case. Imperiously, the Scribe demanded:

"What do you bring Seneschal?"

"A gift from the fortunate dead," returned the Seneschal, "that our unfortunate friend may carry when he returns to the unhappy land of the living."

A thick, oblong case, shaped like an oversized wallet, real meat for hungry eyes!

The utter silence told that all were acquainted with the true contents of that packet, one hundred thousand dollars to be delivered by the famous Louisiana Lottery, famous because in all its history it had never defaulted. This clandestine delivery was being managed under the mummery of the Knights of Hades, whose pretence of ill-luck would be the best luck of some person's lifetime!

"A mere token," spoke the Scribe, "but it would please His Mephistophelean Majesty, who believes that all should receive all that they deserve. I shall deliver the gift, Seneschal."

The Seneschal handed over the oblong box and retired with a profound bow. Then the Scribe ordered:

"Come, Messenger! Whirl the Wheel of Fate and let us be rid of the fool who will not share our torments! He must be gone before our great King Satan joins us!"

The silence was broken by the clatter of the wheel with the tight pellets jouncing within it. Running his hand into the flow, the Messenger brought out the winning wad and opened it. The hushed guests were clutching the numbered envelopes that contained the similarly numbered invitations and the lottery tickets that they represented.

Opening the number, the Messenger showed it to the Scribe, who announced it:

"Eighteen!"

A happy cry stabbed the disappointed murmur and a frail man in a Harlequin costume pressed forward waving the winning envelope and all that went with it. He was nervous this winner, until his numbers were checked; when the box was placed in his hands, he began to gulp thanks that the Messenger promptly abbreviated.

"Begone!" The Messenger pointed a skeleton hand toward the door. "The Seneschal will show you to your carriage, fool who prefers life to death!"

Looking around, Margo saw the uniformed Seneschal standing at the outer door. It dawned on her that the carriage could only be the Humpty Dumpty float that was waiting in the street. Then with a regretful sigh that marked the passing of a hundred thousand dollars, Margo decided to enjoy what fun, if any, the coming festivities might provide.

Much was to happen, though not under the head of fun. The first person to realize that was the winning Harlequin after the Seneschal bowed him out into the alley and closed the door.

Anxious to reach the waiting float, the frail man took a few quick paces, only to stop warily and look back toward a little side gate that flanked the doorway of Hoodoo House. The Harlequin fancied that he had heard a slight clink from that iron gate.

Imagination, probably, but it quickened his pace and that in turn made him stumble. Then, from the blackness came part of it that lived, unseen hands that clutched the faltering Harlequin, stifled his startled cry and whirled him into the doorway of a deserted house, a side door, just within the mouth of the blind alley.

More happened swiftly.

Dazed by his spin, the Harlequin was bound and gagged by frills ripped from his own costume. They weren't the sort of bonds that would survive a healthy struggle, but they would last long enough for the unseen personage to travel far with the box that he had plucked from Harlequin's failing grasp.

All that the captive Harlequin heard next was the closing of a door, but there were others who were treated to some of The Shadow's rapid tactics. In the big room where the mummers from the float were sitting bound and gagged, The Shadow paused long enough in the darkness to loosen one prisoner's bonds.

Neat, this, to start the release of those prisoners while he dealt with the men who had trapped them, but The Shadow's mode of dealing with the imposters on the float was rather unusual too.

Doubling around through the alley, The Shadow arrived openly in the glare of torches that had been lighted by the phony float crew. His appearance started consternation that threatened violence, judging by the way hands went for their guns.

Only The Shadow himself was gunless. All he carried was an oblong box that he waved quite joyously and the gang that had taken over the float remembered that this was Mardi Gras where anybody might masquerade in any character—even that of The Shadow.

Quite a coincidence that the lottery winner should have chosen such a costume, but that merely added to the irony of it. They were smirking beneath their masks, these thuggish imposters, as they politely opened the Humpty Dumpty egg and bowed The Shadow indoors.

The egg clanked shut with the sound of steel, not the dull thud of papier mache, the usual material used in Carnival float construction. Then the false mummers were on board and the mules were lumbering ahead, inspired by the flames that the torch bearers waved in their faces.

From within the hollow egg came an unheard laugh, the sardonic mirth of The Shadow, foretelling that this Mardi Gras would witness the unscheduled excitement of frustrated crime.

The Shadow intended to take a personal hand in that frustration, although he had planned it so his services would not be too badly needed. Indeed, The Shadow wouldn't have come along if he'd known of something more important to be settled.

Which proved that The Shadow's present calculations didn't include an analysis of what was going on behind the Mask of Mephisto!

IV.

The gloom that followed the departure of the lottery winner was not dispelled when the Seneschal returned into the Devil's Den, clicked his heels and saluted first the Scribe and then the Messenger.

Even Margo shared the general envy of the lucky Harlequin whose luck already was undergoing a rapid change that none of them knew about, although that change was to prove for the better. Glumly the guests accepted skull mugs that the guards passed around, while the Seneschal remained at the outer door and the Scribe stood with folded arms. It was the Messenger who furnished the index to the next event.

The man with the skull hood was staring toward the stairs as though expecting someone who had so far purposely refrained from joining this scene where merriment was lacking.

One thought was general: The Krewe of the Knights of Hades would have to furnish something startling in the way of entertainment if they hoped to enliven these guests, whose interest at least had gone very, very dead.

The silence gripped even the orchestra, which remained idle on its platform, and through the hush came the muffled beat of mule hoofs that faded from the front street. A dozen seconds later, the watchful eye of the Messenger detected a stir from the stairs and he raised a skeleton hand in signal.

A cymbal crashed from the orchestra platform. A drum began a rattle that ended in an even louder smash and with it, a descending huddle of crimson spread suddenly upon the landing in the shape of the awaited master of the coming ceremonies, His Satanic Majesty.

Though Margo had seen such resplendence earlier, she felt the same chill as the other guests. It was highly dramatic, this entry of Mephistopheles into his own Devil's Den. The lights were arranged to accentuate the crimson of the costume that shimmered from the landing and the man who wore the Mask of Mephisto was an actor who could play his part.

Even to the trousers that showed below his knee-length cape, King Satan was complete in ruddy dye, as though he had gathered the flames from his favorite fire-pit and used them to permanently tint his costume.

King Satan was wearing gauntlets, long red ones, of some material that had the same sheen as his spreading cape, and with each forward step that he took down from the landing, the fingers of those hands writhed, as though seeking something suitable for their scarlet touch.

Instinctively, the guests drew back and away, forming an awed semicircle, while the Scribe, as if in their behalf, stepped cautiously forward with a cringing bow. The Scribe's voice came plaintive:

"If it please your Devilish Highness—"

Interrupting with a majestic sweep of his shimmering arm, Mephistopheles pressed the Scribe aside.

"But these guests are of the dead." The Scribe tapped a record sheet to prove it. "We have found the lone scapegoat who belonged among the living."

King Satan turned to the Messenger as though demanding that he prove it. The living skeleton bowed and made a gesture toward the lottery wheel.

"His number was called and he was unchosen." The Messenger reared back his skull-face and spread his painted arms. "Oh, Ruler of these Nether Regions, you may strike me living if I speak not true."

The lines that the Messenger recited were so stilted that Margo decided it would be a favor to strike him dead instead of living. So did the man in the Mask of Mephisto.

Without a word, the impersonator of King Satan drew a revolver from his carmine cape and fired three shots into the body of the skeleton-clad Messenger.

People stared as though they expected a rattle of bones when the Messenger struck the floor. What he did was thud and roll over.

It was somewhat ludicrous the way the Messenger sprawled. What proved it wasn't all in fun was the way the white-painted bones on his costume began to take on splotches of color that were too much like the sheen of Satan's cape.

This was murder, committed in the presence of half a hundred witnesses!

It was the bearded Scribe who started the hue and cry. Wildly, he pointed to the doorway toward which the murderer had started only to be blocked by the uniformed Seneschal. He was raising his smoking gun, this Satan who was living the part, when he saw that the Seneschal wasn't to be cowed. Turning, the man with the Mephisto Mask dashed for the stairs, took them with long strides and was around the turn of the landing by the time people began to follow. The bearded Scribe led the rush in that direction, while the bold Seneschal, seeing the route was crowded, dashed across the floor and beckoned the guests to a rear stairway that offered a chance to cut off Mephisto's flight.

Completely lost in the rush, Margo didn't have time to philosophize how brave people could become after someone else showed them how. Practically everybody had chased upstairs, by one route or the other, and the Seneschal, back at the outer door, was waving to bring back the few who had fled in that direction. Who those few were, Margo didn't know, because so many had preferred to pursue the Satanic murderer.

It was something of Margo's business to check on facts, since Cranston wasn't here. Besides, she wasn't anxious to stay around with nobody but the dead Messenger for company.

The stairs were long and by the time Margo reached the top, results had been gained. The Scribe's crowd were smashing at a door which gave suddenly to pitch them into a room where a door on the other side was cracking to admit another valiant horde that included the Seneschal.

This room was scarcely more than a hall where the front and back stairs joined; it had a window through which the murderer might have pushed the Mephisto head, but certainly couldn't have squeezed himself after it. The Seneschal was quick to recognize that fact, for he was doing more than beckon now. He was shouting for the rest to follow him up the joined stairway to the third floor front.

There, the only handy window opened above the alley, but there was a sheer drop of thirty feet and nothing in the way of a hanging rope or other device by which the murderous Mephisto could have made it. There was a ladder leading to a cupola atop the house, while bolted doors offered access to windows that led out to the side roofs of adjoining buildings. His fugitive Majesty could have taken any of those routes after barring the way behind him, so people began to climb the ladder and bang down doors in order to overtake him.

By then, Margo was on her way downstairs. From the second floor she could hear the sound of a car pulling away along a rear street but she was sure the murderer couldn't have reached the ground that soon. In fact it was all so puzzling that Margo felt there was only one person who could crack the riddle, if he happened to be still around.

That person was The Shadow.

Margo went out through the front alley to hunt for the cloaked figure that she should have realized could not be found in darkness, when she ran into an old friend—or enemy, providing how you felt about somebody who had outdrawn you in a trifling matter of one hundred thousand dollars.

Margo felt friendly enough when she saw the fellow's plight. He was the Harlequin who had won and lost. His costume was tattered and his mask was gone, revealing a drawn, long-jawed face that suited his frail figure.

The frantic Harlequin gasped his story to Margo.

"I've been robbed!" he panted. "I've been robbed and it's terrible! I wouldn't think it could have happened!"

"Look in there." Margo steered the Harlequin into the Hoodoo House, straight toward the Messenger's body. "You'll see somebody who's been murdered and that's even more terrible. He didn't think it could happen either!"

Rushing out to the street, Margo heard shouts from roof tops, delivered by searchers who thought she was Mephisto in full flight. Heedless of those calls Margo looked for the mule-drawn float, but wasn't surprised to find it was gone. There still was a chance that The Shadow might have followed it.

The streets were clear now, for all the maskers had gone to Canal Street and other points from which they could view the Comus procession, which Margo was going to see after all. Yet all she hoped was that she could find The Shadow and tell him what she knew of murder.

It was a long chance, longer than the odds against winning the Louisiana Lottery, this hope of finding The Shadow out of all the costumed spectators who were watching the big event of Mardi Gras. Still, there was an element that favored Margo's quest.

If you saw trouble, you could probe into the thick of it and generally find The Shadow. Such trouble was due along the path of the Comus parade.

The Shadow had done more than ask for it!

V.

There were twenty-one floats in the Comus parade instead of the advertised twenty, but comparatively few of the spectators checked that difference. The first float in the parade was the title car, listing the names of the eighteen that were following the king's car, and by the time the last float passed, most people had forgotten some of the titles.

The squatty Humpty Dumpty, perched upon his mammoth egg, was so in keeping with the theme of Mother Goose that it brought huge rounds of applause. Indeed, the only fault with this topic was that it was too good, and the fake maskers who had taken over the spurious float were quite aware of it.

They were arguing that point as they flung good luck trinkets to the crowd.

"It's time we were mooching out of this," one masker said. "Like we mooched into it. When we get to the review stand, they'll know we're phoney."

"Only we ain't going past the review stand," returned another. "We're keeping right ahead the next time this caravan turns."

"Yeah, but what's the crowd going to think?"

"Nothing. There's always a chance that a float is going to fall out of line. That's why a repair truck rides along with the coppers up front of the parade."

"Then they'll be sending the truck back to help us out—"

"Yeah, only when it gets back, nobody's going to find us. Listen, we ain't any phonier than the phonies we took over from and we know how they had it figured."

The figuring was easy.

This float had joined the parade simply to lose itself, or rather cover its own trail. The revivers of the Louisiana Lottery had planned it as a special service for the winner of their illicit game, something which they could well afford, since they had sold more than double the number of tickets needed to pay off the grand and only prize.

By easing into the parade, then out again, the fake float was supposed to reach some unknown destination where the occupant of the boiler-plate egg could depart in peace and security with his precious box of funds.

Such was the original plan and in forestalling it, the present oc-cupants of the float were simply adapting it to their own purposes.

They too intended to ride to some unstated place with their charge, but when or if they sent him on his way, he would go without the money. The fact that the prize winner was masquerading as The Shadow had jarred this faction only briefly; indeed they were possibly less worried than their predecessors might have been. The Lottery racket was illegal from the start!

There didn't seem much that The Shadow could do to remedy his present situation, considering that he was clamped in a metal con-tainer and if he tried to pry his way out, he would give his identity away. These maskers who had taken over weren't going to give The Shadow a chance to start anything.

So they thought, not realizing that The Shadow had already started all that was needed.

Just as the parade was turning a corner, about the time when the middle of the procession had made the swing, the thing happened.

A group of maskers who looked like fugitives from a Comus float came hustling through the crowd that thronged the corner. They were using the old New Orleans system which the younger set thought was sport; they were coming as a human chain, hands locked as they whip-lashed through the crowd.

Once such a string got under way, its own momentum carried it. If the head of the chain struck too tight a cluster of people, the back-wash cleared it. This sort of horse-play was annoying and quite un-seemly during the grand parade of Comus, but it served its purpose.

The crowd suddenly parted and the lined maskers plunged through, practically into the parade itself. Torch bearers scattered, the horses of the Comus Knights reared madly and the general con-fusion might have ruined the parade if the roisterers hadn't veered away and gone barging back to the rear of the cart-wheeled flotilla. So it all looked like a happy ending until they reached Humpty Dumpty.

There these madcaps turned into a veritable pirate crew that swarmed on board the egg exhibit with intent to capture it. So far, maskers on the other floats had repelled these trouble-makers with fistfuls of thrown trinkets, but the Humpty Dumpty guardians were better equipped.

They drew guns, as did the attackers and in a trice the whole float was a riot of slugging and shooting. One tough crew was seeking revenge on the other. They were canceling each other out, due to The Shadow's foresight!

Somebody lashed the mules and away they went, past the last float that was clearing the corner. Things were jammed long enough for the crowd to open a path so the mules could rocket straight ahead, taking the float battle out of circulation. Quite a spectacle in itself, the fugitive float drew a mad rush of spectators after it, and they saw the climax of the furious fray.

Muffled shots went unheard within the pill-box that was shaped like an egg, but the smoke from a gun muzzle curled out through the cracks. The Shadow had broken the lock with those shots; now, a human instrument of double vengeance, he was springing out to settle the balance of the battle to the misfortune of both sides.

The trailing populace saw this cloaked avenger clout down fighters impartially until the float was strewn with dazed maskers; then, seizing the discarded reins, The Shadow lashed the mules and fired a few shots past the pair on the right. The stampeded steeds veered left, around a narrow corner. The float couldn't make its turn and Humpty Dumpty took his great fall, egg, float, and all, flinging the battle-weary maskers to the flagstones.

All the crowd had to do was pick them up and turn them over to the police, a task that The Shadow seemed to indicate by a parting, sweeping gesture, as he sprang lightly from the crashing float and disappeared along the narrow street leading into Frenchtown.

Only one person followed The Shadow. She was a Columbine whose trim legs were built for speed as well as looks. Hearing shooting, Margo Lane had gone to look for The Shadow and found him.

Suddenly blocking the Columbine's path, he halted her with a whispered laugh and again was piloting Margo among the narrow streets.

Margo was too breathless to talk until she found herself in an upstairs cafe on Exchange Place, that single block where the night spots were so popular that they were forced to double-deck themselves. There, his slouch hat removed, his black cloak thrown back, Lamont Cranston was again his complacent self.

"Lamont!" Margo panted the name. "I must tell you—something."

"Don't tell me that the grand prize disappeared."

"It did, but that wasn't all." About to go into the news of murder,

Margo halted abruptly. "But how did you know about the money?"

From the draped cloak, Cranston brought the sealed box that Margo had last seen in the hands of the prize-winning Harlequin. For the moment, Margo was too astounded to think of anything else, so Cranston took a table-knife, cut open the heavy seals and lifted the lid of the compact treasure chest.

Margo gave a grateful sigh, since one thing at least seemed settled, but that sigh turned to a gasp, accompanied by a stare of amazed alarm.

Mystery was only beginning in New Orleans. Instead of containing a bundle of tight-packed currency, the oblong box was empty, lacking even a trifling souvenir from the Krewe of the Knights of Hades!

VI.

Police Captain Selbert listened in stolid style to the excited testimony that he was hearing in the midst of Hoodoo House. Jim Selbert missed seeing the Comus parade, but he'd been expecting something to happen here in the French Quarter where he was in charge.

Something always happened in the Vieux Carré on Mardi Gras Night and Selbert couldn't have looked forward to a more bizarre setting than this old Hoodoo House which had once been the temporary residence of the famous Dominique You, a lieutenant of that once-renowned pirate, Jean Lafitte.

And right now, Jim Selbert was getting the inside story on the Krewe of the Knights of Hades, whose ways were known but whose identities until now had never been revealed.

The Scribe, deprived of his Druid gown and whiskers, was none other than Tourville Talbot who pronounced his name with a round "O" and an absence of the final "T." Older than he looked, Talbot was known to everyone as Tourville because he'd refused to grow up. Selbert wasn't surprised to find Tourville as Scribe of the Knights of Hades. The old boy simply couldn't wait for Mardi Gras to come around each year and he'd grown jaded attending the functions put on by Comus, Rex, Aparomest, Mithras, Oberon, and all the rest of them.

The Seneschal in real life was Hubert Aldion, a rugged but rather handsome young chap who had probably done much to finance the

Hades Krewe, since like Tourville, Aldion had inherited some money but hadn't found time to sink it in sucker investments. In contrast to Tourville, who was shaky and distressed, Aldion was grim and determined. Tourville could only talk about the murderer's flight, while Aldion was chiding himself for his own failure to overtake the killer.

In death, the Messenger proved to be Louis Chardelle, a middle-aged gentleman of very checkered history. Some people had said that Chardelle had his ups-and-downs; others termed them his ins-and-outs. It was all one and the same, because definitely Chardelle was now down and out, to stay that way.

The skull hood, peeled back, disclosed Chardelle's dead face as a wan one, its eyes still carrying the look of a schemer in their glassy bulge, the lips opened wide in a grimace of surprise which Chardelle had evidently felt when he saw King Satan bring out the gun that delivered those fatal blasts.

The uniformed guards were unimportant in the opinion of Jim Selbert, but he intended to check them just the same. He knew their names when he heard them; they belonged to some of the older families of New Orleans, by marriage at least, and they were just the sort of young chaps who would join up with an outfit like the Krewe of Hades on the chance that it would some day develop into an outstanding Carnival society.

As for the guests, Selbert had simply blocked them in the corner of the room where he intended to question them later. Right now, Jim wanted to know who King Satan was, so he put the question bluntly.

The guards looked at Aldion, who looked at Tourville, and the elderly Scribe decided that his Oath of Hades could be waived at the demand of the law.

"You've heard of Frederick Ferrand," said Tourville. "He was supposed to play King Satan."

Selbert turned to Aldion, who nodded, as did the guards. Then in hard tone, Selbert demanded:

"What do you mean supposed to play King Satan?"

"It was Ferrand's office," explained Tourville. "He was the head of the Krewe of Hades. But I couldn't swear that it was Ferrand who murdered Chardelle."

Selbert wheeled on Aldion.

"Could you?"

Aldion shook his head, as did the guards.

"Why not?" snapped Selbert. "Granted that he was masked, didn't he go through the proper mummery?"

"More or less," conceded Aldion, "but I can't understand why he would have murdered Chardelle. I didn't see the actual shooting"— Aldion thumbed across the room—"because I was over by the outer door, and there were too many people in between. But it was all very crazy."

"Perhaps not," grunted Selbert. "Any of you might have murdered Chardelle on account of the Lottery."

Aldion stared blankly.

"What lottery?"

Bluntly Selbert gestured toward the wheel and Aldion's face, furrowing in new surprise, gradually relaxed into a deprecating smile.

"Why that was just part of the flubdubbery," declared Aldion. "We always banish one of our guests with some souvenir. This year we were giving a pen and pencil set, weren't we, Scribe?"

With his question, Aldion turned to Tourville, who nodded. As for Selbert, he wouldn't have credited Aldion's ignorance if Tourville hadn't corroborated it. Even yet, Selbert doubted.

"You mean you don't know what was happening here tonight?" demanded the police captain. "You did know that you were fronting for the Louisiana Lottery?"

Old Tourville stared; then cackled:

"It's been years since that Lottery was held, Captain!"

Checking the faces of the guards, Selbert found them as puzzled as those of Tourville and Aldion. Swinging to the unmasked guests, Selbert demanded why they had come here and a chorus answered that they had come to participate in a prize drawing of one hundred thousand dollars.

To emphasize that feature, Selbert brought forward a dapper man in tattered harlequin attire who answered to the name of Howard Shorke and asked why he had come all the way from Buffalo.

"I wanted to win the big money," declared Shorke plaintively, "and I did. Only somebody took it away from me—"

"We'll get to that," interrupted Selbert. "Meanwhile"—he swung back to the group that represented the Krewe of Hades—"I want to know why you're all so ignorant."

As Scribe, old Tourville was looking over the list of guests and he couldn't find Shorke's name on it. When Tourville said so, Selbert took the list and called off the other names. None of them tallied with the persons present, a point which impressed Selbert.

"Who prepared this list?"

"I did," replied Tourville, "and I gave it to the Messenger so he could deliver the invitations."

Over the list, Selbert stared down at Chardelle's rigid body.

"So it was your racket, Chardelle," mused Selbert as though speaking to someone who could still hear. "I might have known it, considering some of the deals you were mixed in. But it still doesn't add up."

Wheeling to the living members of the Krewe, Selbert snapped a fresh challenge.

"Chardelle was dealing with some really big shots," asserted Selbert. "He couldn't have risked letting them down and he must have known it. His only way to be safe was to cut you fellows in on the deal!"

"Except that we wouldn't have listened," expressed Aldion, indignantly. "As Seneschal, I'd have voted against such a thing!"

"As Seneschal, you would have no vote," reminded old Tourville, "nor would I as Scribe." Producing a scroll, Tourville passed it to Selbert. "Read by-law 5-A, Captain, and you will see that King Satan has complete say on all matters of policy concerning the Krewe of Hades."

"But this would be different," argued Aldion. "It doesn't come under the head of policy—"

"All lotteries are policy," interrupted Selbert, "and without intending to be funny, I'd say that Scribe Tourville is right. All that Chardelle had to do was take it up with King Satan, which meant Ferrand. You fellows didn't count. The most you could do was quit."

Tucking the scroll in his pocket, Selbert went into another tack.

"When did any of you last see Ferrand?"

Tourville shook his head and Aldion shrugged. Then Aldion stated:

"We haven't seen Ferrand for some time. He's been moping, you know, over girl trouble."

Selbert raised his eyebrows to show he didn't know.

"Ferrand was going down to the bayou country, the last we heard," added Tourville. "I instructed Chardelle to find out if Ferrand would be back in time, and Chardelle assured me that he would."

Another idea was growing in Selbert's mind.

"You gave a lot of orders to Chardelle, didn't you, Tourville?"

"As Scribe of the Krewe of the Knights of Hades," returned Tourville, with dignity, "I am special deputy to His Majesty, King Satan. It is my prerogative to assign certain tasks to the Seneschal, and lesser details to the Messenger."

"We'll take over your duties," asserted Selbert, a trifle sarcastically, "and it would please us, Scribe, if you would tell us where His Murderous Majesty might happen to have gone at present?"

"King Satan is answerable to no one but himself." Tourville was still taking his mummery seriously. "But it is his wont on Mardi Gras night to appear but briefly at the functions of the other Krewes."

"Good," decided Selbert, "we'll start a man-hunt or a devil-hunt, just in case he's showing nerve enough to go through with the old routine."

Turning to instruct the few police who were present with him, Selbert was pleased when the door opened and more arrived, including a few plain clothes men who were dressed as masqueraders since Carnival costumes were the equivalent of plain clothes on this final evening of Mardi Gras.

These arrivals were bringing news of massed battle on a Humpty Dumpty float, and by questioning survivors they had learned that it traced back to the Hoodoo House that operated as the Devil's Den. Paramount was the account of a cloaked masker who had cracked loose from within a steel egg and gone his way into the night.

"Somebody masking as The Shadow—"

Before the informing detective could go further, the man named Shorke made an excited interruption.

"He must be the one who took the prize money!" Shorke's plea was addressed to Selbert. "I couldn't see him in the dark so he answers the description."

Waving for silence, Selbert inquired:

"Any reports on The Shadow?"

"He was seen earlier," informed a detective, "when he ran into a man with a Mephisto Mask up toward Canal Street."

Selbert's eyes narrowed.

"Go on."

"And there was a girl with him," added the detective. "She was wearing a Columbine costume. Short skirts and long legs—"

"She's the one who was here!" broke in Shorke. "When I told her I'd been robbed, she didn't wait around!"

"Any further reports?" queried Selbert, briskly. "I mean on the Devil, The Shadow, or Miss Columbine?"

The detective nodded.

"Somebody saw the girl over at Exchange Place."

"Then what are we waiting for?" demanded Selbert. Turning to his own squad, he waved for them to take charge; then to the rest, he ordered: "Come on!"

The hunt had started and which it produced first, The Shadow or King Satan, Jim Selbert didn't seem to care!

VII.

Item by item, Lamont Cranston had connected the details that Margo Lane remembered from her gruelling experience in the Devil's Den. On the table-cloth, Cranston had drawn a complete plan of the neighborhood around Hoodoo House as well as the interior of the building itself, the latter copied from Margo's descriptions.

Carefully, Cranston was marking crosses and dotted lines to represent various participants and their courses, when the sound of a police siren reached him. They just couldn't seem to get along without sirens, even in New Orleans.

So rapidly that Margo wondered what it was all about, Cranston came up from his chair and whisked her behind an open door.

"Stay there," he warned, "until after they all come through. Then go out the front way, because they'll have forgotten all about it. Here"—Cranston whipped away the table-cloth with its penciled evidence—"throw this over your head and shoulders and masquerade as a ghost until you get back to your hotel. Then get out of that Columbine costume and hide it!"

Footsteps were pounding up the stairs while Margo was enveloping herself in the white drape and Cranston similarly was robing himself in black as he resumed the costume of The Shadow. Instead of looking for some place of concealment, he started for the door, showed himself in full light, and wheeled in the opposite direction.

Shouts from arriving police were drowned by the crash of a window. Next, the officers were storming through the deserted cafe on the trail of someone who was making as remarkable a flight as the one that Margo had attributed to King Satan.

Almost as remarkable but not quite.

No one had caught a glimpse of the crimson-clad Devil who had flown from Hoodoo House, but there were plenty of fleeting glimpses of The Shadow, despite his black attire.

That in a sense made The Shadow's trail more remarkable.

The Shadow intended to draw pursuers after him. He was spotted when he dropped from a low roof to the street; seen again when he cut diagonally to another sidewalk. Through a narrow alley which had once been a rendezvous for fencing masters, The Shadow showed a suitable technique by parrying the police clubs that swung at him.

Once through the alley, The Shadow evaporated. He had drawn the whole man-hunt, including Captain Selbert, along his own course, leaving nobody to witness the departure of an improvised ghost from the upstairs cafe back in Exchange Place.

The man-hunt then switched to terms of King Satan, though the man who wore the Mephisto Mask didn't realize it. Ken Langdon, bedecked in flowing crimson, was completing the tour as indicated on the typewritten time-sheet.

He'd paid his respects—or disrespects—to Comus, Rex, the Druids and the Zulus, though it was hardly more than a token courtesy—or discourtesy—considering that the evening parties thrown by those Carnival associations had been hardly under way when Ken called by as Mephisto.

At least people could testify that he'd been there and now, to give the Devil his real due, Ken was making his final stop at the Borneau Mansion where the Greater Carnival Association was holding a reception.

This was a new group whose aim was to encourage a bigger and better Mardi Gras in keeping with educational standards. New Orleans already boasted a school children's parade which went under the title of the Krewe of Nor, and the Greater Carnival Association felt that this should be the standard for future adult Krewes. Obviously the Association was diametrically opposed to any secret and unsavory groups like the Krewe of Hades, no matter how prominent their members might be.

Which was probably why King Satan was to include the Borneau Mansion on his calling list, and knowing nothing about any of it, Ken Langdon stalked right into the sacred preserves of the city's most stodgy aggregation of ultra-conservative stuffed shirts.

The Association members were in costume, but unmasked, since they were strictly interpreting the rule that all masks should be off by sunset, an ordinance which the populace had been ignoring of late years. So the entry of a full-fledged Mephisto, clad cap-a-pie in crimson, devil's head and all, was something that should have created consternation.

There was a girl who foresaw this, a vivacious blonde who was wearing a Dutch costume. She clattered forward in her wooden shoes, clutched Ken's shimmering sleeve and stopped his Mephistophelean stalk with the ardent protest:

"Fred! You shouldn't have come here!"

Tilting back his head, Ken looked down the Mephisto nose and turned to resume his stride. Then, something that even his obstructed vision had observed caused him to pause and reconsider the girl's plea.

She was really worried, this girl was, and the flash in her violet eyes carried something soulful that Ken wished was meant for him instead of somebody named Fred.

"It isn't right, Fred!" The girl's protest was heartfelt. "You know how these people are trying to improve the Mardi Gras. They didn't send the police to raid that secret Krewe of yours, so why should you impose upon them?"

Apparently the girl didn't know that the police had taken over the Krewe of Hades with all its Mystic Knights, but neither did Ken, so that made it mutual. Ken muttered something that might have passed as Fred's voice in the hollow depths of the Mephisto Mask, but it only complicated the situaion.

"I'll call Rolfe," the girl said. "He'll see that you get home all right. He won't tell anybody who you are and I'm sure he'll be reasonable when he finds out that you're connected with the Krewe of Hades. You know that Rolfe doesn't approve of such organizations—"

Ken interrupted with a mutter consigning Rolfe, whoever he was, to the particular realm belonging to the character that Ken was impersonating instead of Fred. Meeting a girl like this was something Ken didn't want spoiled by anybody named Rolfe and since Fred was being blamed for staging the Mephisto act, Ken didn't care about him either.

What Ken chiefly wanted was to conclude this imposture within an imposture and collect for services as rendered. He turned away and strode in Mephistophelean majesty straight through the middle of the reception, leaving a rooted flock of astonished conservatives in his wake.

Such behavior was just too much for the blonde. Turning away, she started fleeing, only to run into a young man who was wearing a Colonial costume with fancy knee-breeches.

"What's happened, Joan?"

"It's Fred," the girl choked. "You must stop him, Rolfe, before he unmasks. If they ever find out who he is!"

"Why, he's Fred Ferrand," returned the Colonial gentleman, "and I'm Rolfe Trenhue, his best friend. Or didn't you know?"

"You still can't understand, Rolfe!"

"But I do understand. Why shouldn't Fred Ferrand come to a reception to meet Joan Marcy? Everyone knows that you two are engaged, so where one is invited, the other ought to be."

"But Fred was sent here by the Krewe of Hades as an insult. He's wearing a Mephisto Mask and he's probably been flaunting it all over town."

"Calm yourself, Joan." Rolfe Trenhue steadied the girl and helped her out through the door to a garden bench. "It can't be Fred. He's gone down to my hunting cabin among the bayous. He told me he intended to stay there."

"But he didn't tell you about the Krewe of Hades?"

Trenhue shook his head and his dark, round face showed a puzzled expression.

"What is the Krewe of Hades, Joan?"

"Of course Fred wouldn't tell you," returned Joan, "knowing you don't approve of secret clubs. Go find Fred and ask him. Get him away before he makes fools of us as well as himself. You'll find him in the Devil's own costume."

The girl buried her face in her hands and Trenhue, disturbed by her sobs, decided to go and learn what the Mephisto menace was all about.

Meanwhile, the menace had disposed of itself. Ken hadn't unmasked because his time sheet didn't call for it. He strode out through a far door and found the most convenient street for the finish of his tour.

It was very simple from now on. The last stop was to be Moubillard's, back in the French Quarter and about a dozen blocks from the Borneau Mansion. At Moubillard's, Ken would leave the costume and go on his way.

Everybody knew Moubillard's, including Ken, although he'd never patronized the place. Henri Moubillard specialized in all sorts of fancy costumes and his business was big during Mardi Gras—so big that Moubillard always celebrated Mardi Gras Night himself. By then all his costumes were out and there was no use staying open.

Always, too, Moubillard left his shop wide open on this night of nights. He boasted that he did this to prove that he had rented all his costumes; that if anyone entered the shop they'd find nothing to steal. But rumor had it that Moubillard left the door open because he wouldn't be able to unlock it even if he didn't lose his key, which he was likely to do, considering how thoroughly he celebrated on this annual splurge.

Ken knew therefore that Moubillard's would be open and he was glad of it. As he strode along the streets, Ken could hear the wail of police sirens and if there was trouble in the neighborhood, he didn't want any part of it. If any maskers had become too riotous, the police were likely to blame the first they found, so Ken gave the sound of sirens a wide berth.

Moubillard's at last.

The shop was deep beneath an ancient balcony and true to custom the door was wide open. As usual there wasn't anything to be stolen, the show window so generally filled with the peering faces of grotesque masks, now being entirely empty.

Nevertheless it wouldn't do to just fling the Mephisto costume and forget it. Since Moubillard was keeping open house, even when absent, it would be better form for Ken to leave the costume in the office where the proprietor would surely find it. Besides, there was a chance that this might be the place where Ken was to pick up the other half of the hundred dollar bill.

Taking off the big Mephisto head, Ken Langdon saw his way through the gloom and reached the office. There he set the mask on a chair beside the desk and started to remove the gaudy crimson cape. Even in the faint light, the material had an intriguing shimmer, but Ken no longer cared about fancy costumes.

Striking a match, Ken looked around the desk to see if the half-bill had been left there. Then, as the match flame neared his finger tips, Ken extinguished it with a shake. It might be all right to be here in Moubillard's office, and again it might not be.

The thing that caused Ken to consider the latter prospect was the sound of footsteps entering the shop. Whoever the arrival was, Ken didn't want to meet him. What Ken wanted was a way out and a quick one.

If Ken Langdon had guessed all that was coming, he'd have wanted an exit that was double quick!

VIII.

It was strange, the sense of menace that moment of silence could produce when they served as prelude to new sounds which could not be identified.

Ken Langdon felt this as he waited in Moubillard's tiny pitch-black office, wishing he was back in his own studio on the other side of the Vieux Carré which was the natives' name for French Quarter.

Small wonder that Ken should be thinking in fancy terms considering the aura of phantasy that he had spread around New Orleans while stalking majestically as King Satan. Maybe some of the Devil's own faults were catching up with him right now!

The sounds that came were creeping footsteps, yet so irregular, so uncertain that Ken could not define them. Somehow, they seemed like echoes of Ken's own footfalls that had brought him through the shop to this box-like office that formed a hollow, windowless cell.

Maybe this was a trap, planned as a conclusion to the bizarre but senseless mission which Ken had so foolishly accepted for a sum that now seemed a pittance!

If Ken Langdon had known of the Krewe of Hades and what had happened in the Devil's Den, he would have realized that the web was tighter, more purposeful than anything he could imagine. Yet though his impressions were vague, Ken was almost sensing the truth behind it, as he crouched there in the tiny office, awaiting the unknown.

Footsteps here, footsteps there—occasionally quick, then hesitant, or blundering. Ken's own footsteps creaked as he worked toward the door, hoping better to define the sounds from the shop proper. It struck him then that the sounds might represent two people, one baiting the other. Perhaps the place was haunted by the spirits of the grotesque masks that Moubillard had rented out—a thing which Ken was almost ready to believe!

At moments Ken thought he could trace fleeting forms against the dim window or the black shape of the door. Then suddenly he realized that footsteps were very close, almost creaking the floor boards on which he himself stood. And from outdoors came sounds that so far Ken had only taken as a background; the whines of halting police sirens, the brief shrills of whistles.

They were very close, too. Across his turning shoulder, Ken thought he could see the outer doorway obliterate itself with blackness as though something had completely filled it!

Then Ken was at the desk, reaching for the Mephisto Mask, hoping to add it to the cape which he had half removed from his shoulders. If people were playing a game called "Scare Me" as a variant of hide-and-seek, Ken felt he still had a chance to prove that he was "It."

The chance vanished with a click.

Flooded instantly with light, the room revealed a crouched man with a quick eye and wizened face, old Henri Moubillard. He'd come back earlier than expected and he hadn't celebrated too heavily, otherwise he wouldn't have handled the situation so smartly.

With his first glance, Moubillard proved that he didn't rate Ken as an ordinary thief, nor even as some prankster who was literally interpreting the policy of the open door. Suspicion, understanding, and finally denunciation registered themselves in almost instantaneous procession across Moubillard's crafty crab-apple features.

And the reasons were plain.

Moubillard saw the Mask of Mephisto and recognized it, along with the cape of crimson sheen. He also saw Ken and didn't recognize him, which to Moubillard meant something more. Moubillard himself was costumed in an old Spanish garb with ruffled collar and to Ken, the wizened man seemed to represent some Inquisition, so thoroughly accusing was his stare.

If he'd trapped an actual King Satan, Moubillard couldn't have been happier, and now he was conniving some way to hold his prisoner. While Ken stood rooted, Moubillard moved backward, intending to hop through the door, slam it, and clamp it from the other side.

Before that could happen, Ken saw a red gauntlet snake through the doorway from the darkness beyond. With it came a mass of flowing crimson that might have been the reflection of Ken's own costume. Red fingers reached the light switch and clicked it off.

In the darkness, Ken heard Moubillard's excited snarl as the old costumer wheeled. Ken too was on the lunge, realizing that here was a new menace that might convert Moubillard into an ally instead of an enemy. Ken's guess was right but his action came too late.

Muffled shots greeted Ken's arrival in the doorway. Until he reached there, Ken didn't know that the stabs had been aimed straight his way. The thing that had muffled them also stopped them.

That thing was Moubillard.

Tripping over the costumer's sagging body, Ken locked grips with someone who for all he knew, might really be the Devil, here to wreak vengeance on those who had collaborated in his impersonation. Then, as they grappled, Ken found that his opponent wasn't so formidable, for in snatching at the gun, Ken gained it.

Only that was a mistake.

Jogging Ken's gun arm upward, his foe took him by the throat and began to choke him. Writhing, Ken heard a laugh, fierce, challenging, but low, which he thought came from the man who harried him.

The challenge was voiced by an invisible arrival who wasn't even hazily outlined in the blackness of the costume shop. The Shadow was here to settle this case impartially and his laugh was set to an obbligato of police whistles that were converging upon Moubillard's, attracted there by the shots.

Ken's present antagonist was speedy and lucky in meeting The Shadow's challenge.

The fists that choked Ken flung him with a twist and with the departure of those gripping gauntlets, Ken was whirled squarely against The Shadow, stopping the cloaked combatant's drive. Thinking that both adversaries were one and the same, Ken slugged valiantly with the captured gun and after landing a glancing blow, tried to punch a bullet home, as fair due to a murderer.

That error was anticipated by The Shadow. His sweeping arm sent Ken's gun-hand upward; the bullets merely nicked some of Moubillard's empty shelves. A jab from The Shadow's other elbow clipped

Ken's chin and flipped him back over Moubillard's body into the office.

It was too late though for The Shadow to go after the missing Mephisto. Outside Moubillard's, police saw a man in red mask and cape dash out, then double back through a narrow alley that led to the rear of the costume shop, clanging an iron gate as he went by. Others spied him from the rear street and saw the crimson figure dart back through the alley. Coming through from both directions, those from the front pried open the alley gate while the others were discovering an open window into Moubillard's.

All this aided The Shadow. He had stepped into the office and closed the door behind him. Turning on the light, he bolted the door and studied Moubillard's body, with Ken Langdon sitting dazed beyond it.

The Mask of Mephisto was resting on the desk. The shimmering cape had dropped from Ken's shoulders. The red gauntlets included in his costume was drooping from his hands and beside the right lay the empty gun with which a murderer had finished Moubillard and with which Ken had failed to shoot The Shadow.

Footsteps were pounding from the shop. Looking upward, The Shadow saw a heavily clamped trap door in the ceiling of the office. Seizing the desk, he turned it on end, dumping the Mephisto Mask. The heavy jounce of the desk was echoed by a hammering at the office door, along with a shouted command that had something to do with the law.

The gauntlets dropped from Ken's hands as The Shadow brought him to his feet and started him climbing a chair to the elevated desk end. Realizing that a friend had found him, Ken cooperated groggily. The Shadow clicked off the light and followed Ken to the desk perch; there, restraining Ken's sway with one hand, The Shadow used an automatic with the other, to blast the clamps from the trap door.

The ripping creak of the lifting trap was drowned by the battering-ram smashes that drove through the panel of the office door. A dozen seconds later, the door itself was smashed, but at that moment the ceiling trap was settling in place.

No longer costumed, Ken Langdon was feeling somewhat himself again, as the sweep of night air revived him. The Shadow was steering him across a roof top to reach an adjacent balcony. From there, they worked through an empty house, down to an alley, and finally to a corner where Ken read the name Dauphine Street.

There, Ken heard a parting laugh from a cloaked friend who seemed to fade with the remnants of the breeze and with the tone, he could have sworn that it called him by name, gave his address, and told him to go back there.

That was the last seen of The Shadow on this Night of Mardi Gras. Having nowhere else to go as his cloaked self, he skirted Moubillard's neighborhood with its deluge of police, and headed for a place where costumes were optional and masks taboo.

This was the reception at the Borneau Mansion, conducted by people who advocated a tamer Mardi Gras as a better Mardi Gras. Arriving there as Cranston, The Shadow found the setting so delightfully conservative, that he decided to call Margo Lane and have her come there in an evening gown instead of her Columbine costume.

During his phone call, Cranston missed an incident that had some bearing on the case in hand.

A serious-faced young man in Colonial costume was meeting a Dutch blonde who was coming into the mansion from the garden door. The anxiety on the face of Rolfe Trenhue brought a similar reflection from the violet eyes of Joan Marcy.

"I couldn't find Fred anywhere," reported Trenhue, "so he must have gone out while I was looking around. Anyway, he didn't unmask."

"You're sure, Rolfe?"

"Positive. I asked people who the Devil was and nobody knew." Trenhue relaxed with a smile. "Most of them said he could go to himself for all they cared."

"He may be doing just that," said Joan, uneasily. "I haven't been able to understand Fred lately, Rolfe."

Trenhue gave a sympathetic nod. Then:

"I went out to my car intending to drive around and look for him, but the police seemed to be stopping everybody, so it wasn't any use."

New anxiety flashed from Joan's eyes.

"They couldn't have been looking for Fred?"

Rolfe Trenhue gave a heartfelt laugh that banished the girl's qualms. After all, Joan had to agree that whatever the faults of Frederick Ferrand, he wasn't the sort to run afoul of the law.

Maybe The Shadow would have held a different opinion, had he heard of a young man named Frederick Ferrand.

IX.

It was the day after Mardi Gras and New Orleans had taken on a mill-stream quiet. In fact, somebody once said that the reason the Crescent City lay deep below the level of the diked Mississippi was because it settled a foot after every Carnival.

Certainly the crowds had done enough tramping to wear down the city somewhat and the existing calm was like a sober regret for too much merriment. And this was one time when merriment wasn't all to be regretted.

For one thing, the police were getting right to the bottom of the Louisiana Lottery.

Too many things had happened on too many beats patrolled by too many individual cops. Such wasn't right in New Orleans, where, to some degree, police officers were like little lords in their own domain instead of being mere underlings who might be shifted willy-nilly.

The individual police had been tolerant of Lottery gossip until now; therefore they were able to gather a lot of facts. Brought to the higher-up officials, this had led to the summoning of a bulky gentleman of political ambitions named Elfreth Queed, along with a suave, sallow character of the water-front known as Kip Tarlan.

Captain Jim Selbert was present at the hearing, as were members of the Greater Carnival Association. Along with the latter came a man named Lamont Cranston, who was in a position to supply some information.

Big Queed, as he was known to his small-time faction, sat sullen while the municipal authorities reviewed his case; then suddenly, he burst into a tirade that contorted his fat face.

"Sure I was behind the Lottery," asserted Queed, "and why not? Everybody in New Orleans wants it and always did. Why in the old days some of the biggest men in the city took the Annual Policy and the state took its share of the receipts. I brought it back and I intended to run it on the square, the way it always was."

Nobody offering an objection, Big Queed resumed.

"That's why I talked to Louis Chardelle," Queed declared. "I knew he was tied up with the Krewe of Hades and that they had the right sort of people in their group. Chardelle told me he'd take it up with them, and later he said he had. They liked it, Chardelle said."

Waiting for comments, Big Queed received a question from Jim Selbert.

"How much did you pay Chardelle?"

"Five grand," replied Queed. "That was for his whole crowd. I thought it was enough for one night's work."

"And you gave Chardelle the hundred thousand?"

"That's right. How else could it be handed to the winner?"

"Maybe it wasn't handed to the winner."

Selbert's comment was sound, as one witness could have testified. The calm-faced Mr. Cranston studied the police captain with well-concealed approval. That empty box which The Shadow had so kindly borrowed to relieve Howard Shorke from responsibilities, fitted perfectly with a theory that was growing in Selbert's mind.

"You mean Chardelle was a double-crosser?" Big Queed came heavily to his big feet. "Say—if I thought he was—"

"Just what would you have done?" queried Selbert, as Queed paused, fuming. "Gone in for murder?"

That question deflated Queed. He sank back so hard his chair creaked; then shook his head.

"Talk to Kip Tarlan," suggested Queed. "Murder is in his line, not mine."

"Yeah?" snarled Tarlan, without waiting to be prompted. "What gives you that idea, Fat Guy? You hired a lot of lugs to fake a carnival float and come around to take away the winner, only when you found you could get other boys cheaper, you took them instead.

"The first guys squawked to me and I figured they were right. The job was theirs, so I told them to take it. Maybe we would have asked this fellow Shorke for a nice hunk of his winnings, but why not? The way you'd squeezed profits from the Lottery, you could have afforded to pay him back."

From then on, Queed and Tarlan took the floor together and the committee let them have it. Queed had played the big shot and Tarlan was the muscler who had tried to nick the racket, so the more they argued, the more the facts. It developed that both were right, in that neither had wanted to go in for violence.

Tarlan's gang had managed Queed's hirelings quietly, but when the latter had been released, they were in a mood for revenge, not discretion. That accounted for the battle on the Humpty Dumpty float, though Queed tried to condone the behavior of his men by saying that they had been hired as private bodyguards and were therefore performing a public duty in going after Tarlan's high-jackers.

This cleared the local angles where the Lottery ring was concerned, but it meant that Queed and Tarlan would be turned over to the Federal authorities. Along with them went an affidavit signed by Lamont Cranston, who had checked on the sale of lottery tickets in New York and who had come to New Orleans to learn if the sponsors of the illegal business really intended to go through with it.

Being so well acquainted with the lottery situation, Cranston automatically was invited to a discussion of the murder case which Captain Selbert was investigating. They went to Selbert's office, where along with several detectives, Jim reviewed Chardelle's death in detail.

On Selbert's desk were diagrams as exact as those which Cranston had drawn on a table-cloth that had later vanished along with a Columbine costume. As witnesses, Selbert had Shorke present, along with some of the guests who had gone to the Ball of Death.

"Big Queed is a rat," was Selbert's preamble, "but when a rat squeals, you can take his word. We know that Queed only talked to Chardelle. If Chardelle had wanted to grab the prize money, he wouldn't have stayed in New Orleans. So it wasn't Chardelle who pulled the double-cross."

"How do you know there was any double-cross?" put in Shorke, plaintively. "They gave me the box with the prize money and somebody took it—"

"And that somebody was The Shadow," interrupted Selbert. "You've heard of him, haven't you?"

Shorke nodded. Then:

"Maybe it was just somebody masquerading as The Shadow. Have you thought of that, Captain?"

"I have," returned Selbert, "and I'm telling you right now that nobody but The Shadow could have staged what he did. And from all I've heard of The Shadow, if the cash was in that box, he'd have shipped it right here to my office, tied in ribbons with a thank-you note."

Selbert looked straight at Cranston, feeling he'd get a corroboration from this gentleman whose intelligence had already been acknowledged. Cranston didn't nod, but his calm reception of the statement seemed to certify it.

"Anyway, Chardelle was the link," continued Selbert, emphatically. "If that money turned up missing, he'd have to answer for it. Only Chardelle is dead, so he can't talk and we all know he was murdered by someone wearing a Mask of Mephisto.

"That brings us to another murder, done by the same killer. Henri Moubillard was slain probably because he knew who was wearing that costume. We saw the murderer double back toward the shop and we found the costume in the office. The killer cracked a trap door and went out by the roof."

It was so good a summary that Cranston didn't raise the objections that he could have. The fact that Ken Langdon, and not the murderer, had discarded the costume which the police found in Moubillard's office, was something for future consideration. Ken's costume was at present hanging in a corner of Selbert's own office, so the police captain gestured to it dramatically.

"And the man who wore that costume," announced Selbert, "was Frederick Ferrand, the King Satan of the Krewe of Hades! Frederick Ferrand is a double murderer!"

The door was flinging open as Selbert voiced that denunciation, and on the threshold stood a man in hunting costume whose glaring eyes were wilder than his unshaved face was woolly. With a bellow loud enough to be heard back among the bayous from which he had come, this arrival roared:

"That's a lie, Selbert, and I'm here to prove it!"

X.

They were much alike, Fred Ferrand and Jim Selbert, although they differed on a question of murder. Specifically they differed on who had murdered whom, not who might want to murder whom.

For Ferrand was exhibiting the very inclinations that Selbert had attributed to him. Back from the bayou country, Ferrand had brought his shot-gun with him and in rough and ready style, he was shoving the double muzzles in Selbert's direction, with possible intent to let him have both barrels.

As for Selbert, he was drawing a police revolver, indicating that he meant to settle with a murderer and consider the evidence later. The police captain came up from the desk, faster than Ferrand could follow him with the shot-gun.

Shaking only a trifle of his complacence, Cranston intervened by blocking Selbert's aim and gesturing the revolver aside. Before Jim could start an angry protest, he saw Cranston's reason. Already two friends had followed through the doorway after Ferrand and were tugging his shot-gun upward.

One was Rolfe Trenhue, the other Joan Marcy. Trenhue had been at the previous hearing and had evidently met Joan afterward to bring her here. Their arrival in Ferrand's wake was therefore quite timely.

Ferrand could have flung off a pair of men like Trenhue, for the latter, though wiry, was mild of brawn compared to the big boy of the bayous. However, Joan was supplying more than the needed share because Ferrand was reluctant to become too rough with her. The net result was a clatter of the shot-gun and Ferrand, sullen rather than enraged, was letting his arms stay gripped as he still glared at Selbert.

With a nod of thanks to Cranston and the others, Selbert put his revolver away. Then:

"All right, Ferrand," said Selbert. "Tell your story. I'll listen."

"I don't have a story," gruffed Ferrand. "I just didn't get back to town for Mardi Gras, that's all."

"Why not? Your friends were expecting you, weren't they?"

"I tried to reach them," returned Ferrand. "Only they were all out when I phoned."

"Where did you phone from?"

Ferrand hesitated at answering the question, and finally said:

"From a place down near Yscloskey."

"Not very far away," commented Selbert. "Less than fifteen miles, Yscloskey."

Ferrand let that estimate ride.

"What were you hunting, Ferrand?"

About to reply, Ferrand decided on silence.

"Let's keep it to New Orleans then," decided Selbert. "Our rec-

THE MASK OF MEPHISTO 43

ords show"—Jim was referring to a little book—"that you ordered a special costume with a Mask of Mephisto, from Moubillard's Costume Shop."

"Suppose I did?" queried Ferrand. "I wasn't here to wear it. Besides, why couldn't somebody else have gotten a costume and played the Devil?"

"Because you were the only person who could have known about the Louisiana Lottery money. Chardelle would have told you."

"Only Chardelle didn't. Why should he?"

"Because you had full say in the affairs of the Krewe of Hades."

"As long as I reigned as King Satan, yes," conceded Ferrand, "but when I wasn't around—and I wasn't—the Scribe had charge. So it was up to Tourville."

Shaking his head, Selbert brought a scroll from the desk drawer and unrolled it.

"Evidently you don't know your own by-laws," Selbert told Ferrand. "It says here that in the absence of King Satan, or during his inability to rule, the majority vote of the other officers shall be needed to appoint a substitute or successor."

By the other officers, Selbert specifically meant Tourville, Aldion, and the defunct Chardelle, who as Scribe, Seneschal and Messenger were recognized officials of the Krewe. Not having Chardelle's body handy to confront Ferrand with it, Selbert did the next best thing.

The police captain pressed a buzzer; a door opened and both Tourville and Aldion were ushered in from another room where they had been kept in temporary custody. But if Selbert expected this surprise to produce results, he was guessing very badly. Tourville and Aldion nodded amiably but warily to Ferrand who returned the greeting in his usual abrupt style, then turned to Selbert and demanded:

"What do they have to say?"

"Only that they knew nothing about Chardelle's deal with the Lottery," returned Selbert. He paused, to add casually: "I'm rather inclined to believe them."

"Then why not believe me?"

"Because Tourville and Aldion were accounted for at the time of Chardelle's death," declared Selbert. He tapped a diagram with his pencil. "Tourville was here beside the orchestra platform and Aldion was at the outer door."

Ferrand stared at a big letter "M" which marked the beginning of a curved line that trickled into a row of dots.

"I suppose the 'M' stands for Mephisto and is supposed to mean me."

"It might," said Selbert drily, "and we'd know for sure if you traced the rest of the line for us. We're sure you must have gone as far as the third floor, but where you went after that, we don't know."

"Suppose I couldn't tell you?"

"Do you mean couldn't or wouldn't, Ferrand?"

"Both," retorted Ferrand, "since you want to be obstinate about it. You seem to think that I was lurking upstairs in the Mephisto costume, that I came down, shot Chardelle, fled upstairs again, jumped on a saddle-pigeon and flew back to Bayou Yscloskey."

Ignoring Ferrand's humor, Selbert studied the diagram.

"You couldn't have dropped to the front alley," Selbert decided, "but you might have doubled around through there after coming down from a side roof. There's a passage around Hoodoo House, leading through a gate into the alley. Doubling back seems to be your specialty, Ferrand.

"You doubled back through Moubillard's shop"—Selbert's eyes lifted and fixed steadily on Ferrand—"although you could have taken a side alley to another street. There's a gate alongside of Moubillard's too. Maybe you're forming bad habits, Ferrand."

Of the many eyes that were on Ferrand, the steadiest were Cranston's. He wanted to get the bearded man's reactions and with good reason. Cranston knew that Selbert was playing a wrong hunch in talking about doubling back. That trail at Moubillard's hadn't been reversed by the man who murdered the old customer.

Whatever Ferrand knew, he didn't betray it. Instead, he seemed inclined to keep Selbert guessing and did so. There were other eyes that gazed questioningly at Ferrand, a violet pair belonging to Joan Marcy. Then, rather than stare too long, the girl let her gaze drift, and she noted how closely Cranston was watching Ferrand.

Joan's chance observation stirred a curious recollection that was to produce immediate results.

"Don't tell us you couldn't have gone to Moubillard's," Selbert was saying to Ferrand. "You were seen at the Borneau Mansion earlier and we checked the time. It gave you just the right number of minutes to get over to the costume shop—"

"I was seen at the Borneau Mansion?" interrupted Ferrand. "Why, I wasn't within miles of the place. Who says they saw me there?"

"Miss Marcy, for one."

Ferrand wheeled so savagely toward Joan that she stepped back quickly past Trenhue's protecting arm. Before Ferrand could question Joan, Selbert did it for him.

"Tell us, Miss Marcy," said Selbert. "Didn't you see somebody in a Mephisto Mask at the Mansion?"

"Why, yes," admitted Joan. "Only—"

"Only what?"

"Only I'm not sure it was Fred."

"Didn't you speak to him?"

"Yes, I did."

"And he answered, didn't he?"

"In a way, yes," Joan conceded, "but I couldn't swear it was Fred's voice."

"Trying to disguise it, was he?"

"I don't know." Joan frowned, then brightened suddenly. "Yes, frankly I think the voice was disguised. In fact I have an idea who might—"

The last words were lost, drowned by the ugly snarl that Ferrand hurled Joan's way. Fred was calling the girl a double-crosser, but he spent a while getting to the term, due to a supply of preliminary adjectives. This time, however, Ferrand was reckoning rightly with Captain Selbert.

Coming around from his desk, Selbert caught Ferrand off guard and by the shoulders, spinning him with a twisty shove that landed Ferrand in a chair that broke and deposited him in its wreckage. Facing Joan, Selbert demanded abruptly:

"All right. Are you sure or aren't you as to the person in that mask?"

Joan's reply was to Selbert, but her eyes were elsewhere. The girl was looking straight at Cranston when she said:

"I am not sure."

Old Tourville and young Aldion were helping Ferrand to his feet, promising him their moral support as well as physical, but Ferrand wanted none of it. Delivering a contemptuous snarl in Joan's direction, Ferrand faced Selbert in challenging style.

"Since I need an alibi," declared Ferrand, "I'll give you one. Come down to the bayous with me and talk to the people there. We'll find somebody who will remember seeing me some time last night."

"I'll make the arrangements," agreed Selbert, tactfully. "Meanwhile everyone else is free to leave. Only I'd like you all to be on call, particularly you two."

By "you two" Selbert meant Tourville and Aldion, as he indicated. A pair of detectives took custody of Ferrand while the rest of the group filed out, Cranston included. There were two persons, however, who paused outside the door of Selbert's office.

Cranston noted them: Joan Marcy and Rolfe Trenhue. But it wouldn't have been good policy to have stayed and eavesdropped on their conversation.

Besides, Cranston had a good idea what it was all about and the accuracy of his surmise was to prove itself quite soon. His whispered laugh, unheard as he departed, was more than vaguely reminiscent of The Shadow's.

XI.

Oysters Rockefeller formed a tasty dish that delighted Margo Lane, particularly the kind that were served in a certain French restaurant just within the borders of the Vieux Carré. At present however, Margo was neglecting this specialty to furnish Lamont Cranston a bit of tidy news.

"Don't look now," undertoned Margo, "but there's an old friend of mine who doesn't know me when he sees me. He must think he's going to collect some prize money that he didn't get or he wouldn't be so interested in local blondes."

Cranston looked, by way of a restaurant mirror, and gave Margo a nod.

"I know who you mean," said Cranston. "Howard Shorke."

Margo stared, a bit puzzled.

"You've met Shorke?"

Cranston had, but he didn't say so. Instead, he replied:

"I've met the blonde."

Such a revelation would have put Margo in a fighting mood, if it hadn't occurred to her who the blonde in question was. Margo recalled her as a girl in Dutch costume that had made her look considerably different.

"But what does Joan Marcy see in Shorke?" queried Margo.

"Nothing," replied Cranston. "It's what she wants to hear from him."

"You mean details about last night's fiasco?"

"The police called it murder, Margo, and they've put the blame on Ferrand. Joan probably wants to clear him."

"And why? I understood they weren't clubby any more, and from the way you said Ferrand acted—"

"Ferrand's actions are Joan's main reason," interposed Cranston. "She wants to clear the book. Trenhue stayed at headquarters, probably just to tell Ferrand that Joan was doing all she could for him."

"And is she?"

"I think so." His tone extremely confidential, Cranston explained why. "Joan has listed her own candidate for Suspect Number One in the Mephisto murders."

"Do you know who he is?"

"You're looking right at him, Margo."

Since she was looking right at Cranston, Margo continued to stare, her eyes wide with disbelief.

"It was rather odd that I should show up at the Borneau Mansion," reminded Cranston. "If Mr. Mephisto had time to get from there to Moubillard's and toss off a murder, I for one had time to get back to the Mansion. Besides, nobody has asked me where I was at the time Chardelle was killed."

"But Lamont! Of all the nerve!"

"That's a mere side issue, Margo. I think I'll go the rounds and maybe run into Tourville or Aldion, to hear their opinions. When you're clear, you might phone young Langdon and tell him that it would be advisable for the missing Mephisto to stay under cover a while longer."

With that, Cranston passed Margo an envelope which had dropped from Ken's pocket during last night's trip across Moubillard's roof. It bore Ken's name and address to which Cranston had thoughtfully added a pencilled phone number.

From the corner of her eye, Margo watched Joan follow Lamont's departure. If she hadn't learned the truth, Margo would have classed the blonde's gaze as a designing one. But then Margo was over-suspicious of blondes, just as she underestimated the intelligence of such milk-toast gentry as Howard Shorke.

While Margo was watching Joan, Shorke was watching Margo. Turned slightly from the table, Margo was resting one knee upon the other and Shorke, who had an eye for mirrors too, was catching the reflection of some very sightly legs that reminded him of the trim limbs of a Columbine.

When Shorke leaned over to say something to Joan, Margo supposed it referred to Lamont instead of herself. She finished the last of the fancy oysters and sauntered from the restaurant, planning to do a little shopping and then to phone Ken.

Right then, a phone call wouldn't have found Ken Langdon at home. Behind his outward manner, Ken was a much more jittery person than even The Shadow supposed. With afternoon waning, Ken had decided on a course that was utterly foolish.

Ken had decided to go to police headquarters and talk to Captain Jim Selbert.

How far Ken had taken matters into his own hands, he didn't fully realize. Certainly The Shadow wouldn't have approved this notion, and Ken himself would have later cause to rue it. Nevertheless, Ken's folly in seeking Selbert was counteracted by the luck he had in not finding him.

Not wanting to be disturbed, Selbert had left word to send up the names of any visitors before admitting them to his office. So a detective came in reading Ken's card and announced:

"There's a guy named Kenneth Langdon wanting to see you, Captain—"

That was as far as the detective got. Answering a phone call with his other ear, Selbert wheeled to Trenhue, who was sitting in the office.

"It's about Ferrand!" Selbert stormed. "He's pulled a fast one! He's slipped the officers who went along with him and headed off into the bayou country!"

Trouble clouded Trenhue's rather bland face.

"Do you think he can get out of the state, Captain?"

"Get out!" retorted Selbert. "We'll have more work finding him if he stays in! Why a man could hide for weeks among the marshes. There's one chance, though"—appeal strengthened Selbert's tone— "and that's if you could locate Ferrand for us."

Slowly, Trenhue shook his head.

"You wouldn't be going back on a friend," argued Selbert. "Anyway, Ferrand went back on you, mixing in with that Hades Krewe although he knew you were opposed to such organizations."

"I'm not so sure," debated Trenhue. "Every man has a right to his own opinion, and should guide his actions by it."

"Suppose Ferrand is innocent," suggested Selbert. "It will be all the worse if he is hounded and hunted. He'd need a friend to assure him that we'll give him a fair trial. You're coming with me, Trenhue."

"All right," decided Trenhue, "but I'll have to call my house, so they'll know where I've gone. Maybe if we stop by there we can pick up some of those bayou maps."

"Bayou maps?"

"Yes, old ones that particularly interested Ferrand. I thought once he was going to buy up property down there; that's why I was really surprised when I learned he had sunk money in the Krewe of Hades—"

"Forget the Krewe of Hades," broke in Selbert. "Do your phoning while I'm arranging for a car."

Trenhue had made his phone call by the time Selbert returned. The car was ready, but Jim took time out to see that the office was in order, something that he always did. He noted that the Mephisto costume was hanging in its proper corner, with the grotesque Mask above it. Then Selbert and Trenhue were on their way, with only one slight delaying incident.

Just outside the office door, Selbert ran into a rather haggard young man who had the look of an artist. Whoever he was, Selbert hadn't time to talk to him. All Jim said was:

"We'll be back late. Better come around tomorrow. If it's too important to wait, tell it to somebody else."

Good advice if there had been any one else to hear the story. But Selbert's men were going along with him, so Ken Langdon was stranded in the vacant corridor outside the office door that Selbert hadn't locked. Dusk was filling police headquarters which meant that it was getting late, and Ken had a fairly long trip ahead to the Vieux Carré.

So long that Margo Lane reached Ken's studio ahead of him. The reason she went there was because the telephone didn't answer. When she called information to check on Ken's number, she found he didn't have any. Of course Margo had been calling the number in the little renting office across the patio from Ken's studio, but she didn't know anything about that arrangement.

Thus Margo found herself looking into a tall but not too sizeable studio that contained an imposing statue, towering almost to the ceiling. It was a strange statue, representing a curious, forceful creature with bedraggled hair and tattered robe, tilting forward and staring straight ahead with determination written all over its plaster face.

Wondering what the subject of the statue was, Margo became more intrigued by the problem of how it could be gotten out of the studio. Looking from door to statue and back again, she tried to compare the dimension. Still dubious, Margo gauged the statue again, and then turned to the door.

Immediately, the problem changed.

It wasn't a question whether the statue could be safely removed from the studio. It was a question whether Margo Lane would be able to remove herself!

XII.

Blue-cold was the revolver muzzle that covered Margo and the violet eyes behind it had acquired something of the same hard cobalt glint. The gun wasn't very big, but it was just the right size for Joan Marcy, the girl who owned the gun and looked as though she knew how to use it.

In miniature, Joan's expression resembled that of the bulky statue. It spelled determination plus.

The door was swinging shut from a flip of Joan's free hand. As it slammed, the blonde stepped forward, warily keeping enough range to hold Margo entirely helpless. Then, in a calm, decisive contralto, Joan spoke her piece.

"Coincidences just don't happen twice," declared Joan. "That goes for a certain Mr. Cranston and yourself. Or should I call you Mephistopheles and Columbine?"

"You might," returned Margo, "but you'd be wrong."

"Just how wrong?" quizzed Joan. "Half?"

Margo didn't answer that one.

"Half then," Joan summed. "But which half?"

The answer seemed to hang in Margo's mind. It wasn't the difference between truth and falsehood, because such didn't matter when somebody demanded one or the other and used a gun to back the request. The important thing was to nullify the gun threat.

Still, that wasn't the full answer.

Presuming that whatever Margo said would be used against her, the thing to say was whatever would hurt less. On that basis, truth was preferable.

Cranston hadn't played the part of King Satan; therefore it would complicate matters to say that he had. Whereas if Margo admitted she had been Columbine, she would only be revealing something that might be found out anyway. So Margo admitted:

"I was Columbine."

To Joan's credit she accepted it very nicely which briefly changed Margo's opinion regarding blondes. Being frustrated on the Cranston theory, Joan popped a new one.

"Now I understand," declared Joan, sagely. "You were working with Kenneth Langdon, the man who has this studio. He was masquerading as Mephisto."

In fitting a half truth, Joan had struck upon a whole one, so far as the masquerade was concerned, but she was very far from accurate on a question of murder. However the proposition had now reached a state where Margo could no longer dispute it without getting in deeper.

A buzzer sounded, postponing an answer. Someone had pressed a button on the board down in the archway, where Ken's name was listed.

Gesturing her gun at Margo, Joan said:

"Answer it."

Now there was no door down in the archway and therefore no reason why anyone should ring for admittance. Probably the proper response was simply to step out to the railed balcony and call down to the courtyard. Not knowing the New Orleans custom, Margo was quite at loss, but there was still Joan's gun to be considered.

Margo compromised by stepping to the studio door and turning the knob very gingerly, just so Joan would see she didn't intend to make a sudden dash. It couldn't be Ken Langdon, ringing to inform someone that he was coming back to his own studio, more logically it would be Lamont Cranston, letting Margo know that he had arrived.

There was also a chance that it might be The Shadow, for darkness had settled by this time and it would be like Lamont to switch to his black garb. Margo hoped so, at least, because she wanted to surprise Joan. So it wasn't until she felt the knob turning from the other side that Margo let the door come open.

It was indeed a surprise for Joan and Margo shared it. In through the doorway stepped a crimson-clad Mephisto, mask and all!

Out of the hideous hush that followed, the silent night itself seemed to deliver the horrendous cry:

"Murder!"

It could mean nothing else, this new manifestation of the masked Mephistopheles. Mardi Gras was over and to stalk the New Orleans street in costume was the most conspicuous act possible. Of course this intruder could have put on his costume in the secluded archway, but why should he risk such a course at all?

Of all possible maskers who might still be celebrating Carnival, anyone who wore the Mask of Mephisto would be an utter fool.

If Margo had known that Fred Ferrand had slipped the guards who had taken him on the bayou trip, she might have understood this foolery, since Ferrand was wanted anyway. Her only other conclusion was that Ken Langdon had deceived The Shadow as well as others, and was really the King Satan who dealt in murder.

Whichever the case, Margo wasn't on the spot, at least not yet. The crazy tilt of the Mephisto Mask was an index to the gaze of the eyes behind it. The man in red was here to find Joan Marcy and to prove it, he whipped out a gun and sidled it past Margo in order to aim at the startled blonde who was back by the big statue.

Whether Margo took the right course or the wrong one was a question, but it proved to her advantage. By right, she should have tried to dodge past the man in the Mephisto Mask and let him blaze away at Joan, but that wouldn't have been sporting. Besides, it didn't seem good sense to take chances with a gun behind you, so Margo wanted to discourage Joan's fire.

The best way was to take sides with Joan against Mephisto, so Margo did, hoping to win the blonde's confidence.

Grabbing at Mephisto's gun, Margo was rewarded with a swing that flung her half across the studio, but the man in red didn't fire. All he did was snarl, or its equivalent, the hollow head making the tone sound like a bellow. That gave Joan a chance to fire a few shots, but they were wide despite the cramped surroundings. The reason was that Joan was trying to dodge behind the statue while she used her gun, and the two plans didn't mix.

Angered by the shots, the masked man spurted a few in return but the only toll they took was plaster from the statue. By then, Margo was on her feet, grabbing for the man's gun, shouting for Joan to rally to the cause. Maybe that was where Margo was really wrong, for she was inviting Joan out into the open, but it no longer mattered.

As suddenly as he had entered, the man in red wheeled and sprang out through the doorway to the balcony. People were peering from other doorways and they saw him dash down the stairs to the archway. Just to discourage Joan's fire, Mephisto wheeled from the stairs to send a few shots back, and by then Margo was in again.

Right in where she shouldn't be, in a line with the murder's aim! And the venom that this killer had shown toward Joan was something that he was now quite willing to transfer to a meddler named Margo.

Halting too late at the top of the steps, Margo tripped forward straight toward the looming gun muzzle, only to see blackness rise en masse and lift a clump of crimson regalia into a somersault, mask and all.

Maybe other witnesses thought that Mephisto merely tripped, but not Margo. Nobody could trip with a bound that carried them six feet upward. Looking down the steps, Margo saw exactly what happened, and knew why. That blackness was The Shadow, coming up just in time to meet Mephisto on the way down.

As the crimson menace landed by the arch, The Shadow was busy halting Margo's sprawl. By rights, Mephisto should have been there when The Shadow turned to aim at him, but the Devil's own luck was still with the impersonator. He had landed like a cat and he was away like one, out through the arch.

Clutching the curved rail by the steps, Margo thought her eyes were fooling her. She saw blackness streak along Mephisto's trail, but peculiarly gun-shots sounded from beneath the darkened arch before its blackness swallowed The Shadow's form. Either there were two Shadows, or the only one was gone before Margo saw him leave, and neither of those theories seemed credible.

True, The Shadow often dealt in the incredible, but this was too much of it.

Then, jogged along by Joan who was coming down the stairs, Margo reached the archway and saw two figures there, one helping the other to his feet. There was enough light from the street to recognize them: Lamont Cranston and Ken Langdon.

Since one was The Shadow, the other would have to be Mephisto, but the latter didn't hold.

Grabbing Cranston's arm, Ken gestured to the street and urged this friend to come along.

"I nearly stopped him!" Ken voiced hoarsely. "Anyway, he didn't clip me with those shots of his! Come on, we've still got time to overtake him!"

There wasn't time. King Satan had made good his escape. What with alleys, overhanging balconies, deserted houses and other peculiarities of this narrow street in the Vieux Carré, there wasn't a sign of Mephisto, hide nor hook, when they looked for him out front.

Again a murderer had vanished, but this time death was absent from his trail.

XIII.

One mind at least was still fraught with suspicion and that mind belonged to Joan Marcy. Joan's ways were firm when it came to making up that mind of hers, but to her credit she could also change it.

First, in regard to Lamont Cranston.

Being a friend of Margo, who had already taken Joan's part, Cranston no longer rated as a possible Mephisto.

Next, Ken Langdon.

Never having met him, at least not to her knowledge, Joan could only regard him as another victim of circumstance like herself.

Furthermore, since neither of these men had a sign of a Mephisto costume between them, both were cleared. Certainly one would not have been so tolerant of the other, if either had been doubtful.

There was a costume that Joan didn't notice, a black cloak and hat that were bundled on a narrow ornamental ledge inside the arch. Cranston had perched them there when he assumed his present personality. Too late to overtake the fugitive Mephisto, Cranston had dropped The Shadow role in order to help Ken, who had arrived back just in time to tackle Mephisto and miss. Cranston's real help was a sort that Ken didn't quite yet recognize. He was really giving Ken an alibi; that point came out after Ken had chatted a bit with his neighbors and heard their version of the gunfire and Mephisto's flight. That done, Ken went with Cranston and the girls to one of Frenchtown's quiet restaurants and there began this serious summary:

"It was lucky I came along when I did." Ken felt quite proud about it. "If I hadn't, nobody would have believed anything you people told them. Since they took you for friends of mine, everything was squared. But if I'd only gone after that fellow in red!"

"You would have," put in Cranston, calmly, "if I hadn't held you back."

Ken stared narrowly at this complacent friend of his. There was something of anger in that look, emphasized by the thrust of Ken's square chin.

"You did just that," recalled Ken. Then, deciding that Cranston must have had a reason, Ken let his feeling subside. "All right, I like riddles. Answer that one."

"Somebody was trying to frame you again," explained Cranston. "You were lucky during Mardi Gras, getting rid of that Mephisto Mask before the police found you in it. They might have caught up with you at the Borneau Mansion, you know."

There was a slight gasp from Joan as she leaned forward to study Ken's face, which was rather laughable since all she'd seen of him was the Mephisto Mask. Looking into Joan's eyes, Ken saw appeal in their violet tint; they seemed to be asking for the truth and hoping it wouldn't be too bad.

"Yes, I was a fall guy," admitted Ken. Then to Joan, he said: "I met you at the reception when I was rigged out as the Devil, but I hope you'll believe me when I say I'm not the man the police are after. I'd never heard of the Krewe of Hades and as for the Louisiana Lottery, I was working for a lot less than it paid off."

Tossing the torn half of a hundred dollar bill on the table, Ken added the typewritten schedule and leaned back with a shrug.

"There's what I got," he said, "and there's what I did. I'm still wondering who has the other half of that bank note."

While Joan and Margo were studying the trophies, Ken turned to Cranston.

"Getting back to what you just said. How was I being framed tonight?"

"Your neighbors heard the shooting in your studio," replied Cranston. "They saw somebody dash out in that Mephisto costume. The next step would have been to hunt you up, wouldn't it?"

"Of course."

"And what would you have said?"

"Why, that I hadn't been around. In fact, I might have shown up while people were still looking for me. Maybe a few of them would have been foolish enough to think I was the man in costume—"

With that, Ken caught himself. His eyes opened in a reflective stare.

"Say!" Ken exclaimed. "They'd have asked me about last night, wouldn't they?"

Cranston nodded.

"I couldn't have told them I'd played Mephisto," mused Ken, "because they wouldn't take my version of it, the way you did. If I didn't account for last night, I'd be without an alibi."

"This evening," reminded Cranston, "you have an alibi. You came in too soon after Mephisto went out. You wouldn't have had time to shed the red regalia."

"But if I'd chased Mephisto," acknowledged Ken, "none of my neighbors would have known that I was back. No wonder that character was in a hurry. He was really out to pin it on me!"

By this time, Joan's interest was more than roused. She was remembering a score of her own.

"Maybe I know too much," affirmed Joan, "or maybe I've talked too much. Anyway, Mephisto was trying to add another murder to his list, and I was the intended victim. There's only one man vindictive enough to feel that way about me and that's Frederick Ferrand!"

There was a defiant sparkle in Joan's eyes; it softened, only to regain its fire, and the girl's next words explained the changing of her moods.

"I once thought Fred cared for me," Joan said, "until I learned that my money was my main attraction where he was concerned. Fred let it slip; then he tried to reconcile the two: love and money. He said we'd have to have money to be happy together, so why did it matter whose money it was?"

Looking around, Joan waited a few moments and then answered her own question.

"It didn't matter," she declared. "It was just the way Fred put it. Finally he said he'd find a way to make his own fortune and that I could go to the devil for all he cared." Joan's eyes suddenly became startled. "Odd, wasn't it, that Fred should say that? But those were his exact words."

"How long ago was that?" queried Cranston.

"A month or more," replied Joan. "After he'd been down among the bayous."

"Where he is now," put in Ken, "and a hard time they'll have finding him."

"I don't suppose Ferrand will lose himself," remarked Cranston. "Not with a pair of deputies handcuffed to him."

At that, Ken snapped his fingers.

"Of course!" he exclaimed. "You couldn't have heard! Ferrand slipped those deps somewhere along the way to Bayou Yscloskey. Selbert and Trenhue were starting out to hunt for him when I was over at headquarters."

Startled exclamations resulted from Joan and Margo who began exchanging glances that had a mutual thought behind them; namely, that Ferrand might have been the Masked Mephisto who had invaded Ken's studio. But Cranston was more interested in something concerning Ken.

"You went to headquarters, Langdon?"

"Why, yes." Ken became apologetic. "You see, I was getting jittery there in the studio. I couldn't take an interest in Wingless Victory—"

"You came directly back?" interrupted Cranston. "No stops anywhere?"

"Straight back."

Calculating where he had been during Ken's journey of perhaps a quarter hour, Cranston tallied a few facts.

"I stopped in to see Hubert Aldion," stated Cranston. "At his office, just off Canal Street. That must have been just about the time you were leaving headquarters, Langdon. It's only five minutes' walk from Aldion's to your studio, but I went around past the Talleyrand

Club, to see if Tourville Talbot was there. He was, but I didn't want to disturb his chess game."

On a pad, Cranston drew a long line, representing Ken's trip back from police headquarters to the Vieux Carré. Near the end that represented Ken's studio, Cranston tagged another pair of x's to represent Aldion's office and Tourville's club.

"Did you talk to Selbert, Langdon?"

A head-shake from Ken.

"Very good," decided Cranston. "But was there anyone in his office after he left?"

"I wasn't in Selbert's office."

"Then you wouldn't have seen what was hanging there, even if nobody had borrowed it."

"What was that?"

"A very fancy red costume," announced Cranston, "complete to the Mask of Mephisto."

Leaving Ken gaping, Cranston went to the telephone and called headquarters. Returning, Cranston stated:

"They are all three back in Selbert's office."

"Selbert and Trenhue are two," tallied Ken, "so I take it they caught Ferrand, since he must be the third."

"Not Ferrand," declared Cranston cryptically. "By the third, I mean the Mask of Mephisto!"

XIV.

New Orleans was noted for its men of mystery and now the long and time-mellowed list was boasting a new member. His name was Frederick Ferrand and whether he was in town or not, he belonged to New Orleans.

In fact, most men of Ferrand's present classification had been famous because they were away from the city when anybody wanted them. For Ferrand now rated with the celebrated pirate Jean Lafitte and others of the ilk, who also favored the bayou region as the place to spend their spare time.

The hunt had been on for nearly a week and was still getting nowhere. Jim Selbert had about reached the state of waiting for the murderer to return to the scene of his crime, for Jim was seen quite often in the vicinity of the Hoodoo House. On this particular night,

Selbert was just coming from the alley when he ran into a visitor who was still in New Orleans.

Jim Selbert was rather glad to see Lamont Cranston. The police captain suggested a stroll in the direction of Jackson Square.

On the way, Cranston inquired: "What luck?"

"None," was Selbert's verdict. "I've been through that Hoodoo House from top to bottom, so often that I probably know it better than Dominique You ever did, if he lived there long enough to count."

They were passing a large and antiquated house to which Selbert gestured by way of contrast.

"That place, for instance," Jim stated. "It was actually owned by René Beluche, captain of a smuggling ship called *The Spy*. And around the corner here are a couple of other places, the Café des Refugées and the Hotel de la Marine. They were really pirate hangouts."

Selbert pointed out the buildings as they passed; then returned to the theme of the Hoodoo House.

"No trap doors," he muttered, "no panels, not even any secret fireplaces. I've done everything except roll up the old cement floor in that room the Hades Krewe called the Devil's Den."

Cranston's slight smile was unnoticed in the dark.

"You don't like to miss a detail, do you, Jim?"

"Not me," coincided Selbert. "It's easy enough to figure how Ferrand got in there in the first place, without benefit of hidden passages. Being the bigwig of the Hades Krewe he might have been there waiting. He said he was floating around on a bayou, but we don't believe that."

No comment coming from Cranston, Selbert continued.

"That upstairs hall is the stickler," Jim confided. "Ferrand bolted both doors and that gave him a little time. Aldion busted through one and hauled open the other—"

"Which one?" interposed Cranston. "And which other?"

"It doesn't specially matter," returned Selbert. "Aldion was quick to go after Ferrand, which made me a bit suspicious of old Tourville Talbot. He's the guy who likes his first name better than his last, like Dominique You did in the old days."

Smiling slightly at this historical digression, Cranston decided not to interrupt.

"Only Tourville is an old guy," granted Selbert, "so he couldn't get upstairs as fast as Aldion. Anyway, Tourville wasn't able to either stop or help Ferrand in that murder of Chardelle, so that's that. Particularly because nobody else was around when Ferrand killed off Moubillard, unless—"

The pause was when Selbert glanced at Cranston. Jim had been about to mention The Shadow, in complimentary terms, but decided not to confuse the issue. If at Moubillard's, The Shadow had certainly done his utmost to block the murder; of that Selbert was sure.

What Selbert wasn't sure about was why he didn't want to talk to Cranston about The Shadow. Maybe it was because the two were much alike in that they were so completely different. Cranston was a man of advice, The Shadow a person of action. You could always find Cranston when you needed him; The Shadow always found you, when needed.

Those were just a few of the points that made the two personalities as opposite as the poles. What Selbert didn't consider was that since Cranston and The Shadow were so far removed, nobody ever expected to meet them both at once.

"What gets me," resumed Selbert, back on his major theme, "was the nerve Ferrand showed in doubling back to headquarters after I left there with Trenhue. Taking the costume was plenty; bringing it back, even more."

Cranston wanted to check that point.

"You're sure it wasn't gone before you left, Jim?"

"Positive. I came back to the office just after Trenhue finished calling his house. I saw the costume hanging there and Trenhue went out ahead of me. By the way, we ought to be seeing Trenhue around here."

They had reached the old French Market, with its long array of sheds and stalls. At one end, trucks were unloading shrimp and people were watching from the tables beside one of the famous coffee stands. Trenhue was there and with him Aldion; seeing Cranston and Selbert, Trenhue invited them to sit down.

"Wasteful, isn't it?" Trenhue referred to the way the truckers were tramping over loose shrimp, as they shoveled big masses into baskets. "Shoveling shrimp like coal makes men become careless. Let's see—" Trenhue tilted his head to calculate—"at the restaurant figure of five cents a shrimp, those chaps have mangled at least twenty dollars worth. That would be one hundred dollars on a five day week—"

Trenhue paused to laugh lightly, with a nudge at Aldion, whose face was very sunk. Then, sobering his own expression, Trenhue declared:

"I'm glad you came along, Selbert. Have you finished with the Hoodoo House?"

Jim nodded and let the process lift his eyebrows.

"Aldion here put up half the money for it," explained Trenhue, "and Ferrand posted the rest. Only Fred didn't have the money, so he borrowed it from me and Aldion went his note."

"How soon is the note due?" queried Selbert.

"Past due," replied Trenhue, "and for the first time I'm learning why Fred borrowed the money."

"It was a rum trick for Ferrand to play," conceded Aldion, "but I assure you, Trenhue, I didn't know you were so opposed to secret organizations like the Krewe of Hades. Fred never even mentioned it."

"Fred wouldn't," said Trenhue, bluntly, "but we didn't know his true colors—or lack of them—until now."

"Imagine it!" Aldion was protesting glumly to Cranston. "Ferrand using Trenhue to finance the Devil's Den! And now—well, I'm stuck for all of it. I deserve it; the question is, can I pay it."

"That won't be necessary," decided Trenhue, generously. "Since the Krewe of Hades is no more, I am willing to take half ownership of Hoodoo House. But you know, if Ferrand had told me he intended to buy the place, I wouldn't have been surprised."

It was Aldion who was surprised.

"Why not, Trenhue?"

"Because he was interested in anything that concerned the one-time pirate Dominique. That's why Fred visited the bayous so often. They were Dominique's stamping ground."

From his pocket he brought a sheaf of old papers and handed them to Selbert.

"Some more Dominique data, Captain," stated Trenhue. "Stuff that Ferrand collected. If you piece enough of it together, you may be able to track him among the bayous."

Finishing his coffee, Trenhue shook hands all around and waved away the effusive thanks that Aldion repeated over Trenhue's kindness in taking the half share in the Hoodoo House. The two walked a short way together and as they parted at a corner, Cranston, watching from the coffee stand, commented:

"Nice of Trenhue to see Aldion through on that bad deal of Ferrand's."

"Nice if he can afford it," returned Selbert. "Only Trenhue is no better fixed than Aldion."

"You mean the property will prove a loss?"

"What do you think? Hoodoo *will* mean hoodoo around the Hoodoo House after that murder that took place there. Still, they may get out what they've sunk in it."

Selbert's final sentence brought a reflective gaze from Cranston, something that Jim didn't notice over his coffee cup.

"This was really nice of Trenhue." Selbert tapped the bundle of papers. "I've about given up on Ferrand coming back to town; soon it's going to be a question of going after him, and the more data that shows how his mind works, the better our chance of finding him."

Lamont Cranston looked as though he hadn't heard a word that Jim Selbert said in reference to Trenhue's documents. To Cranston, the most potent of all Selbert's phrases was one that the police captain had voiced in an off-hand way:

"They may get out what they've sunk in it."

XV.

Margo Lane was getting tired of reading up on a man named Dominique whose name was short for Dominique You. In her opinion, Dominique was the least picturesque of all the Baratarians, those swashbucklers headed by Lafitte and who were termed pirates or smugglers, according to the point of view.

Those bullies of the bayous dated back more than a century. They had reformed long enough to help win the Battle of New Orleans; then they had gone back to their questionable ways. All except Dominique; he'd become a ward politician in New Orleans.

Margo expressed her disappointment to Joan.

"What a tame ending for an adventurous career!"

"You don't know our ward politicians," rejoined Joan, sweetly. "If you're really thinking of tame endings, consider those who left

New Orleans and wound up among the bayous." Joan's sweet tone had grown bitter, word by word: "Like Fred Ferrand!"

Margo looked across the courtyard. She and Joan were doing the Dominique research in an empty studio just off Ken's patio. From where they were, they could see Ken working on Wingless Victory, whose bullet wounds had long ago been plastered.

Following Margo's gaze and noting that it contained no envy, Joan queried softly:

"Do you think I'm right?"

"If you mean because you've gone sculptor-minded," returned Margo. "Yes."

"Ken is a realist," considered Joan. "Take his Wingless Victory. He decided that Victory needed a head more than wings, so he swapped. I like that."

"Wasn't Fred a realist?"

"If you mean because he bayed around the bayous, I suppose he was. But let's forget Fred."

"What about Rolfe Trenhue?"

Joan shook her head.

"If you must bring up comparisons, Margo, I suppose I'll have to analyze them for you. Let's take the Krewe of Hades as the balance point. Can you think of anything sillier than sponsoring a thing like that?"

"Off-hand," admitted Margo, "I can't."

"Well, I can," retorted Joan. "Starting such stupid organizations is bad enough; trying to stop them is worse. That sums Rolfe."

Margo admitted that it did. Then:

"Tell me, Joan," queried Margo. "What do you think of a man who spends his time looking at old coins but never buying any?"

"If you mean Lamont," returned Joan, "I'd say he's just trying to avoid something worse, like doing research on Dominique."

"I'm not so sure," said Margo. "Old coins are getting scarcer and therefore worth more."

"But Lamont isn't buying any, is he?"

"He isn't and that's the funny part about it. Maybe the business is only booming locally. Still, old coins ought to be a good investment."

Remembering something, Joan went through a batch of clippings and found the ones she wanted.

"Speaking of investments," she said, "Dominique was a bad hand at them. He was practically broke when he died and that's a real mystery."

"I'll tell Lamont," decided Margo. "He likes mystery, though I can't say he's been working at it lately."

Right then, Cranston was really working at it. In a secluded courtyard behind the old Hoodoo House, he was helping Jim Selbert reconstruct a crime, though the police captain didn't know it. In Selbert's opinion, they were merely adding to the intricacies of an existing mystery.

Cranston was standing directly below the tiny window of that little second floor hallway where pursuers had barged in from two directions to find that Mephisto had continued along his way, which could only have been further upstairs.

In the window itself, Selbert's head and shoulders were framed with little space to spare.

"Here's a question," called down Selbert. "Ever hear of a midget who was a contortionist too?"

"Can't say that I have," Cranston called up. "Why do you ask?"

"Because nobody else could have squeezed through this window," Jim decided. "Well, it proves one thing. The murderer must have gone up to the cupola or the roof. Come around to the front door and I'll meet you there."

Coming around to the front door was easy. Cranston simply went around the side of the house, through an adjacent passage, and opened the unlocked iron gate that brought him to the front door of the old stone house. He was there before Selbert had time to come downstairs and since the door was open, Cranston entered.

Men were at work hacking the cement floor of the Devil's Den with pick-axes. When Selbert came down the stairs, Cranston asked:

"What are you doing? Hunting for Ferrand? I thought you said that he wasn't hiding here."

"Not my idea." Selbert shrugged in the direction of the workmen. "Improvements, that's all."

"Who ordered them?"

"Trenhue or Aldion; maybe both. They've got to liquidate this architectural horror in order to get back their investment."

"They're going to tear down the house?"

"No, indeed." Selbert seemed outraged by the suggestion. "That's no longer being done in New Orleans, now that historical landmarks are running out. They'll just remodel the place and rent it out as studios or apartments." After watching the workmen hack away a while, Selbert decided to go outdoors. From the front alley, he surveyed the Hoodoo House again and gave a puzzled head shake.

"If it had been The Shadow," Selbert said to Cranston, "I could understand it. The disappearing stuff is his specialty. But I can't see how Ferrand dropped out of sight so fast, if he did drop."

With the final comment, Selbert looked up to the roof to make sure that it was as high above the alley as it always was. Satisfied that the mad escape of the Masked Mephisto still rated as a superhuman achievement, Selbert decided to let it rest at that.

"There's something I want to ask Miss Marcy," Selbert told Cranston. "Let's go over to the studio and see her."

Questions from Selbert had become part of Joan's daily dozen, so she wasn't surprised when the police captain arrived in the recently formed bureau of research that was devoting itself to data concerning Dominique.

Nor was Margo surprised when she saw Lamont. He'd said he would stop around to learn how the work had progressed. Nevertheless, Margo was interested in what Selbert was asking Joan, but it turned out to be the usual routine. Selbert wanted to know where Joan had been at every odd minute on Mardi Gras Night and all the persons she had seen. He was still trying to get some trifling fact that would lead to Ferrand.

Joan tried to help, but managed it only in a negative way.

"I've told you I expected to meet Fred," she declared. "Rolfe was looking for him, too. Only I couldn't tell Rolfe that Fred was going to the Hades meeting. Rolfe wouldn't have believed that there was such a thing as the Krewe of Hades."

"Be specific," insisted Selbert. "What happened and at what time?"

"Rolfe left me at seven—"

"That was just when the guests were coming into the Hoodoo House," tallied Selbert. "Since Ferrand was already there, Trenhue couldn't possibly have found him. Nobody could enter the Devil's Den without an invitation and then only as a guest. Go on."

"Well, I couldn't find Fred either," stated Joan. "I was supposed to meet Rolfe at seven fifteen, at the coffee stand in the old French Market."

"Which coffee stand?"

"The one on the side toward the Cabildo, but I went to the other one first, by mistake. You see, I was walking through Frenchtown, while Rolfe was driving out to Fred's apartment and back—"

"But why were you walking through the Quarter?" broke in Selbert. "Be specific, please."

"Because Fred was so often around there," explained Joan, patiently. "He had a favorite drinking place in nearly every block."

"And you looked into all of them?"

"Yes, but no Fred. Anyway, at about seven thirty, Rolfe found me. He'd parked his car at the other end of the Market and had been waiting for me there. Only he had sense enough to decide that I'd gone to the wrong stand. So we drove out to the Borneau Mansion."

"And?"

"And that was all. You've heard the rest a dozen times."

Deciding that he'd heard all that was needed, Selbert went his way and Joan resumed her filing of the Dominique data. It was Cranston who put the next questions and his were addressed to Margo Lane.

"Speaking of time elements," said Cranston, "how soon did you get out in front of Hoodoo House after that Mephisto murder?"

"Soon enough," replied Margo. "If Friend Fiend had come that way, I'd have seen him."

"People were still chasing up to the roof?"

"Yes, and to the cupola. You know, Lamont"—Margo's expression became quite wise—"if the murderer could have squeezed through that tiny second floor window, he might have gotten away."

"Only he couldn't make the squeeze," modified Cranston, "but what makes you think he'd have gotten away if he had?"

"Because a car drove away from out back. Now if Ferrand had dropped out that window—"

"He'd have done it in pieces," Cranston interposed, "which he didn't. He was very much together when we saw him later. Ever hear of a midget contortionist, Margo?"

"Why, no!"

"Neither did Jim Selbert. Find one and you'll have a murder suspect. Only he would have to be twins to fill the Mephisto costume. So Selbert is still looking for Ferrand."

Dusk was closing in, the time when Lamont Cranston could become The Shadow and do some expert searching on his own. That was exactly what he planned, for his low laugh, heard only in the archway as he left the patio, marked the advent of another personality cloaked in black.

As Cranston, The Shadow had learned much; far more than anyone else supposed. Selbert's questions to Joan, plus those Cranston had asked Margo, were fitting some important pieces in murder's jigsaw.

Frederick Ferrand was still the man to find and perhaps The Shadow could accomplish it here in New Orleans while others were wasting time in their search of the bayou region.

XVI.

The chronicles of crime teem with instances of murderers who have returned to the scene of their deed, but the purpose behind that folly has been attributed to reasons more foolish than the thing itself.

Some analysts have attributed it to a killer's conscience, as if murderers were commonly burdened with such a handicap. Others claim that some horrible fascination is the cause, bringing the killer back to mope or gloat, according to his peculiar inclination.

Such theories, of course, belong to fiction, something in which The Shadow had never dealt.

To The Shadow, criminals were men whose game was to outwit the law. The best police officers were those who could outwit criminals at their own game. Therefore the test of a good police officer was how well his mind could duplicate the thoughts of the man he hunted. Hence in this case, Selbert's impressions were an index to Ferrand's.

Now it was neither conscience nor fascination that had caused Selbert to haunt Hoodoo House with the tenacity of a pet ghost. It was just that something didn't quite add up around the place and Selbert wanted to find out why not. Should Ferrand be apprehended

and Selbert find himself confronting the alleged killer in a court-
room, Jim would have to give answers to everything.

The same applied to Ferrand. He would have to prove Selbert's
figures wrong. Maybe Ferrand had calculated everything beforehand,
but that was prior to Selbert's connection with the case.

An exhaustive search of criminal records will produce few, if any,
instances of a murderer returning to a scene of crime until after the
police have been there. That was the nib in Ferrand's case. Guilty
or innocent, he was prey, and like the forest deer, Ferrand would
sniff the camp-fire smoke and from the darkness try to view the
hunter who would be gunning for him on the morrow.

This evening, Hoodoo House was comparable to a camp-fire. From
its windows came a wavery glow, while muffled sounds could be heard
within, as though a horde of ghoulish goblins were hard at work.

The night crew that was hacking up the cement floor looked like
goblins, too, for they were knee deep in rubble and therefore appeared of dwarfish stature. Taller were the two men who watched
the work: Hubert Aldion and Rolfe Trenhue.

They were equally glum. Both were making the best of a bad thing,
for Aldion owed no special thanks to Trenhue for having taken up
Ferrand's share in this questionable piece of real estate. Aldion
couldn't have made good on Ferrand's note and Trenhue knew it,
so the deal was purely automatic.

From the open front door, through which the stone dust drifted,
The Shadow viewed the hazy interior. His ears were alert for he recognized the advantage of the smoke screen that the dust cloud
formed. It would be an excellent lure for Ferrand, should the latter
be about. Jim Selbert was missing his best opportunity tonight.

Guarded footsteps proved it.

Those footfalls came from the mouth of the alley, working their
way along the friendly side wall. As dust swirled, the approaching
sounds halted, then resumed as the cloud gradually thinned.

The Shadow had timed it nicely and managed it neatly. His twist
from the enveloping dusk was responsible for the swirl that improved
the visibility to just the right degree.

The iron gate neither groaned nor clanged as The Shadow manipu-
lated it. The dim light from the dust-shrouded doorway showed the
bars and braces of that gate against a solid background that to all

appearances represented a vacant passage. The Shadow had the qualities of a chameleon when it came to blending with such settings.

Into the dimness came a pale, gaunt face, with hard-glaring eyes. It was Ferrand's face, now shaven, and therefore unrecognizable by his latest pictures, all of which were hunting snap-shots. Instead of the hunter's costume, Ferrand was wearing the garb of the New Orleans waterfront, dungarees with a dark blue cap to match.

What Ferrand saw through the dust encouraged him. Aldion and Trenhue had once been friends of his and still might be, with reasonable reservations. Selbert wasn't around, which eliminated the chief hazard. As for the workmen, Ferrand might have been one of them, judged by his attire, and that gave him confidence.

From his vantage spot, Cranston watched Ferrand's face undergo the evolution that transformed the hunted into the hunter. As the gaunt lips formed a taut smile, Ferrand's hand clutched the one thing necessary to bolster his self-assurance, the gun that bulged in his hip pocket.

Simultaneously The Shadow weighed an automatic, urging its muzzle deftly between the gate bars. One false move from Ferrand and The Shadow's gun would clang the gate. Such a touch would bring the gaunt man full about, too late to outspeed The Shadow in a duel.

Fortunately for Ferrand, he made no false move. Instead, he was merely careless.

Men were coming toward the door and like Ferrand, The Shadow could hear their footsteps and their voices.

Ferrand came into even closer range, back first.

The gate's slight clang occurred when Ferrand pressed his back against it, only an inch from The Shadow's withdrawn gun muzzle. As for Ferrand's revolver, The Shadow could have acquired it from the fellow's hip pocket, for Ferrand spread his arms against the gate to flatten himself further in the darkness.

No trouble was due from Ferrand yet.

Two men stepped from the house: Aldion and Trenhue. They stood outside the front door to hold a conversation that the workmen couldn't overhear.

"They'll be done tomorrow midnight," calculated Aldion, "if we keep them working steady. We'd better stay and watch the job right through."

Trenhue grunted an agreement.

"What about those letters?" asked Aldion anxiously. "You didn't give them to Selbert, did you?"

"He wasn't interested," replied Trenhue, "any more than Fred was. Somehow they both have bayous on their mind."

"Then it was just a coincidence, buying this house?"

"In a way, yes," decided Trenhue, "except that Fred went in for anything that had to do with old pirate tradition. Anyway, I took the letters back to Moubillard's. They belonged to him, you know."

"I know. Fred borrowed old documents from everybody."

"At least I saw that they were kept in their proper envelopes," said Trenhue, with a note of finality. "They'll all be returned to their proper owners when Selbert is through with them."

The two men went back into the house, disappearing through the inexhaustible dust that the stone hackers were producing. As Ferrand turned to the gate and opened it to go through, The Shadow swung back with it.

From then on, it wasn't necessary to trail Ferrand closely, for The Shadow knew exactly where the man would go.

To Moubillard's.

The famous old costume shop was locked and temporarily forgotten, until the appraisers would find time to come around and take stock, which could be almost any time between now and next year's Mardi Gras. But there was still a way into the place which Ferrand had heard about, even though he wasn't the person who had used it.

That way was the trap door through the roof, squarely into Moubillard's office, the place where the now important letters could be found.

Reaching the neighborhood in due course, The Shadow was in time to witness Ferrand's return from Moubillard's preserves. All The Shadow did was pick an observation spot from across the street, one which gave him a view of the space between Moubillard's roof and the hugely ornate balcony next door.

There, The Shadow glimpsed Ferrand's crouchy figure coming back to the balcony, but Ferrand wasn't merely carrying the mail. Or if he was, he was playing parcel postman, for with him he was bringing a light but bulky bundle that formed a double armful.

Letting Ferrand continue his departure unmolested, The Shadow turned and went the opposite direction, his whispered laugh blending like his cloaked figure into the thickness of the night.

Again, The Shadow's restrained mirth carried a prophetic note. Translated, it meant tomorrow—midnight.

XVII.

The dust in Hoodoo House was thicker but finer and it was becoming so troublesome that the workmen were wearing bandanna handkerchiefs around their faces so they could stand it. They weren't complaining, however, because their employers were paying overtime rates in order to get this annoying job finished.

It was most annoying, too, because Aldion and Trenhue were forced to stay up on the third floor to keep away from the dust. That was where Cranston and Selbert found them late the next afternoon, working over plans for remodeling the house.

Selbert coughed from the dust on the way upstairs and commented:

"It's terrible! Next thing, you chaps will be living in the cupola!"

"We have been," said Trenhue in his dry style. "At least at intervals. When we want fresh air we go up there and get some. Want to try?"

Selbert decided not. However, the cupola trip appealed to Cranston, so he climbed the ladder into the window-walled box above the room that formed the present quarters of Messrs. Aldion and Trenhue.

There, Cranston stayed to watch the Vieux Carré adjust itself to twilight.

Here and there came spots of light, not with the jeweled magnificence that characterized the greater city on the far side of Canal Street, but in a furtive style. The light was mostly a reflected glow, since this cupola by no means predominated the scene. There were buildings though that peeked at it, through spaces among intervening walls, and these interested Cranston most.

Definitely, Cranston was sighting toward a certain sector of the Quarter and he seemed pleased because his view of it was restricted. In brief, if Cranston had looked that direction from a higher elevation, he would have seen too many buildings, but from here he could observe only one.

Even better, his view was restricted to just the top floor of that building which he recognized as an ancient apartment house. And the top story was itself restricted, for it was undersized, as if the builders had grown weary and clamped the roof down a little too soon. Just a few pitiable windows, peering out from under eaves, but when a dim glow suddenly appeared from them, Cranston smiled.

All the while, Cranston had been hearing the conversation from below.

Jim Selbert was making most of it. He'd been comparing the data belonging to Ferrand with the much greater mass gathered by the research laboratory to which Cranston had assigned Margo and Joan.

"Take this fellow Dominique," Selbert was saying. "He spent half his lifetime around New Orleans and you'd spend half of yours trying to keep up with You. I don't mean yourself, I mean You—"

"Just call him Dominique," suggested Trenhue. "It will be easier for you."

"I guess You had a hard time of it," laughed Selbert, "and I mean Dominique. But let's switch to the bayou question. I'm not getting results."

"Maybe Ferrand isn't either," put in Aldion. "Anyway, he's probably having a hard time of it."

"I don't think so," declared Trenhue. "Let me tell you why."

Selbert wanted to hear and so did Cranston, though his arrival from the ladder at that moment simply indicated that he'd had enough fresh air.

"Tell me this," said Trenhue to Selbert. "Why did Ferrand spend so much time down in the bayou country?"

"Simple enough," returned Selbert. "He thinks Dominique stashed a load of treasure down there somewhere, before signing off with Lafitte and Company."

"Any evidence in favor of it?"

"Plenty. Take Vincent Gambi for instance. He played pirate too long. He was asleep on a pile of gold when his playmates busted him apart with a broad-axe. That's all told about in the data I've been reading. Dominique was smarter than Gambi, that's all."

"How much smarter?"

"Smart enough to bury his cash."

"Where somebody else would be waiting around when he dug it up?"

Selbert considered Trenhue's question. Then:

"Maybe you've got something," said Jim. "If you're right, Ferrand may have been wasting his time around a lot of empty diggings."

"Perhaps they're not empty any longer."

Selbert's frown was puzzled.

"What Rolfe means," put in Aldion, "is that you haven't found the cash that went with the Louisiana Lottery."

Impressed, Selbert looked to Cranston, who gave the slightest of nods.

"It would be a good way to bury loot," Cranston decided. "Right on the site of a forgotten treasure trove." He turned from Aldion to Trenhue. "Could you think of any better way?"

"I think Dominique did," returned Trenhue, frankly. "I am confident he buried his share right here in New Orleans."

"What gives you that idea?" asked Selbert.

"Because Dominique stayed here," Trenhue replied. "He made a point of it. Why, when he died in 1830 he was one of the biggest men in town. They hung the flags at half-mast."

"I read about it," nodded Selbert. "In that French newspaper, L'Abeille." He turned to Cranston. "It was in the stuff the girls gathered."

Cranston gave a tired nod. He needed more fresh air so he climbed up into the cupola to get it.

"Getting back to date," said Trenhue to Selbert, "Ferrand may have returned from his bayou trip."

"You mean he's put the Lottery cash where we won't find it?" queried Selbert. "That he figures now he can beat the murder rap for lack of evidence?"

"That's what we both think," blurted Aldion. Then, as Trenhue gestured for him to tone down, he added in a lower voice. "It's why we're digging the cement. To worry Ferrand."

Interested, Selbert wanted to hear more. It was Trenhue who glanced up to the cupola, gave a hush-hush gesture and then whispered so that Cranston wouldn't hear:

"That's only one reason. The other is, we think we may come across Dominique's treasure."

Aldion gave a despairing gesture:

"But, Rolfe—"

"It's all right, Hubert." Trenhue's undertone was calm. "We got our break and Jim is entitled to his." Turning to Selbert, Trenhue explained. "Remember those Dominique letters that were in Moubillard's envelope?"

Selbert nodded.

"Political stuff. I didn't read them."

"I did," confided Trenhue. "There was one addressed to the editor of *L'Abeille* when Dominique rigged out the brig *Seraphine* to rescue Napoleon from St. Helena."

Selbert shook his head.

"I don't remember it."

"Napoleon died before Dominique could start," continued Trenhue, "so he never sent the letter. But it happened Dominique thought he was the one who might be dead soon, so the letter was written something like a will."

This interested Selbert.

"There were some flowery phrases in it," recalled Trenhue. "One about New Orleans being a land of treasure—"

"And a man's real treasure," quoted Aldion, as Trenhue paused, "being in his home. That was when Dominique lived here."

Eyebrows raised, Selbert gestured downward with his thumb, meaning the sound of pick-axes that kept persisting from below.

"You mean?"

"Just that," undertoned Trenhue. "Come around after the workmen leave at midnight, in case we find some treasure."

"And in case Ferrand finds us," added Aldion, cautiously. "We figure he may."

"Fifty-fifty," agreed Selbert grimly. "You can have the treasure. I'll take Ferrand."

The looks that Aldion exchanged with Trenhue were accompanied by nods, indicating that they were both right in their estimate of Selbert as a man who believed in duty first, last, and all the time.

The acoustics of the cupola were perfect, at least from Cranston's standpoint. It picked up everything that had been said, like a big mechanical ear; hence Cranston had heard all. But that wasn't exactly why Cranston came down from his temporary perch.

What Lamont Cranston had heard, he had already anticipated. What he had just seen was more important.

The lights in those dim windows beneath the distant eaves had turned off.

Lamont Cranston had another appointment, as The Shadow.

XVIII.

The window slid sideward and The Shadow squeezed through. Windows in this room couldn't go upward, or they would raise the roof. This was the tiny, forgotten apartment that The Shadow had spotted from the cupola of the Hoodoo House.

It went back to Joan's statement to Selbert; when she had told the police captain how she had looked for Ferrand in some of his hangouts in the French Quarter. When a man habituated several places in the same neighborhood, it indicated that he was used to living there.

If Joan had known that Ferrand had some hideaway, she would have said so. There were others who might know without stating it. The Shadow had played that chance. Of all the places in the limited area where Ferrand's hideaway might be, this was the only one that could be seen from the cupola, so The Shadow had resolved to try it.

Lights out meant that Ferrand had left, provided these were really his quarters.

They were.

The Mask of Mephisto said so without words as it stared from a heap of cloth that represented a crimson cape. This was the bundle that Ferrand had brought from Moubillard's shop, following a clandestine visit there. But it wasn't all that showed under the concentrated beam of The Shadow's probing headlight.

Of a stack of letters resting on a battered table, one was open. Its ink was dim, its writing old-fashioned, this letter that bore the signature of Dominique You. Dated May first, 1821, it was addressed to the editor of *L'Abeille* and was couched in the very phrases described by Rolfe Trenhue, the language, of course, being French.

His brief inspection of Ferrand's hide-out ended, The Shadow left by the conventional stairway route and soon appeared in his more prosaic guise of Lamont Cranston. The evening being young, Cranston still had time to call at some of the old coin shops that were staying open evenings because trade was so good.

Margo Lane was spared that ordeal. She had gone to a show with Joan and Ken. They were to meet Cranston later at the coffee stand and on Joan's account, he'd carefully specified which one. Cranston didn't want to stay waiting at the other end of the French Market, the way Trenhue had before he met Joan on Mardi Gras Night.

Cranston bought some old coins this evening. The dealers were quite surprised because previously he'd been selling items of this sort. He was a meticulous collector, Cranston, making very careful records of every transaction, even when he sold at bargain prices.

Tonight, Cranston was still in the last coin shop when it closed and finding that he had time to spare, he rode over to police headquarters to chat with Captain Selbert. In the midst of writing comprehensive reports, Selbert looked up with a smile of greeting, then switched to a disappointed frown.

"Sorry, Cranston." Selbert spoke in the manner of a man who suddenly remembered something. "I'm very busy. Suppose we have lunch tomorrow so we can talk over new developments. I know you're as interested in this Ferrand case as I am, but look at how I'm swamped!"

Spreading his arms to indicate a desk-load of papers, Selbert promptly burrowed into them. This was Jim's way to let a visitor see for himself that there was plenty of work to do. Cranston evidently took the hint, for when Selbert looked up, his caller was gone. Selbert himself left shortly afterward, locking the office behind him.

A satisfied smile accompanied Jim's turn of the key. He hadn't bothered to look in the corner behind the door where the Mephisto costume hung, but he knew it would still be there, now that he had locked the door.

Chance was playing a hand tonight.

Coming from the theater, Joan Marcy lost her gaiety as she and her companions neared the Hoodoo House. Somehow the mere proximity of the place filled Joan with a sense of horror and she said so. Ken Langdon and Margo Lane agreed they didn't have to pass it on their route, so they took a detour to the old French Market.

That was why Joan saw the beardless man.

Though the weather was warm, his face was muffled as he came from a cafe that Joan remembered. Adjusting his coat collar, he inadvertently let his gaunt face show. Joan remembered that face and too well. She lagged to watch where the man went.

Ken noted Joan's absence at the next corner and was worried.

"You'd better go ahead," Ken told Margo. "I can't imagine what happened to Joan." Uneasily, Ken looked along the building fronts and noted the most likely doorway. "I'll find her, though, and soon."

At the coffee stand, Cranston was waiting when Margo arrived there. Finding that she was worried about Ken as well as Joan, Cranston volunteered to find them both. His departure left Margo wondering, considering that disappearances were in order.

There was a reason for those disappearances.

Joan was the first to learn it when she cautiously put her hand upon the door-knob of a top floor apartment where she was sure Fred Ferrand had gone. All the way up the stairs, Joan had been hearing footsteps creak ahead of her. Right now, she wanted another glimpse of the gaunt man to make certain he was Fred.

The glimpse was easy, but the face was different.

Opening suddenly from the other side the door revealed the red-caped figure of King Satan, the mystery sensation of the recent Mardi Gras!

Joan couldn't cry out. Two red gauntlets grasped her neck in a relentless grip that didn't relax until she sagged weakly to the floor. When Joan opened her eyes, she was bound and gagged in a corner and the triumphant Mephisto was bowing an ironical good-night from the doorway.

Only the great Mephistopheles wasn't so devilishly clever as he thought. Beyond him, about to deliver a hard, vengeful lunge, was Ken Langdon. Joan made a funny face, which would have been a smile if she hadn't been biting a gag. Such as it was, the smile didn't last.

A doorful of blackness took Ken so suddenly and silently that he disappeared as though he had fallen through a trap-door in space. Completely baffled, Joan could only stare at the vacancy behind the Devil Man whose costume hid Fred Ferrand. When King Satan turned and stalked from the room, Ken was still missing.

It took another mystery to explain the first. At the end of a few minutes that seemed twice that many hours, the door opened and Ken came rolling in as tightly bound and gagged as Joan. When it came to taking meddlers out of circulation, King Satan and The Shadow were both efficient, but the score was in The Shadow's favor.

This blackness that lived had staged Ken's capture behind the very back of a crimson clad impostor who hadn't the least notion that The Shadow was even around!

Their official meeting was coming later. The Shadow in his guise of black, could travel directly and rapidly to his goal.

That goal was to be the scene where first the Mask of Mephisto had served to cover murder. The stage was set in the Devil's own Den, where a quest for treasure was a bait to lure men to their doom!

XIX.

The last of the workmen had gone from the Hoodoo House, but one it seemed, had reason to return. He was carrying a pick over his shoulder as a bit of realism that didn't fit. First, the pick was rusty, proving it hadn't been used; again, the men who had left the house hadn't brought their tools with them.

Nevertheless, Jim Selbert's disguise of cap and dungarees was good enough to pass muster. What really bothered him was the delay after he knocked at the door. Aldion and Trenhue must have gone upstairs for it was several minutes before they heard Jim's guarded raps and answered.

Recognizing the returned workman, both nodded approval. Leaving the door ajar, they beckoned Jim to the center of the floor, and suggested that he lend a hand. Emerging from the earth was the end of an old coffer that came up heavily under their combined pull. Borrowing Selbert's pick, Trenhue cracked it open.

As the box tilted, from its interior came a shower of gold and silver coins that rattled across the broken paving. Dropping to hands and knees, Aldion began scooping the wealth like the truckers shoveled shrimp, paying no heed to the odd coins that rolled willy-nilly.

"Dominique's treasure!" shrilled Aldion. "The money he left for us to find! It's ours, Rolfe—ours—"

Gesturing for Aldion to calm himself, Trenhue was none too soon. Above the clatter of the coins came the groan of the front door as it swung inward and with it listeners heard a grated laugh that lost nothing by its muffled quality.

King Satan stood upon the threshold of his former domain.

The scene was much like that strange occasion when these premises had teemed with half-awed merrymakers who had been accepting this Satanic masquerade as travesty until it had proved tragedy. Tonight, however, the situation was in strict reverse; if the man in the Mephisto Mask had begun with shooting and on a wholesale basis, it might well have been in keeping with the circumstances.

However, he did not fire, even though his fisted gauntlet held a gun.

Instead, he simply kept people covered, with special attention to Selbert, whose presence was something of a surprise to the man in red. Toward Aldion and Trenhue, King Satan was somewhat disdainful, for they looked quite pitiful, half-crouched above their tilted treasure chest.

Only His Satanic Majesty was taking no long chances. He preferred to reveal his hand. With a sweep of his free gauntlet, he removed the huge disguising head and let his own come into sight.

Revealed, the face of Frederick Ferrand was as hard-set as the chunks of stone that lay in heaps about the broken floor. His eyes showed a glint that rivaled the ancient coins which were spilled from the treasure chest. Ferrand's tone, too, was metallic.

"I am glad you are here, Selbert," announced Ferrand, with a side flash of his eyes. "Perhaps this evidence of a double-cross will convince you of my innocence. Or perhaps"—the eyes turned on Aldion and Trenhue—"perhaps I should term it double-double."

From somewhere in his cape, Ferrand whipped out a sheet of paper and flipped it toward Selbert. It fell at the police captain's feet.

"Pick it up," ordered Ferrand. "Read it. You will find that is a Dominique letter written to the editor of L'Abeille in the year 1821, but never sent. It covers the matter of this treasure which these friends of mine"—Ferrand's gun gestured toward Aldion and Trenhue—"coveted enough to deal in murder."

Appealing glances from Aldion and Trenhue were directed toward Selbert, who boldly took up their defence.

"Nobody had to murder Chardelle to get this treasure," declared Selbert. "The same applied to Moubillard. He didn't even know what was in this Dominique letter and he didn't even have it because it was with the stuff you left with Trenhue."

Ferrand didn't even sneer.

"Go on," he said coldly.

"Chardelle let you in on the Lottery deal," analyzed Selbert, "so you knocked him off and then went after Moubillard, because he knew too much about you."

"No more than anyone else did," put in Ferrand. "I was scheduled to play King Satan, but I told Chardelle not to count on me."

Selbert's eyebrows lifted; then he questioned:

"Why didn't you tell Tourville?"

"Because Chardelle was the Messenger," returned Ferrand, "and it was his business to inform Tourville, who served as scribe. Only I don't think Chardelle did; he was too crooked. Somebody mooched into this game, somebody who played Mephisto in my place, and I'd suggest you talk to a chap named Kenneth Langdon."

Now Selbert had been thinking somewhat along those very lines, but in a trifling way. Knowing how trifles could build up to greater factors, Jim listened.

"Maybe Langdon was just a front," conceded Ferrand, "but he's interested in more things than sculpture, Joan Marcy for one. Understand, I'm not blaming Joan. She and I were quits and most of the fault was mine. But getting back to my own case; after I found this costume at Moubillard's, last night—"

"At Moubillard's!" broke in Selbert. "And last night! Why it was in my office only this evening. The only reason I wasn't surprised to see you walk in wearing it, was because you were smart enough to borrow it from my office once before."

From Ferrand's cold stare it seemed he didn't believe any of this. It took the quick wits of Aldion and Trenhue to supply the simple answer.

"Langdon was fronting all right!" exclaimed Aldion. "He was fronting for Ferrand!"

"In another Mephisto Mask," added Trenhue, "so Fred here would have an alibi."

"Only Fred couldn't wait to kill Chardelle—"

"Maybe he was trying to toss the crime on Langdon. Now we're getting the right answer!"

That theory clicked with Selbert, particularly because it awoke Ferrand's rage. Of course anger was a common thing with Ferrand, but he was a rough man when his temper ruled him. And now, glaring unmasked from the crimson collar of his Mephisto cape, Ferrand's face was demoniac in the lantern light. His rage showed all the venom of a murderer's as he wheeled toward Aldion and Ferrand.

They weren't to be taken by surprise, the way Chardelle had been. They'd provided for this very emergency by dint of their successful treasure hunt. They dropped, not just behind the money coffer, but down into the pit they'd dug it from. Drawing guns, they were set to wither Ferrand from their improvised foxhole.

The complication was Jim Selbert.

With Ferrand's wheel, Selbert lunged. Not wasting time to draw his own gun, Jim was going after Ferrand as the most efficient way to prevent new massacre and at the same time gain a needed weapon.

Before either Aldion or Trenhue could aim at Ferrand, the grappling had begun. Two brawny men were stumbling about the up-heaved floor, with Selbert doing right well by himself. So well in fact, that Selbert hoped to take Ferrand alive and therefore was using craft as much as strength.

There was one point, though, that Selbert overlooked. Aldion and Trenhue, half up from their fox-hole were waiting only until Ferrand twisted in their direction, before letting their guns rip. Then the interruption came.

It was a hollow laugh, almost a replica of the Satanic mirth that Ferrand had himself delivered, but it came from the high stairway echoing from the very landing where a crimson murderer had made his first entrance on Mardi Gras Night.

Hearing such defiance, Aldion and Trenhue turned. There stood the living proof of the double Devil game, another King Satan clad in crimson, his features hidden within the ample scope of a duplicate Mask of Mephisto!

Arms folded, crime's new candidate seemed to regard himself the real master of this show, but Aldion and Trenhue were no respecters of persons—or demons. Anyone who wore the crimson garb of murder was entitled to quick death. As guns swung up toward the stairway, the crimson menace seemed to realize it, for he flung himself forward in a titanic dive toward the broken floor below.

Guns blasted the hurtling Satan and amid the hail of bullets, His Hellish Highness disappeared completely in mid-air!

XX.

It was the impossible realized.

This new candidate for Satanic honors had lived up to his part.

It seemed that he had plucked aside a curtain in space and let it swallow him. Not only were Aldion and Trenhue nonplussed; Selbert and Ferrand forgot their struggle and froze like a posed movie still.

Out of somewhere came an echoed laugh, no longer hollow. It rose to a chilling taunt and with it, there appeared another figure from the semi-gloom of the stairs. He was cloaked in black, visible when he reached the spot where the flying Satan had evaporated. By then, his guns were visible too, and they were big ones, automatics of .45 caliber.

The Shadow was holding the whole scene static with those looming muzzles. When he reached the bottom of the steps, he kicked something that had wedged from sight between two upturned chunks of cement. Bouncing across the rough floor, the object revealed what it was.

The costume of the vanished King Satan!

Now for the first time, Jim Selbert was realizing the chief feature of such a costume. The great head was attached to the cape collar, the long gauntlets hooked to the flowing cuffs. The lining of the cape was black, of cheaper stuff than the crimson satin that formed the outside.

A matter of economy, such a lining, but it served another purpose when required.

An upward peel of the cape and the whole thing not only turned inside out, but could gather the Mask of Mephisto within its folds! There was the evidence on the floor, where The Shadow had kicked the bundle apart to let the Mephisto Mask peer from the reversible cape.

More potent still was the thought that drilled through Selbert's mind, as though The Shadow's laugh, as well as his cloaked garb, inspired it.

Because of its ample head and sizable cape, the Devil's costume allowed the wearing of another masquerade beneath! The Shadow had demonstrated it, though his attire was not strictly a masquerade. He'd come down the stairs layered as Mephisto; his whip-fling of the crimson costume had left him as himself. The hurl had turned the red cape inside out, swallowing the Mask inside it.

No wonder the Devil had disappeared amid the flay of bullets! No eyes had followed the downward fall of the black bundle, any more than they had looked up to probe the higher gloom wherein The Shadow had remained.

But The Shadow's laugh told more. Catching the inference, Jim Selbert relaxed as he stared at the half-spread bundle.

"So that's how the Devil went!" exclaimed Jim. "Out through the little window on the second floor! All that had to go was the costume, but somebody else stayed."

Wondering who else, Selbert decided to ask the only person who had been here at the time of Chardelle's death. Jim turned to Hubert Aldion.

"Who was it?"

"—I wouldn't know," stammered Aldion. "I was the Seneschal, you know. I was wearing a blue uniform and I was over by that door." Gesturing toward the outer door, Aldion added suddenly:

"Ask her, she knows."

The person in question was Margo Lane. Tired of hunting everywhere else for the friends who had deserted her, Margo had finally come to the Hoodoo House.

"Yes, the Seneschal was standing over here," acknowledged Margo, slowly, "but his costume wasn't entirely blue. The coat was blue; the trousers were red."

The Shadow's low laugh showed that he appreciated that fuller description. So did Jim Selbert.

"Red to match the Devil's costume!" Releasing Ferrand who stood by with lowered gun, Selbert approached Aldion. "When you chased up to the second floor, which way did you go?"

"Why—the quickest way." Aldion was much confused. "I helped smash one door—"

"And you yanked open the other," put in Selbert. "But which door was which?"

Aldion tried to answer, but hesitancy gripped him. The Shadow's laugh, supplying its same low tone, prompted Selbert to turn his quiz into direct accusation.

"You won't say which," Selbert told Aldion, "because you know the witnesses will disagree when I get around to asking them. They all remember you opening one door, so they think you crashed the other." Looking toward The Shadow, Selbert caught the glint of burning eyes beneath the hat brim. Realizing he was right, Jim drove home the final point. "What you did was peel the Devil's costume and chuck it through that window; then you yanked both doors open. You were the killer in the Mephisto Mask!"

Almost wilting under the accusation, Aldion finally rallied and gestured feebly to Margo.

"She'll tell you I was by the outer door. I was standing there when Chardelle was murdered."

"Somebody was standing there," conceded Margo. "Somebody costumed as the Seneschal. Only I don't know how he got there in the first place; I just remember that he started outside."

"After the murder?" queried Selbert.

"Yes," replied Margo. "Then next, I saw him upstairs. The Seneschal, I mean, or someone in such a costume. I wonder—"

The Shadow wasn't wondering. His laugh supplied the difference and Selbert grasped it.

"Wondering if there were two Seneschal costumes," declared Jim. "Why not? There were two Masks of Mephisto. You've clinched it, Miss Lane. Aldion must have gone upstairs while everybody was watching the Lottery pay off. Another Seneschal took his place inside the door!"

"And later went around through the little gate!" Margo exclaimed. "Why it could have been his car that I heard leave in back!"

Looking straight at The Shadow as she spoke, Margo was recalling Cranston's earlier interest in the matter of that departing car. Another idea struck her, but Selbert was first with it.

"That car was parked under the little window," decided Jim. "The costume and the Mask landed right in it. Whoever drove away took it with him—"

There was a pause, as Selbert's chain of thought continued. This time it was The Shadow who supplied the climax by completing the sentence in a strangely sinister tone:

"—And wore it when he murdered Henri Moubillard, who unfortunately saw Ken Langdon come in with the other costume."

That brought a quick response from Fred Ferrand.

"I get it now! They were using this Langdon chap to put the frame on me! But they were playing it two ways. If my bayou alibi held, they could switch the works on Langdon. Since there were two of them, why not have two of us. Two of them—"

Pausing with his repetition, Ferrand heard the approving laugh of The Shadow. The term "two of them" held, because Aldion hadn't been at large to murder Moubillard as a follow-up to Chardelle's death.

And if Hubert Aldion was one, Rolfe Trenhue must be the other.

All eyes were on Trenhue as The Shadow spoke the accusation that had grown in every mind.

"You were late in meeting Joan Marcy," stated The Shadow, "because you were needed here, Trenhue, to double as Seneschal. From the Borneau Mansion you drove to the costume shop, murdered Moubillard, and sped back again. Brief though the interim was, you have no alibi to cover it."

Trenhue hadn't and he knew it. He was afraid to argue the point, because he saw mistrust in Aldion's gaze. These partners in murder could each expose the other and both knew it. The best Trenhue could do was voice something that might help them mutually.

"How could we have known about the Lottery money?" demanded Trenhue. "Let's hear someone answer that."

"Chardelle told Aldion," returned The Shadow. "That gave them the majority vote over Tourville, since Ferrand was too busy hunting treasure to play the Devil for the Krewe of Hades. Then Aldion told you, Trenhue."

"I would have been a fool!" broke in Aldion. "What would have made me double-cross Chardelle?"

"One hundred thousand dollars," announced The Shadow. "You took the prize money from the box before you sealed it. You needed a partner to stage what you thought would be a perfect murder. Chardelle's death was necessary to keep the Lottery ring from learning that he took you into his confidence."

Jim Selbert was stepping forward with Ferrand's gun. His feet were clinking loose coins from the treasure coffer as he queried:

"Where did you two stow that prize money?"

The Shadow's low laugh joined the jangle of the coins that were answering for Aldion and Trenhue. Stooping, Selbert picked up some of the loose gold and silver.

"Old coins," spoke The Shadow. "Collectors' coins. Check them at the local shops and many of them will be identified, Selbert. Of course the dates are long enough ago. Aldion and Trenhue wouldn't have overlooked that when they liquidated the Lottery money to turn it into treasure that Dominique never buried.

"Dominique's letter is better evidence, Selbert. It won't take an expert to prove it a clever forgery. Dominique couldn't have addressed it to the editor of the famous *L'Abeille*, because the newspaper was not founded until six years after the *Seraphine* was fitted for the cruise she never took."

So impressive were The Shadow's words that Selbert reached for the letter. To get it from his pocket he placed the gun beneath his arm, since his other hand was full of coins. Up from their pit came Aldion and Trenhue; flinging Selbert from their path, they drove for the outer door.

Despite its warning, The Shadow's fierce laugh spurred the fugitives instead of halting them. His gun would have spoken next; he was waiting only until the murderers bottlenecked each other at the door. But at that moment, Ken Langdon made a most untimely arrival, with Joan Marcy right behind him.

Seeing guns muzzle-first, Ken flung Joan away from them. Turning to block the fugitives, Ken was grabbed by Aldion, who flung him in Trenhue's path. Unobstructed, Aldion sprang through the door as Trenhue sprawled across the threshold. There, Trenhue heard the taunt of The Shadow's approaching laugh, half-triumphant it seemed, because one murderer had remained within his reach.

Trenhue saw that it wasn't only one.

Coming to his feet Trenhue lunged through the doorway, blasting shots ahead. He'd stop Aldion, the man who had left him to his plight, rather than turn and face The Shadow. Stop Aldion Trenhue did, and a few moments later Trenhue was racing past his floundering partner.

From the cobbles where Trenhue's bullets had dropped him, Aldion raised himself on one elbow and gave the final say in this game of each man for himself. Aldion said it with bullets too and his dying grip did not destroy his aim. As Trenhue telescoped across the curb beyond the alley, Aldion sagged and lay equally still.

They were murderers to the finish, those two Mephistos, even when they were no longer wearers of the Mask. As they had canceled each other, so did they write off themselves, with The Shadow's laugh their deathknell.

The next day, Jim Selbert had a problem for Lamont Cranston when the latter stopped at his office to say good-bye.

"It left me woozy," expressed Jim, "the way that Shadow guy disappeared. He must have taken the Devil's costume that was here in the office and right from under our noses, too. Because we know that Ferrand was wearing the duplicate that Aldion and Trenhue planted in Moubillard's shop, hoping Ferrand would wear it and make himself a goat, which he did.

"But here's the problem. Who took the costume that was hanging here, the day the Masked Mephisto popped into Langdon's studio and tried to murder Joan Marcy? It couldn't have been Trenhue; he went along with me. Aldion wouldn't have had time to get out here from his office and back to Langdon's studio."

Cranston considered the problem briefly. Then:

"It was Aldion," he decided. "Wearing the duplicate costume, he had plenty of time to work it that way."

Selbert smiled wisely.

"I thought you'd say that," he nodded. "But how did Aldion know that Ferrand had slipped the deputies and that Langdon had made a dumb trip out here? Unless he knew, he wouldn't have tried another of those double frames."

"Remember the phone call Trenhue made to his house?" queried Cranston. "Before you started out to look for Ferrand?"

"Why, yes. It was about some papers. I wasn't here—"

Cranston didn't have to interrupt. Selbert did it for himself.

"He called Aldion instead!" exclaimed Jim. "The duplicate costume must have been in Aldion's office, so when Trenhue slipped the dope about Ferrand and Langdon, the rest was a cinch."

"Any other questions, Captain Selbert?"

Jim Selbert had none. He and Lamont Cranston just shook hands and said good-bye. Grinning from two corners of the office were two great empty faces that seemed to enjoy this parting scene.

They were the Masks of Mephisto.

THE END.

PART TWO

MURDER BY MAGIC

I.

From the street the sign read:

Cigam was a neat name for a magic shop, even though it wasn't the name of the man who ran the place. Spelling Magic backward to form the word Cigam, was an old gag, perhaps, but it was new to the general public.

And Cigam was making a play for the general trade, even to demonstrating tricks in his second floor front window, which drew attention—and customers—from the street. He was rather clever, this drab proprietor who called himself Cigam.

Only today, Cigam wasn't working in the window.

It was six o'clock and the shop was packed because this was a Saturday afternoon. Usually though, the crowd began to thin before six, which was the closing hour, but today Cigam couldn't get rid of the customers.

Maybe it was because this Saturday fell on the full of the moon, or possibly it was on account of the show that the Universal Wizards Association had scheduled for tomorrow night. Some of Cigam's customers were at least buying tickets for the show, even though they weren't purchasing any of the magical apparatus with which his shelves and counters were full.

Yes, Saturday was just a big headache for a magic dealer.

Youngsters in short pants were gawking into the glass-topped counters trying to guess the purposes of the gimmicks they saw displayed there. Others, a few years older, were dropping billiard balls and thimbles as they tried to show each other their pet sleights.

Over in a corner, Val Varno was performing deft one-hand cuts with a pack of cards, winning enthusiastic acclaim from an adolescent gallery whose quick-change voices tempted Cigam to sell them ventriloquist dummies instead of magical apparatus.

What bothered Cigam even more was the private conference between Glanville Frost and Zed Zito. Suave and persuasive, Frost was a manufacturer of magical apparatus who looked as though he could sell anything. Blunt, challenging Zito was a performer who didn't want to be sold. Nevertheless, Cigam didn't like to have other people doing business in a shop where he paid the rent.

Then Cigam forgot his lesser troubles because of Wade Winstrom.

Big, imposing, firm of eye and jaw, Winstrom looked like the business magnate that he was. Brushing through the juvenile customers as he would a flock of office boys, Winstrom arrived at the counter, laid down a bundle of currency, and gave Cigam a steady stare.

"Sorry, Mr. Winstrom," Cigam apologized. "I haven't had a chance to pack the stuff you want. If you can only give me until Monday—"

Winstrom looked around the shop and its confusion caused a sympathetic smile to appear on his broad lips. Waving for Cigam to keep the money, Winstrom gave an obliging nod, and turned toward the door. He was blocked off by a squad of whipper-snappers who were pouncing for the counter telephone, only to have Cigam intervene.

"No phone calls, boys!" declared Cigam. "The shop is closing right away."

That brought an argument.

"We're only calling Demo Sharpe—"

"So we can try the new phone trick you sold us—"

"The instruction sheet says to call him any time after six o'clock—"

"And he'll name any card we think of—"

Cigam ended all that by banging the counter.

"If it's six o'clock, this shop is closed," he asserted, "and that's official. Use the phone in the lunch room across the street. I charge a nickel for all calls you make here anyway."

Across the street a calm-faced gentleman was sitting in the window of the lunch room finishing a cup of coffee while he idly studied Cigam's second floor shop, or as much of it as could be seen through the upstairs show window.

The gentleman's name was Lamont Cranston and he could easily have learned all that was happening in Cigam's by going up there, but in that case he would have missed something else that was happening in the lunch room.

Two rather obnoxious characters were also keeping their eyes on Cigam's without realizing that Cranston had them under observation.

Familiarly, these two characters were known as Louie the Grift and Side-face Sam and they represented what might have been termed in better circles a renaissance of the gangster epoch in American history.

Louie the Grift saw Mr. Winstrom come out the street door beneath Cigam's shop and get into a chauffeured limousine that promptly drove away.

"There goes the big dough customer." It was the Grift who said it. "I'll bet he left a sheaf of moola with Cigam for some of the junk the guy peddles."

"Peel an eye upstairs," suggested Side-face, speaking from the side of his mouth that he wasn't feeding with a ham sandwich, "and you'll win your own money."

The upstairs window showed Cigam opening an old-fashioned safe which had a door that unfortunately opened in the other direction. Cigam was equally unfortunate in counting his cash slowly and twice before putting it away. The long-distance witnesses could see that it was plenty.

Having seen all they wanted in Cigam's window, neither Side-face nor the Grift bothered to watch the lights go out. It was the astute Mr. Cranston who studied that procedure and later saw Cigam come out the street door with three of his professional patrons.

Those three were recognizable at a distance, even in the dusk. From left to right they were:

Val Varno, master manipulator, whose offer of five thousand dollars to anyone who could duplicate his skill at sleight of hand had never been challenged, chiefly because it was known that Varno didn't have the money.

Glanville Frost, creator and manufacturer of more magical tricks and illusions than any other inventive genius, including all persons whose ideas he had appropriated.

Zed Zito, hypnotist, mentalist and manager of the famed Miss Libra whose uncanny faculty had baffled every scientist who had witnessed her amazing performances which by a peculiar coincidence had never excited scientific investigation.

Cranston didn't blame Cigam for locking the street door. Only

Cigam should have had more judgment than to use a type of padlock
that anybody could open with one of the gadgets that Cigam himself
sold for fifty cents.

These masters of mystery, Cigam included, didn't bother to come
across the street and learn how Demo's telephone trick was working.
They simply parted and stalked away in their various directions.

Maybe they took it for granted that Demo was naming the cards
that people called for. In fact Demo was, much to the annoyance
of two lunch room customers.

"If them punks would lam," sidemouthed Side-face, "we could
start working on that joint across the way."

"Give 'em time," returned Louie. "It ought to be a little darker
anyhow."

"It's dark enough now. For me, anyway, providing you stick here
to flash copper if one comes along."

"Okay, only let's wait until the dead-pan guy fills up on Java. I'd
rather see new faces before we move."

The "dead-pan guy" was Cranston and he became obliging a few
minutes later. Maybe he'd just been waiting until Cigam's younger
customers had finished letting Demo baffle them with his telephone
mystery. Whatever the case as soon as the cluster had gone from
around the telephone, Cranston strolled out too and moved leisurely
away along the almost-deserted street.

Only Cranston didn't walk far.

Half way down the block, he stepped into a darkened doorway
and opened the bottom of a special brief case that he carried. From
between the inverted V of the two partitions, Cranston brought out a
tight-packed black cloak and a flattened slouch hat.

As Cranston put on those garments, he adjusted a brace of automatics that he already packed beneath his business suit in their
well designed holsters. Then, a gliding shape of blackness, this transformed personage edged forth into the thickened dusk.

It was rather magical, the way Lamont Cranston became The
Shadow.

II.

Louie the Grift didn't have one of Cigam's fifty-cent gadgets.

What he had was a revolver and one whack of the butt did a complete job with the street door padlock. Turning around, Louie blocked all sight of that damage and looked over at the lunch room. Side-face Sam kept working on another sandwich. He saw nothing to worry him and neither did Louie. The grunt Louie gave meant that if the street had become dark enough for Side-face, it was dark enough for Louie too.

Only it happened to be too dark for both of them.

Close enough to touch Louie with a ten foot pole and have three yards to spare was a figure so black that it passed as part of the wall against which it stood. With a simple reach of his gloved fist The Shadow could have stopped Louie's first move toward burglary.

Only it wasn't The Shadow's policy to frustrate people like the Grift until they neared their ultimate objective. Crime was coming back and The Shadow recognized it; therefore he needed a few examples to prove properly that crime did not pay. Tonight was an excellent opportunity for such an object lesson.

To trap Louie actually at Cigam's safe and phone the police to round up Side-face as a preliminary would be a feather in The Shadow's cap. But he would prefer to divide the feather between a police inspector named Joe Cardona and a reporter, Clyde Burke, who would give the incident due publicity and thereby discourage similar endeavors by lawless characters.

So when Louie opened the street door, The Shadow let the Grift enter unmolested. In fact he gave Louie considerable leeway. The Shadow was timing his own entry until he saw Side-face begin to look upward at Cigam's window. However small Sam's chance of glimpsing The Shadow, it wasn't worth the taking while a moral issue was at stake.

That was why Louie the Grift had little trouble reaching Cigam's upstairs door and not much more in cracking that second barrier. For the door that said CIGAM—MAGIC had a glass panel and by cracking a chunk from the corner, Louie was able to reach through and turn the knob on the inside.

Closing the door behind him, Louie looked around a trifle warily. Street lamps that didn't show the lower doorway did manage to give the shop a glow and Louie had never seen any more of this shop than the area visible through the show window.

And a magic shop was a rather uncanny place to anyone unused to it.

The counters weren't so bad. They contained small items like silk handkerchiefs, packs of cards, small canisters, miniature billiard balls, glasses, odd-looking coins that weren't money, and small nickel-plated tubes and boxes.

What impressed the Grift were the shelves behind the counter. There he saw boxes big enough for rabbits, portable tables with fancy drapes, big dice that would half fill a hat, fancy trays, bowls, and clusters of peculiar looking flowers.

One rack in particular commanded full attention. It formed a sort of wall beside a door leading to a back room and on its shelves were exhibits of magic as it used to be.

At the left of one tall shelf hung a curious clock dial made entirely of glass and furnished with a long flat pointer like a single hand. Over at the right, past a pyramid of small square bird cages was an upright metal rod set in a pedestal. On this rod was a large ball, pierced through the center to allow the passage of the rod. The surface of the globe was studded with fancy stars.

It was the large clock dial that captured Louie's eye and with good reason, for the pointer suddenly began to spin as though actuated by some invisible hand. Creeping toward the counter, Louie planted his hands there, forgetful of such minor things as fingerprints, and simply gawked.

That whirring pointer was making Louie's own wits whirl. He hadn't expected Cigam's shop to go magic on him!

Outside the shop door, blackness was looming up the stairs from below, its approach a symbol of coming trouble for Louie the Grift. But Louie was too busy wondering about Cigam's mysteries to be thinking in terms of The Shadow.

It wasn't just the clock dial that was behaving oddly now. The big ball was starting to move up and down on the rod finishing each drop with a sharp click as though counting off the seconds that the one-hand clock wasn't registering.

In the hallway The Shadow halted, his cloaked form barely outlined against the thicker blackness of the wall. The Shadow could hear those clacks from the spirit ball and for the moment was at a loss to define them.

The Shadow wasn't expecting Louie to be watching magic. Right now, the Grift should have been working at Cigam's safe. Not only were the sounds coming from the wrong direction; they weren't the sort that a safe-cracker would make. The Shadow paused to reconcile those noises with the circumstances.

And now The Shadow was missing the feature of the show.

Between the spirit clock and the mystic ball, a larger piece of antique magic towered above the pint-sized bird cages. It was a big grinning mask with horns that made Louie mistake it for a devil though actually it represented a satyr. The thing was mounted on a single pedestal and it was of more than human size, grotesquely lifelike with its bulging eyes and grinning mouth.

The satyr was coming to life!

First the head rolled its eyes as though looking Louie over and the huddled crook shied away. Then, classing the eyes as mechanical, Louie reared half across the counter and snarled at the satyr's head. At that moment the satyr wiggled its horns and Louie, suddenly infuriated, decided to throw something at the mechanical head.

All that was lying handy on the counter was a pack of cards, but Louie decided it might be enough to stop the works of this self-acting gadget.

As Louie's arm went back for the throw, the gloved hand of The Shadow was coming through the broken corner of the door to turn the inside knob, but Louie wasn't looking around behind him. Instead, Louie was throwing the pack of cards directly at the satyr's face.

The flying pack splashed all over the big head and the eyes stopped their contortions. The horns were frozen too, but Louie hadn't put an end to the magic. Instead, he'd actually played stooge to the climax.

From among the flutter of descending cards, four stood out. They were the aces from the pack, standing balanced in a slightly curving row on top of the weird head, directly between the horns!

The outer door had opened silently, but Louie hadn't turned to see it. The crook's face was as rigid as the satyr's until, a moment later, Louie's jaw sagged of its own accord as a token of sheer amazement.

At that moment, Louie was half across the counter, balanced on both hands in the exact position that had marked the finish of his fling. The bulge of the satyr's eyes seemed a copy of Louie's own. To make it perfect, the leering face had only to drop its own jaw, which it did.

Though inside the shop, The Shadow hadn't a chance to stop the thing that happened even if he'd expected it.

From the satyr's opening mouth came a tongue of flame accompanied by the sharp report of a gun. The stab was downward, straight toward the chest of Louie the Grift.

With a shriek the crook reared upward, staggered back and lost his balance, flattening supine on the floor!

Even before Louie landed, The Shadow was clearing the counter at the left, dropping there with a crouch that turned into a forward drive. He was out of sight behind the sliding doors that lined the rear of the counter and therefore as good as out of range.

His drive however was a quest for a close-range meeting for whomever stood behind the satyr, for The Shadow's route was straight past the display rack where the clock hand was slowly ending its spin, the metal ball having earlier ceased its rise and fall.

Through the doorway, The Shadow reached Cigam's back room, a dimly lighted place stacked with filing cabinets, assorted boxes, desk and shipping bench. There was nothing large enough to hide a human being, so all indications were that the murderer had gone through the window at the rear, which furnished the back room with what light it had.

Reaching the window, The Shadow established that theory when he found that the sash was unclamped. It came flying up with the whip of his hands and in the same gesture The Shadow was through the window and out across a ledge from which he made a twirling drop to the ground behind the building.

This was one way to take up a murderer's trail, except that it proved too precipitous for The Shadow to conceal his presence.

Even as The Shadow landed, a chunky figure came flinging upon him, swinging something that had the glint of a revolver. Only The Shadow, even during his rapid drop, had been thinking in just such terms.

The gloved hand that swept upward from the folds of The Shadow's cloak carried the dark bulk of a gun-metal automatic that stopped the descending revolver in mid-air. Sparks flashed from the clashing weapons, preliminary to the more spectacular fireworks that were to follow.

For as The Shadow wheeled one way, his antagonist the other, the man with the revolver let loose with the wild sort of shots that The

Shadow expected. In return came The Shadow's taunting laugh, as though commending such wasted fire. With his mirth, The Shadow whirled still further in the dark to gain the vantage of an alley that he knew led to the front street. Another foolhardy stab from his opponent's gun and The Shadow would wing him with a single.

Only the man with the revolver didn't choose to use it.

He knew this backyard better than The Shadow and he made the most of it. All that The Shadow heard was the wild clatter of footsteps making off through another passage to a side street. By the time The Shadow cut across the yard, found the narrow cleft and probed it with two shots to discourage any return fire, the passage was empty. The fugitive, whoever he was, had reached the street and was away.

Windows were clattering all around. Shouts were accompanying the cautious sweep of flashlights. From somewhere a police whistle shrilled and a siren responded not too far away.

It wasn't The Shadow's policy to stay around and take the blame for somebody else's crime. Speeding back to the alley that he preferred, he continued through it and seemed to evaporate somewhere in its gloom.

When Lamont Cranston, a calm stroller who carried a brief case, stopped in front of a little lunch room to join the curious throng that watched the police going up to Cigam's it was only natural that he should glance into the lunch room too.

There was no sign of Side-face Sam.

In death, Louie the Grift had lost the services of the side-kick who had been willing to help him out in life. Like an unknown murderer, Side-face had decided to become scarce, leaving the riddle to the police—and The Shadow.

III.

"Yes, my name is Demo Sharpe."

Pete Noland said it over the telephone in the half-sepulchral tone that so fitted Demo's style that it had taken Pete a long while to rehearse it.

Somebody put a query over the wire and Peter answered without changing voice:

"I know you are thinking of a card. You have that card in your hand, of course."

The person didn't have the card so Pete told him to get it and concentrate, then write the name of the card upon a sheet of paper. All this was done without the person stating the card aloud; that part was up to Demo, or rather Pete.

"You have concentrated enough," announced Pete in that same impressive tone. "Your card was the five of clubs."

There was an amazed gasp from the telephone receiver but Pete was used to all that. Besides, somebody was knuckling at the window pane, so there wasn't time to waste listening to a customer's reaction to the phone trick.

Pete simply hung up the phone and opened the window. It was Demo of course, since he was the only person who entered his own apartment by that route. For the first time, Demo seemed unnerved by his crawl along the twelfth story ledge.

Demo went to pour himself a drink, which was unusual.

"Why don't you quit this fool stuff?" queried Pete in the frank style that went with his looks. "This steeplejack act will throw you, if you don't throw yourself. Taking a drink is bad, if you're intending to go out again—"

"Only I'm not going out again." Demo shoved his face up from the chunky shoulders that supported it. His face had the same squarish look. "Not tonight, I mean."

"Then why go out at all?"

The phone bell interrupted and Demo gave a jerky gesture.

"Answer it, Pete."

It was somebody else wanting to know a card so Pete went through the usual routine and named it. Eyes eager, Demo listened to Pete's copy of his style and nodded approval.

"I'm fed up, Demo," argued Pete, in his own tone, as he clamped down the receiver. "If we're going to be partners in this telephone gag, let me be myself at least."

Demo shook his head.

"It won't work that way, Pete. I've been selling those instruction sheets under the title of Demo's Own Mystery. Nobody's going to buy them if I make it common."

"Then handle the works yourself." Pete went to the closet to get his hat and coat. "I'm leaving and not by the window. Good luck, Demo."

Frantically Demo threw his hunched form across the door to block

Pete's departure. Demo looked really wild with his gasping lips, his blinking eyes, and the tangled hair that strewed down across his forehead.

"You can't walk out on me, Pete."

"I'm doing it." Pete's handsome face had clouded, though not in a too unfriendly way. "Sorry, Demo."

The telephone rang.

"Answer it, Pete. Just once more. I'm still shaky."

"All right, Demo, for the last time."

Pete almost botched Demo's own, because his mind wasn't on the telephone mystery. Vague thoughts and troubled ones were cluttering Pete's mind regarding the in-and-out act that Demo had been staging every evening, leaving Pete to double for him in the apartment. So when he finished this last call, Pete wheeled and demanded:

"Out with it, Demo."

Demo nodded and took the telephone off its hook. To Pete, Demo said:

"That will cut off those calls for a while. Shed your hat and coat so you can listen. Remember, I said we'd go fifty-fifty. That goes for more than just the take on the telephone trick."

Demo wasn't forgetting the phone trick, though, because he made his story rapid and brief, so as not to keep too many customers waiting. Besides, Demo was thinking of an alibi.

"Here's the whole story, Pete," declared Demo earnestly. "I asked you to stay up here evenings and fake like you were me answering calls on the phone trick I've been peddling at two bucks a throw. My sneaking in and out by the ledge to the roof next door may have struck you as kind of eccentric, but you knew I was that sort of a guy."

"Until now I thought that was it, Demo."

"Well, I'm still eccentric," admitted Demo, "but in a way that may pay off for both of us. Look at this stuff." Pawing through a desk drawer, Demo brought out some yellowed newspaper clippings, and a few old frayed playbills. "These will give you the general idea."

As Pete began to study the exhibits, Demo glanced at the stifled telephone and became impatient.

"I'll explain them, Pete," said Demo rapidly. "The clippings are about the treasures belonging to the Sultan of Malkara that disappeared from his palace during a revolt of the populace, a good many years ago."

Pete nodded. He'd gotten that far with the clippings.

"The chief harem beauty disappeared at the same time," he added. "Kwana, her name was."

"And later all the stuff showed up," declared Demo, gesturing to the clippings. "Here there and everywhere, with one important exception. None of the sultan's crown jewels ever showed—not anywhere."

That brought a shrug from Pete.

"Perhaps the rabble got them."

"I don't think so," argued Demo. "Look, Pete. How would you guess Kwana got out of Malkara?"

Pete couldn't answer.

"These tell how." Demo brandished the long, old-fashioned playbills. "You've heard of Savanti, the Magician of Many Lands. Look where he was playing, right at the time Kwana disappeared along with the sultan's treasures!"

Staring at the playbill, Pete exclaimed:

"In Grandoq, the capital of Malkara!"

"Right," confirmed Demo, "and here's something more. Look at this billing a year later." He was spreading the other playbill. "Where did Savanti get Mysteria, the Maid of the Himalaya Mists, exotic creature of the higher atmosphere, who floats in mid-air?"

The playbill made Pete smile.

"You mean where did Savanti get the levitation act," he laughed. "Swiped it, I suppose, like he did with most everything in his show. Savanti was notorious for that—"

Stopping short, Pete stared at the playbill, then at Demo.

"You mean Savanti was behind that palace robbery?"

"If you want to call it a robbery," returned Demo blandly. "I wouldn't say that Savanti would go in for that, though. Maybe Kwana had a right to her share of the sultan's wealth. Her deal with Savanti could have been just to get her out of Malkara."

"And Savanti's cut was the crown jewels!"

"That's what I think, Pete."

Chin buried in hand, Pete watched Demo hang the receiver on its hook to resume the answering of card calls. It fitted except for one thing, on which Pete commented.

"Only Savanti died broke, Demo."

"He died on his last world tour," corrected Demo, "before he could get back home where he had stored most of his old apparatus." Demo's eyes narrowed Pete's way. "A lot of Savanti's props have been junked off lately."

"Then you mean the sultan's jewels may be hidden in one of Savanti's old tricks?"

"I couldn't think of anywhere better," returned Demo. "Nobody would steal magic apparatus, and if they did, they wouldn't know what it was all about."

The phone was ringing. Demo answered it personally and by his peculiar system of queries told some lady that she had picked the jack of spades, which proved correct. Then, hanging up:

"There are some smart characters who may have guessed what I have," Demo told Pete. "That's why I don't want them to know that I'm checking on all old apparatus that may once have belonged to Savanti. The best way to keep them from knowing is to make them think I'm here in the apartment every evening."

Now the whole business of the telephone tie-up was clearing itself in Pete's mind, along with Demo's procedure of using the window route instead of the apartment house elevator. No wonder Pete had been called upon to rehearse the part of Demo!

"There's only one man who makes a specialty of buying old apparatus," expressed Pete. "That's Wade Winstrom. He must have a ton of it along with his thousand books."

"And his million bucks," added Demo. "Winstrom loves to waste dough on junk that nobody else wants—or let's call it stuff nobody else wanted until now."

Another phone call gave Pete time to think over that analysis. Then, after Demo had floored somebody who took the two of diamonds, Pete suggested:

"Why not let Winstrom keep buying up old apparatus? Then go around to his place and ask to look it over just for curiosity? He's an obliging sort, Winstrom."

"I thought of that," said Demo. "But I finally decided that I wouldn't be soon enough, going through stuff after it reached Winstrom. Tonight I found out I was right."

Remembering Demo's jittery mood at the time of his return through the window, Pete waited for his eccentric friend to say more.

"Cigam dug out a lot of old apparatus," declared Demo, "and sold it all to Winstrom as a lot. I figured it wouldn't be shipped until Monday so I decided to break into Cigam's and give the stuff a proper preview. Only somebody got there ahead of me."

"Who?"

"I don't know, except that there was some shooting, and I met somebody coming out. I don't know who it was and I haven't an idea what happened in Cigam's shop. I only hope you'll believe me, Pete."

The telephone rang just as Demo's tone became an ardent plea. Deepening his voice to the sepulchral, Demo went into his customary act as he informed some stranger that the queen of spades was the selected card.

By then, Pete Noland had decided to believe Demo Sharpe where tonight's adventure was concerned. A lot of odd things were possible in the world of magic.

After all, Pete hadn't believed that the telephone mystery would work until Demo had demonstrated it and explained the system. Since then Pete had played a personal part in the seemingly incredible.

Pete Noland was only on mystery's threshold. As yet he had never met The Shadow!

IV.

Unacquainted with the secret history of the Great Savanti, Lamont Cranston actually spent a brief portion of Sunday morning weighing the police theory regarding the death of Louie the Grift.

The man who voiced the theory was Inspector Joe Cardona; and it was avidly received by Clyde Burke, the reporter whom The Shadow had hoped to provide with a scoop while supplying Cardona with a living safe-cracker instead of a murder victim.

Here in the magic shop, opened specially for the occasion, Cardona was putting the quiz on Cigam and doing it emphatically. Cardona's theory was that Cigam had been in the shop, plugged the prospective burglar and gone out by his own back window. Joe kept telling Cigam that the law would be tolerant with a man who had resisted invasion of his own premises, but Cigam seemed to doubt it.

Cranston flashed a look at Burke.

"Say, Joe," put in the reporter suddenly. "Wasn't Louie the Grift a great pal of Side-face Sam?"

A furrowed forehead became Cardona's answer.

"Maybe you've got something, Burke—"

"You might have something if you picked up Side-face," suggested Clyde. "Particularly if you got him to talk out the right side of his mouth."

Of course Cranston had relayed that suggestion through Burke simply to get the law working along the right track, only now the law was beginning to do it anyway. For certain of Cigam's friends and customers, reached by telephone, were beginning to arrive. They'd found it rather difficult getting up this early on Sunday morning, about eleven o'clock.

First was Zed Zito, the blunt-faced, rather ruddy man who looked like anything but a magician. There was the showman's air about Zed, though, his dead pan and cold but precise tone giving an effect of authority to everything he said. Zed's hands, though blocky, were the sort that could be deft; moreover they were big enough to hide things. Cranston could tell that when he looked at them, and he particularly noted the purposely slow way in which Zed Zito moved those hands.

Next came Val Varno.

Here was a wizard who looked as clever as he was, maybe more so. Or perhaps Val wasn't too clever, putting up that sort of front. While he listened to proceedings, this sallow, undersized deceptionist kept doing things with his hands, which were as long as Zito's but not as wide.

Varno's left was working the coin roll, making a half dollar run somersaulting across his knuckles in a smooth, uncanny fashion. His right was simply taking his cigarette from his lips between the short, rapid puffs which was Val's way of enjoying a smoke.

Only Val Varno couldn't even take a cigarette from his mouth as the normal human would. He invariably raised his hand palm frontward so that the backs of his fingers pressed his lips when he removed the cigarette. Then by some peculiar flip be made the cigarette do a complete turn-over, so that when he put it back in his mouth his hand was as it should be, the backs of the fingers away from his face.

Just about the time an onlooker was hoping to catch on to this intricacy, Varno's cigarette would get too short for further manipulation, so he would stop the coin roll, pocket the half dollar, and bring out a handkerchief which he laid over his left hand. Poking down some cloth with his right thumb, Varno would drop the cigarette butt in the pocket thus formed, then suddenly spread the handkerchief, showing the cloth unburned, the cigarette butt gone.

Pocketing the handkerchief Varno would reach in the air, pluck a fresh cigarette already lighted and start another smoke, while his other hand came out with the half dollar to resume the coin roll. Only this time, Val varied the process by ending the roll with a spreading movement of his hand which multiplied the coin to two, edgeways between his finger tips. Then each hand took a coin and both were starting that tantalizing roll when Cardona inserted a growled interruption.

"Cut that trickstuff!" ordered the inspector. "All right, Varno, what have you got to say?"

"The same as Zito," returned Val, briefly.

"But you weren't here when Zito testified," argued Cardona. "So how do you know what he said?"

"Because I was here yesterday afternoon when Zito was. That's what you're asking him about, isn't it?"

Cardona growled that it was.

"All right." Varno resumed the double coin roll. "That was all."

"What was all?"

"We all went out together. Cigam, Zito, myself"—Varno clinked the coins into his left hand, vanished them by a simple rub and showed his right hand empty as he gestured it to the door—"and our good friend here, Glanville Frost."

Maybe those polished coins served Varno as mirrors; otherwise Cardona couldn't guess how Val had seen the suave Mr. Frost enter. What Cardona hadn't observed was that two fancy caskets on Cigam's shelf of antique apparatus were polished even more brightly than Varno's coins.

From where Varno stood, one nickeled casket reflected the other and the second mirrored the door. Cranston alone detected Varno's upward glance that gave him that double reflection. But the view wasn't good enough for Varno to see beyond Frost, to the arrival who followed him.

The other man was Wade Winstrom, the extravagant collector who had purchased Cigam's entire lot of antique stuff to add to his already oversized aggregation of obsolete magicana.

Frost had evidently caught Varno's statement for the suave man announced in silky tone:

"Whatever Varno and Zito agree upon, inspector, I can confirm. I was present, as Val says. I presume that Mr. Winstrom will corroborate their statements too."

It was rather subtle of Frost to put it that way, since he would prove either Zito or Varno a liar if the two didn't agree. Particularly subtle since Frost's reputation in the magical fraternity was that of a promiser, which was a polite way of saying he wasn't exactly trustworthy.

As for Frost's added touch, that of involving a man of substance like Winstrom, this was just another evidence of the smooth gentleman's subtlety. Frost was the sort who could have sold magicians palming oil if he'd wanted.

This didn't go with Cigam.

"Don't count Mr. Winstrom in this," Cigam protested in defense of his best customer. "He left before the rest of us did, by ten minutes at least."

Frost only smiled.

"Calm yourself, Cigam," he suggested. "I'm not hurting your business. Mr. Winstrom merely stopped off at my factory to look at an old cabinet illusion which I regarded as a collector's item. That shouldn't annoy you, Cigam. You don't deal in large illusions."

"Neither do I," commented Winstrom, drily. "They take up too much storage room and you can't show them to your friends. Nevertheless I like to see them demonstrated."

"You'll see the Golden Pagoda tonight," promised Frost, in the emphatic tone that meant this was one promise he intended to keep. "I'm doing it at the U.W.A. show." He smiled at Cardona. "Maybe you ought to buy a ticket, inspector. Cigam sells them."

"I'm not thinking of magic shows," grumbled Cardona. "I'm thinking of magic shops and this one especially. When a magic shop gets turned into a shooting gallery, I want to know why."

Winstrom gave Cigam an anxious glance.

"My apparatus," he queried, "is it all right?"

"Except that somebody was fooling with it," returned Cigam.

"They had the clock working and the ball. The same with the big head."

Looking toward the shelf, Winstrom saw the satyr's head with the aces roosting between its horns and the mouth wide in a horrified gape.

"If anything was damaged," began Winstrom, "I won't buy it. If you had shipped that apparatus earlier—"

"I'm shipping it right now," interrupted Cigam, "if the inspector here will let me."

Cardona nodded that he would and turned the same nod into a sign of dismissal for all present. So they filed out with the exception of Cigam, who stayed because he owned the shop, and Cranston who as a friend of the police commissioner, could claim some special privilege.

In fact Cardona was glad that Cranston stayed.

As they stood in the back room watching Cigam take the antique apparatus through openings behind the shelves, Cardona tried out his theory on Cranston.

"If the clock dial and the rising ball were working," declared Cardona, "somebody must have been back here, wouldn't you say?"

Studying the appliances mentioned, Cranston nodded, so Cardona added:

"And the same with the big head. And for one special reason. Look here." He stopped Cigam from turning the satyr's head edgeways to bring it through the space behind the shelf. "The only way the killer could have plugged Louie the Grift, was by shoving a revolver through the satyr's mouth from the back. What's more, he'd have to wait until the mouth opened, which is the last thing it does." Joe turned to Cigam.

"Am I right?"

Cigam nodded soberly, but only Cardona saw him do so. Cranston was looking elsewhere, among spaces between the back room packing boxes and a cranny where the sides of two filing cabinets didn't quite meet.

That gap was right behind the satyr's head. Something glittered from the floor and Cranston shoved a file cabinet aside to pick up the object. It proved to be a black wand with nickel-plated tips.

"Somebody must have put that wand on a file cabinet," said Cigam, "and it rolled down between. Magicians have a lot of trouble with wands rolling off their tables. Sometimes they use square wands so they won't roll."

"This wand didn't roll," commented Cranston. "It couldn't. Look at it."

Looking, Cigam saw a little knob on the side of the wand, set in a slit which actuated a plunger. Amazed, he exclaimed:

"A firing wand!"

"A firing wand?" queried Cardona. "What's that?"

"An improvement over a magician's pistol," explained Cranston. He pressed the knob and there was the sharp click of a hammer. "A wave of this wand, you hear a shot and see a spurt of fire. Now suppose—"

Pausing, Cranston inserted the wand through the back of the satyr's head so that the wand's open tip extended out from the mouth of the big false face. Reaching around, Cranston lifted the satyr's jaw so that the wand stayed in the closed mouth.

"This head is practically an automaton," explained Cranston. "Start its mechanism and it goes through a whole routine of contortions, opening its mouth for a finale."

As Cranston let the jaw drop to illustrate his point, there was another sharp click from the wand.

"A hair-trigger," commented Cranston. "Rather odd for a firing wand. This one can shoot bullets; it's practically a pistol composed entirely of barrel. But it doesn't have the weight of a gun, so the recoil would send it some distance." His hand supporting the wand behind the satyr's head, Cranston gave it a straight, deft backward toss. "Like this."

The wand arrowed into the space between the file cabinets. Cardona pounced after it, exclaiming:

"So that's what killed Louie the Grift!"

Cigam's wits were coming back. Hoarsely he protested that the firing wand wasn't his, that he'd never seen it until the present moment. In fact there hadn't been a firing wand around Cigam's shop during the dozen years that he had owned it, not even among the lot of old apparatus that he had excavated. Firing wands were very rare.

So ardent was Cigam's plea that Cardona was inclined to believe him. Joe looked at Cranston hoping the commissioner's friend would have some more ideas.

Cranston had one. He smiled as he gave it.

"Good-bye, inspector," said Cranston. "I'll be seeing you at the magic show."

V.

The late editions of the Sunday morning newspapers carried a small item about the death of Louie the Grift, but the details were meager. Nevertheless, Demo Sharpe took great pains to show the story to Pete Noland as they sat in Demo's apartment along about the middle of the afternoon.

Such frank procedure gave Demo the opportunity to interpret the case his own way.

"You see what I mean," insisted Demo. "Somebody must have guessed that I was going to crack into Cigam's, only they expected me to use the front way."

It sounded logical to Pete, who nodded. Then:

"Only how would they be expecting you?" Pete inquired. "Everybody knows you're supposed to be up here, answering phone calls on the telephone trick."

"The killer wasn't necessarily thinking in terms of me," expressed Demo. Then, with an odd stare that he used in working out mysteries like his telephone stunt, he continued: "It's known, though, that somebody is going around to all sorts of junk shops, hunting up old magic apparatus. That's what I've been doing evenings."

Things were adding up in Pete's mind. He could picture Demo sliding in and out of obscure stores, keeping himself well muffled as he looked over anything resembling old apparatus that might have belonged to Savanti.

"I've been calling up old timers too," added Demo. "Magicians that most everybody has forgotten. I haven't told them who I was. I've made my voice different just like you've been faking mine. But anyone on the trail of Savanti's stuff may have learned about those calls."

Aloud, Pete began to check the names of persons who might prove to be Demo's rival bidder. Naturally he picked individuals whom he had at some time seen at Cigam's shop.

"There's Val Varno," began Pete, "but he goes in for sleights, so apparatus wouldn't be in his line. Take Glanville Frost, he manufactures apparatus, but mostly he makes illusions for night clubs or stage acts. Zed Zito has a lot of smaller equipment, but his stuff isn't strictly magic. Let's see now—who else—"

"Why?"

Demo put the query so abruptly that it stopped Pete short.

"You mean that's enough of a list?" demanded Pete. "If that's the case, it's my turn to ask why."

"Because those fellows fit my case," explained Demo, simply. "I don't bother with apparatus either. I'm a mentalist, doing mysteries of the mind." He gestured to a stack of typewritten papers on a desk. "Daytimes I'm working on my new book called 'Mental Marvels' and evenings I'm servicing customers who bought my telephone miracle. If I'm smart enough to cover my real interest, so is the fellow who is trying to beat me to it."

Demo's ingenious argument won Pete completely. Pete gave a worried shrug, then reverted to his frank policy.

"I didn't ask for a split on this Savanti proposition," put in Pete. "Why don't you take my share as yours and sound these chaps out, offering a fifty-fifty basis?"

"And put three of them in the market?" retorted Demo. "Not a chance. Where they're concerned my motto is 'All for one and nothing for anybody else'—because that's the way they work."

Again, Demo had nailed his point home.

"Let's keep on playing it my way," Demo insisted. "You stick around and handle the phone trick for me, so I can slide out again tonight."

"You're sure it's safe, Demo?"

"I'm only going to buzz old Professor Del Weird over at the Universal Wizards show."

"But you can't let anybody see you there!"

"I'll get in the back way and talk to the Prof in his dressing room. He just came into town and he doesn't know about my phone mystery. He won't care, either. He doesn't think a trick is any good until it's been tested fifty years."

"Del Weird doesn't use much apparatus."

"He may have stowed some away in years gone by and some of it could have been Savanti's."

Pete's smooth forehead furrowed. He was worrying over Demo's dilemma more than his friend was.

"Wade Winstrom is throwing a buffet supper," reminded Pete.

"Del Weird will be there of course. Why don't you go there to see him before the show?"

"And try to outbid Winstrom on buying apparatus?" snorted Demo. "No, I'll have to see Del Weird privately and get him to hold out on any tricks that may have been Savanti's. I can top Winstrom on a few items, particularly if Del Weird hasn't given him the list.

"Besides"—Demo shook his head reminiscently—"it's hard to break away from Winstrom when he gets in a chatty mood. The last time I was there six o'clock was slipping by before I realized it. Lucky I had you planted over here. What's more, the supper is only for U.W.A. members. You know what that means: 'Usually We're Amateurs'."

Pete smiled at the quip involving the U.W.A. initials. Of the professional magicians appearing in tonight's show, only Del Weird belonged to the Universal Wizards Association; the rest, like Varno, Frost and Zito, had been hired to bolster the bill. So Pete acquiesced to Demo's plan regarding a clandestine interview with Del Weird, Pete's part being to miss the show, which was no hardship, and continue to play Demo's role of the master mind across the telephone.

There were others, however, who considered Winstrom's supper to be a rather important occasion. One such person was Lamont Cranston, who at present was riding by cab to Winstrom's hotel, accompanied by a girl named Margo Lane. Quite intrigued by the thought of meeting a group of magicians, Margo suddenly exclaimed:

"But Lamont! If only magicians are invited to this supper, how can you get in there?"

Cranston smiled. As The Shadow he had ways of getting into places that would have mystified even a magician, but that wasn't the chief reason for his smile.

"It isn't exactly a magicians' party," Cranston explained. "It's being given for the members of the Universal Wizards Association, which happens to be a magical society."

"But they must all be magicians—"

"Not all of them." Still smiling, Cranston brought out a card and showed it to Margo. Bearing Cranston's name, it was a membership card in the Universal Wizards Association. "I joined the U.W.A. this afternoon and paid my five dollars for a year's dues."

"You mean all you need is five dollars to belong to a magical society?"

"They're the ones who need the five dollars," replied Cranston. "The U.W.A. is having a membership drive. Wade Winstrom saw me down at Cigam's, thought I must be interested in magic, so he phoned me at the Cobalt Club."

The cab was stopping at the palatial Hotel Chianti where Winstrom lived and where the Wizards were holding their show in the grand ball room, a coincidence indicating that Winstrom probably had a large say regarding the policy of the U.W.A.

Cranston and Margo rode up to Winstrom's penthouse and found a flock of Wizards there. None of them wore goatees; they were largely a lot of tired-looking business men mostly in their portly forties. Their wives were present in abundance and Margo was promptly swallowed by the ladies auxiliary whose chief topic of conversation was the amount of time their husbands were wasting on that most detestable of hobbies, magic.

In glimpses that she obtained between the shoulders of the broadaxes, Margo was almost inclined to agree. The wizards were fumblers when it came to doing impromptu tricks, turning their backs to arrange special packs of cards when they tried to fool each other. Maybe they found it fun, but it didn't look like magic.

Wade Winstrom, though, was different. For all his austere looks, Winstrom was quite genial and enjoyed it when his fawning guests admired the array of magical apparatus that stocked his spacious living room. Margo joined the group that followed Winstrom into his library where there were shelves upon shelves of magic books that appeared to be in the immaculate condition of jobs fresh from the bindery.

Finding Lamont nearby, Margo remarked upon the fine condition of Winstrom's volumes.

"They should be in good shape," was Cranston's comment. "I've heard that Winstrom never unlocks the book cases, let alone read the books themselves. But you still have a lot to see. Come this way, Margo."

This way led into a windowless room where Winstrom kept his exhibit of playbills. There were a few hundred of them, all in tall narrow frames and many of the specimens were more than a century old, extolling the merits of such historical magicians as the Chevalier Pinetti, Professor Anderson, and Signor Blitz.

However, Winstrom dismissed the playbills with a careless wave

of his imperious hand and ended the gesture by introducing a wizened gentleman who looked like the living relic of the conjurors described in the posters.

"Professor Del Weird," boomed Winstrom. "I know you'll be glad
to meet him, those of you who haven't already."

Old Del Weird bobbed a toothless smile from beside a table where
he was unpacking a lot of fancy glassware from an old battered suit-
case.

"The professor does the wine and water act," announced Winstrom. "The trick baffles me every time I see it. I know it will make
a big hit tonight."

Absent-mindedly, Del Weird was reaching in the various pockets
of his over-sized frock coat. In plaintive tone he spoke to Winstrom:

"I must have left that package in my overcoat. Where would my
overcoat be, Mr. Winstrom?"

"I'll ask one of the servants," replied Winstrom. "He'd know. But
don't worry yourself, professor. It's two hours yet before show time."

Quite relieved, Del Weird regained his senile smile. Then, noting
a lady present, the professor bowed profoundly. Plucking an em-
broidered cloth from his table, Del Weird showed it back and front
and from its folds suddenly produced a glass of red wine which he
tendered Margo's direction.

As the girl gasped at this quick surprise, Del Weird withdrew the
glass and holding it in one hand swept the cloth across it. In the brief
time that the glass was covered, its contents changed from wine to
water.

Margo was still speechless when Del Weird bowed, raised the glass
and drank it as a toast, all without a word. Staring at the others,
Margo met Winstrom's beaming gaze.

"Why—why—" Margo paused to halt her stammers. "Why, it's the
most amazing thing I ever saw!"

"You'll see a lot greater surprises tonight," promised Winstrom. "I
think you'll like magic, Miss Lane."

Cranston too was smiling at Margo's reaction, but the rest of the
Wizards looked bored. They had seen Del Weird's tricks too often
to be impressed.

Nevertheless, Winstrom's prediction stood. People were going to
have a real surprise before tonight's show ended.

VI.

The Chianti ball room was on the ground floor of the hotel and it had a stage that turned it into an excellent auditorium. Only no one was in the auditorium at curtain time; instead, people generally were flooding the large foyer. The same people usually bought tickets to a magic show and they knew that none of the performances began on time.

Besides, the U.W.A. show was being stolen before it even started. To pass the time, somebody had tried Demo's telephone mystery and now everybody was at it.

There was a string of half a dozen phone booths in the foyer and people were using all of them, all trying to get the same number. This bothered Margo so she asked Lamont about it. Looking up from the fancy program he was studying, Cranston said:

"Think of a card, Margo. Got one?"

"Why, yes. The ace of diamonds."

"Grab one of those phone booths," instructed Cranston. "Call the same number as the rest of the people, Anaconda 4-8601. Better write it down before you forget it, because you may be a while putting a call through."

"And then?"

"Ask for Demo Sharpe, tell him who you are and that a friend said for you to call him. He'll tell you what card you took."

"If this is a gag—"

Margo halted, deciding that even as a gag, it would be a good one. She went to a booth, was lucky to get a quick call through. A voice mysteriously responded and heard what Margo had to say. Then the voice announced:

"You took the ace of diamonds."

Margo just stood there, flabbergasted. She didn't even realize that she'd hung up the receiver until the phone bell began to jangle it. Margo answered, wondering if the amazing Demo was calling back to read some more of her mind. It was only the switchboard operator saying there was a call for Professor Del Weird.

At that moment the professor came waddling by, carrying his suitcase flat in front of him so as not to damage the glassware set inside. Margo beckoned him to the phone booth, and finding the call was for him, Del Weird handed her the suitcase, saying to hold it carefully.

So there was Margo standing outside the booth with the professor inside. Still very puzzled, Margo looked up suddenly as she heard Del Weird say through the half-open door.

"Oh, hello, Demo."

Could it be that Demo was really calling back?

Margo was sure she'd heard right, but Del Weird didn't repeat Demo's name again. Instead, he affirmed that he'd sold all his old apparatus and that he couldn't be bothered until after the show. Finally he conceded that he could be reached in his dressing room after he finished his act.

With that, Del Weird came from the booth and without even a thank you, took his suit-case from Margo and blundered off through a door marked "Stage."

Going over to where Cranston was, Margo said:

"Lamont, this is all very puzzling, but—"

"But don't talk about it now," supplied Cranston. "The telephone trick always works and I know it's wonderful. But right now I'm looking for somebody who ought to be here but isn't."

"And I'm telling you about somebody who ought to be somewhere else, but isn't," persisted Margo. "I mean Demo Sharpe."

Cranston's eyes went quizzical.

"Demo called back," explained Margo, "and he talked to Del Weird. But all the while people were in those phone booths talking to Demo. Of course maybe they were just getting the busy signal."

Perhaps that was the answer, but Cranston wasn't letting it pass that simply. Instead, he said something that was very unusual for him.

"I wonder!"

Then, showing Margo the program, Cranston explained what he had found.

"Here's a list of the reception committee," said Cranston. "You'd think they'd all be here; they aren't. A chap named Pete Noland is missing."

"Maybe he couldn't get here."

"There's another reason Noland ought to be around," continued Cranston. "He reviews these shows for a magical paper called *The*

Wivern under the name of Paracelsus Junior. He certainly shouldn't be missing this present function."

"But what has that to do with Demo Sharpe?"

"A lot. I'm not restricting the list of murder suspects just to persons who were at Cigam's yesterday and who happen to be working in tonight's show."

"You mean it was murder at Cigam's?"

"Somebody certainly planted that firing wand too neatly. Whoever did wasn't expecting Louie the Grift. Crooks don't advertise robberies in advance."

"Then the murderer mistook Louie for somebody else?"

"Very probably. Louie's back was to the light. His face couldn't have been seen through that space behind the satyr's head."

Cranston spoke impassively as though he had learned all this today. He wasn't even suggesting to Margo that he'd been in Cigam's at the very moment when murder struck. In analyzing this case of murder by magic, Cranston was not neglecting any magical clues and Demo's telephone trick was looming as one of them.

Checking some time notes that he had made on the margin of his program, Cranston decided on his course.

"I'm going over to Demo's now," he confided to Margo. "I'll have just time enough to get back before Del Weird finishes his act. I'll see you later, Margo."

Cranston went through the door marked "Stage" carrying his brief case with him. Remembering something else she'd wanted to ask, Margo started after. Past the door she saw a group of dressing rooms, off at another angle a wing of the stage where several performers were arguing because each intended to do the other's tricks.

None of them noticed the further door, past the dressing rooms, that Margo saw closing. It was very dark beyond that door, but as the blackness suddenly cleared, Margo saw the glimmer of alley lights.

Then did Margo Lane realize that she'd witnessed one of The Shadow's strange evaporations. Too late with her question, she went back and around into the auditorium which by now was filled with people.

As for Lamont Cranston, now become The Shadow, he took a rapid ride in his own cab, the same cab that had brought him here with Margo, its driver the speediest hackie in New York. The

driver's name was Shrevvy and he clipped about five minutes off The
Shadow's estimated time in getting to the Albuquerque Arms, the
apartment house where Demo Sharpe lived.

This gave The Shadow extra minutes to gauge the location of
Demo's apartment. The Arms was a swank apartment with doorman, clerk and elevator operators, a gamut that The Shadow didn't
care to run as Cranston. What intrigued The Shadow was the much
less pretentious apartment building next door, which nestled up
against the Arms as though the two were a pair of love birds.

There was a ledge that looked too narrow to be even a cat-walk,
but The Shadow knew his ledges and could gauge their proper size
from the street. So he glided into the adjoining building, took the
automatic elevator to the top floor and found an exit to the roof.

Then, navigating the ledge of the Albuquerque Arms, The
Shadow moved like an unseen wraith around the corner and followed his ample path to the lighted window that represented Demo's
apartment.

The telephone mystery was still doing steady business, which
proved that plenty of magicians didn't attend the U.W.A. shows.
But it wasn't Demo Sharpe on the receiving end. The man handling
the apartment's private line was Pete Noland.

One pleasant feature of investigating a magical murder was the
ease with which anyone could recognize whichever magicians might
be involved. One wall of Cigam's shop, opposite the longer display
shelves, was completely covered with autographed pictures of the
local magic. The Shadow hadn't missed a face in that prospective
rogue's gallery while he had been at Cigam's today. The accompanying names had likewise impressed themselves upon his mind.

If The Shadow had wanted to go into the magic business he could
have prepared a memory training system that would have outsold
the popular brand that Cigam peddled at five dollars.

Though Demo's system of telephone telepathy was just a trick,
constant concentration upon it seemed to have stimulated Pete's
extra-sensory perceptions. As he finished naming the nine of clubs
for someone, Pete turned suddenly and stared straight at The
Shadow's window.

Or perhaps it was a peculiar darkening of the window, which
though ever so slight, had caught Pete's tense attention. Now, Pete
saw the blackness unblur and he frowned at the familiar glimmer

of the city lights beyond. Like Margo he had witnessed The Shadow's process of what could be styled evaporation.

Coming over to the window, Pete pulled it open, stared along the blackened ledge. He couldn't see The Shadow now, the cloaked shape was so close to the wall. In a hoarse, anxious whisper, Pete voiced: "Demo!" and then stared downward.

The tinging telephone broke into Pete's fear that his friend had plunged below. Mechanically, Pete went back to answer what might be his last call. His voice came gladly: "Demo!"

Through the open window, The Shadow heard Pete's end of the conversation.

"Guess I was getting jittery, Demo." Pete gave a half-laugh. "Thought you were outside the window just now. . . . What's that? Maybe there is something in telepathy? You might be right. . . . Yes, it was funny I'd think you were here just when you phone. . . .

"You're seeing Del Weird? Kind of risky, Demo. . . . Well, maybe you can make him stay mum. . . . Only I'm worrying what if anybody else sees you. . . . A good stunt for the book? I get it— how to be two places at the same time. . . . But that's one secret you'd better not give away. . . . Good luck, Demo. . . . Better hang up now. Customers are waiting. . . ."

When, after a couple of more card calls, Pete went over and closed the window, the outside ledge was actually unoccupied. The Shadow had learned all he needed at Demo's, at least for the present.

His theory established, The Shadow was on his way back to the Hotel Chianti and further along the trail of magical murder as well.

Only sometimes trails moved faster than the person who followed them. That was something The Shadow knew but he hadn't applied the rule in this case.

At least not yet.

VII.

Margo Lane was getting her first impression of a magic show.

The bill was opened by a dapper amateur who tore some strips of tissue paper and turned them into a fancy party hat. Next he fanned whole packs of playing cards in clever style. Finally he did the well-known trick of clanging a lot of big rings and making them link and unlink.

Next on the bill was Val Varno. He did his short act, just the card fans. Val added a few flourishes that the amateur either hadn't learned or couldn't do.

Another amateur followed with a rapid act in which only three out of a dozen tricks went wrong. Two that went all right were the paper hat and the linking rings.

By then people were beginning to look around the audience instead of at the show. They received smiles, austere ones, from Wade Winstrom, who would have shaken hands too if his reach had been long enough. All the way down from the penthouse and during the half hour that people were around the foyer, Winstrom had been smiling and shaking hands. That seemed to be his idea of a magic show.

The bill spruced up when Zed Zito appeared. He introduced a very attractive blonde whom he called Miss Libra. She could change her weight under Zito hypnotic power, so Zito said. While Zed was getting a committee on the stage, he had Miss Libra do a trick, since this was a magic show.

Miss Libra did the paper hat.

Margo saw some people sneak out from the audience. They were going to have a smoke in the foyer and try the telephone to see if Demo could still name cards in his uncanny way. Demo's trick could stand repetition that others could not.

Deciding to sit through Zito's act, Margo was well-rewarded. The act was really good. When Zito said "Heavy!" strong men found themselves unable to lift Miss Libra. When he said "Light" she became as a feather. To prove it really happened, Zito had Miss Libra stand on a scales. Her weight went down to twenty-five pounds at his command of "Light" and rose to two hundred and fifty when he thundered "Heavy!"

For the finish, Zito hitched Miss Libra to a rope which ran up over a big pulley above the stage. Three men took the other end of the rope and with no effort hauled the girl a dozen feet above the stage. Zito commanded "Heavy!" and Miss Libra came straight down while the surprised committee men went up on their end of the rope, all three of them at once.

It was really very good and the audience remained patient even when Glanville Frost, suave and sleek, appeared and started his act with card fans. Quite smooth, Frost won real applause which faded suddenly when an assistant brought him a stack of linking rings.

Frost talked the audience down. He said that his version of the rings was the correct Chinese edition, taught to him by Ching Ling Foo. Even Winstrom seemed to swallow that, though his own play-bills upstairs would have proven that Ching went back to China when Frost was only three years old. But Frost, the clever showman, held his audience by adding that the rings were a necessary introduction to his finale, the famous Golden Pagoda, now to be shown for the first time.

Under his breath Frost might have added "in fifty years" but if he did, nobody heard him.

Frost was bowing from an armor of tangled rings when the curtain rose disclosing the famous pagoda. It was a miniature pagoda meas-uring about four feet every direction and it stood on a little platform so that people could see beneath it. Shaking himself free of the rings, Frost opened the whole front of the pagoda and showed it empty; then he and the assistant wheeled it around.

Closing the pagoda, Frost recited something in Chinese, there was a puff of smoke and flame, the pagoda sprang open, top and all, and a girl in Chinese costume rose to take a bow. It was a really startling illusion and everybody applauded heavily, particularly when they saw that the girl was Miss Libra and that Frost had been forced to do the other tricks to give her time to change costume.

Then Professor Del Weird came on and Margo Lane gave up. If after fifty years of wand wielding, Del Weird hadn't learned a better opening than the paper hat trick, Margo didn't want to watch him. Besides, those were the inevitable linking rings hanging over a T-stand behind the table where a pitcher and a row of glasses were set for the wine and water specialty.

Margo wanted more than a smoke, she wanted a drink if the cock-tail lounge was still open, and she was so sick of magic she didn't even care about testing Demo's telephone mystery. So she started out to the foyer only to find herself stopped by a man who wore a badge that said "Committee."

"You can't interrupt Professor Del Weird—"

"That so?" queried Margo. "Well if he turns those torn papers into a hat, I'll scream and that will really interrupt him."

Another committee man decided in Margo's favor. Already she

had drawn considerable attention at the back of the house and among the persons who stared her way was Inspector Joe Cardona. He had an expression that resembled the Great Stone Face and was obviously annoyed because he had come here at Cranston's suggestion only to find Cranston himself absent.

Seeing Cardona brought Margo's mind back to stark reality. When she reached the foyer, she threw a look at the door marked "Stage" and saw a muffled man entering it. He had rapid striding legs under a coat that was hunched up over his shoulders and his hand was across his mouth holding a cigarette from which he blew a heavy cloud to hide his face.

That was hardly necessary, considering that his hat was tipped down over his eyes, but he could still see well enough to notice Margo looking his way. Increasing his already rapid pace, the man went through the door, slamming it behind him.

Margo gathered a very good hunch that this was Demo. She went through the stage door too and saw the muffled man bob out of sight into a dressing room. A girl's voice gave an excited protest and the man came out again.

"I'm sorry," Margo heard him mutter. "I was just looking for Professor Del Weird."

A girl's arm pointed from the doorway.

"That's his dressing room over there!"

The girl was Miss Libra draped in a hastily arranged towel. Two doors closed as Margo neared them, one admitting Demo Sharpe to Del Weird's dressing room, the other declaring that Miss Libra wanted no more unannounced visitors.

Now Margo knew that the man was really Demo. His voice, losing all disguise, had been identical with the tone across the telephone!

On stage, Del Weird was doing the wine and water. Margo stopped for a view from the wings. It was much more elaborate than the simple trick the professor had done earlier. He was filling glasses from the pitcher, some wine, some water, then pouring them back into the pitcher, which suddenly became all water.

Yet that same pitcher was pouring wine and water again, alternately. Mixed, the various liquids turned to wine. Yet from a pitcher full of wine, Del Weird poured only water, half a dozen glasses of it!

This was so amazing that Margo stood enthralled, forgetting all about Demo. And now a great, hollow buzz came from the audience.

Professor Del Weird was about to prove that his demonstration had been truly magical. As Del Weird picked up the linking rings, he pretended to remember the thing he hadn't forgotten. With a bland smile, he turned, picked up the last glass in the line and raised it to his lips.

Del Weird was going to drink the result of all his transformations to prove that it was truly harmless water. Margo could hear the words "He drinks it!" repeated by various persons amid the stir of voices.

The professor drank it.

That audience was spared another demonstration of the ring trick.

Knees caving instantly, Professor Del Weird hit the stage so flat and hard that everybody knew he must be dead.

VIII.

To say merely that pandemonium reigned would not have been doing justice to what pandemonium really could make of itself.

The audience went wild with screams that were drowned by the clatter of the folding chairs used to turn the ball room into an auditorium. Nobody had to ask if there was a doctor in the house because there were plenty, all amateur magicians. They flooded the stage as fast as the performers from the wings.

It was Glanville Frost however who reached the spot first and seeing the rush of arrivals, Frost had the presence of mind to pick up the table beside which Del Weird lay and start to carry it off stage before anyone could upset it and ruin the precious glassware.

Frost was coming directly toward the wing where Margo stood when Zed Zito, arriving from an angle, blocked him in rather bulky style.

"Where are you taking that table?" Zito demanded. "Better put it over there by your pagoda and leave it alone!"

To prove his point, Zito practically scooped the table from Frost's hands, since the latter wasn't in any position to interfere. Momentarily it looked as though Frost intended to use his hands to punch Zito, but the blunt-faced hypnotist balked him by swinging around, thus blocking him off with the table itself.

For some reason this registered oddly with Margo and she looked around as though asking the advice of other witnesses. There was only one and that Val Varno who had sauntered from a dressing room and was watching proceedings with a casual eye while practicing his coin roll with his left hand.

It was then that the door of Del Weird's dressing room opened, just a chink it was true, but enough to catch that keen eye of Varno's. With a nudge of his free hand, Varno called to Frost:

"Better find out who's calling on Del Weird. There's somebody in his dressing room!"

Zito heard Varno's words too. In fact he couldn't have heard better if Val had timed it, for Zito was just turning from the wing where he had placed the professor's table beside the golden pagoda. As if neither wanted to be the last, Frost and Zito came lunging from the stage while Varno stepped aside to let them pass.

Neither got far, for by now a stocky man was arriving from the foyer door. This was Inspector Cardona, taking the shortest way back stage and Joe didn't intend to let anyone get off these premises. Impartially judged, Frost and Zito gave the impression that one was trying to get away while the other stopped him; which was which could be decided later.

Behind Cardona came others, among them Wade Winstrom who motioned people back, then rushed ahead to help Cardona. Smiling blandly at the commotion he created, Val Varno seeped back to a niche in the wall and began slowly placing hand over hand so that his animated coin could continue a perpetual waltz from one set of fingers to the other.

A horror was gripping Margo that the man in Del Weird's dressing room might not be Demo Sharpe!

If one person could fake Demo's voice, so could another. Lamont was due back by this time and perhaps he was trying to beat Demo at his own game, whatever that was. It could be that the mysterious caller was actually Cranston, for Margo had known him to try odder stunts than this.

And Margo wasn't taking any chances, not with murder again infringing upon magic!

While Varno was watching Cardona tangle with Frost and Zito, Margo took advantage of the moment to rush for Del Weird's dressing room. If Winstrom saw her, she wouldn't care; it might be all the better, since he'd know she hadn't started there until after the cry of suspicion had been raised.

If Margo had given a thought to the alley door, she could have forgotten her needless trip right then. That exit was opening, with blackness its impelling force. The very blackness that meant The Shadow, if Margo had only looked!

The girl who looked was Miss Libra, coming from her own dressing room in the tangles of a kimono. She saw blackness mold itself into a cloaked shape that was vaguely human and this time her screech carried more of horror than surprise. An instant later, the cloaked figure was gone, the exit slamming automatically.

And people, a flock of them, were coming in Margo's direction, thinking that Miss Libra's frantic gesture was indicating Del Weird's door.

Already in the old Professor's room, Margo was finding that she'd taken a big chance after all.

The man who had ducked back was half way through the window. He wasn't Lamont, his form was too hunchy. Besides, it wasn't Cranston's voice that came hoarsely, savagely though withal forced in tone.

"Stand back! Stand back or I'll shoot!"

Whether it was Demo, Margo couldn't tell for the dressing room was dark except where the light from the corridor hit it. Not dark enough though to hide the big gun that the intruder brandished in his hand, an old-fashioned, one-shot pistol that belonged to Professor Del Weird and had the look of a blunderbuss.

Caught half off balance Margo couldn't turn about, so there she was, wondering if the antique gun could be loaded and hoping that it wasn't. That kind of cannon could blow the dressing room apart at this close range if the savage man let go with it. Shouts were almost at the door and even if Margo tried to stand back, she'd be swept off her feet.

Then the menace ended.

It ended when the man at the window went backward, outward with a snarl waving the gun as he went. It was blackness that took him, living blackness that could only be The Shadow.

Now Margo was sure that the man must be Demo since The Shadow, popping into the picture, had eliminated her silly theory about Lamont. Demo was slashing at something using the ancient pistol as a bludgeon. A chunk of gloved blackness stopped Demo's arm in mid-air and the pistol left his hand, scaling in through the window and landing almost at Margo's feet. Margo jumped away, but fortunately the gun didn't strike on its trigger and therefore it didn't go off.

But was it fortunate?

That question was to become a moot one, very promptly.

Cardona and three or four other men came piling into the dressing room as the pistol landed and saw the open window to the courtyard where The Shadow had intercepted Demo. Shouting something about the law and all it stood for, Cardona rushed to the window and squeezed through. One man followed him; the others, being bulkier, started around the other way.

That struck Margo as a good idea. On the way, however, she intended to look for Zito and Frost, who had somehow been left behind in the rush. But before Margo could even glance along the passage, every light back stage was suddenly extinguished!

There was another deluge of excitement and somewhere from its distance Margo had the faint impression of the tinkle of breaking glass. Then out of the hubbub she heard Winstrom's strong voice urging everybody to be calm, to stay where they were or walk—not run—to the nearest exit.

Probably most of the people couldn't guess where the nearest exit was, but Margo wasn't bothered by that complication. Her nearest exit was right at hand, the alley door, and she reached it at something faster than a walk. Closing the door behind her, Margo cut off most of the confusion; then listened to sounds from the courtyard which formed a sizeable cul-de-sac around a corner of the building.

Sounds came first; then the sweep of flashlights. Evidently Cardona and his coterie weren't faring well in their hunt for an unknown intruder who happened to be Demo. Odd too that they didn't find him, for by now The Shadow certainly should have overpowered the man who was leading a peculiar double life.

Then the thought struck home to Margo that perhaps The Shadow didn't want to capture Demo. This was supported by the sounds that Margo heard of someone stealing out through the alley to the street. The Shadow wouldn't make that much noise, so it could only be Demo.

But where was The Shadow?

Peering boldly around the corner Margo watched the play of flashlights in the courtyard. One gleam suddenly moved upward, climbed the wall and swept along a third floor cornice that topped a low extension wall. Below the cornice was an upright oblong, the black outline of a window against the white wall.

As the flashlight focussed there, the outline spread like an increasing blot which curiously continued upward like grappling hooks seeking a hold. That blot was The Shadow, reaching to grasp the overhanging cornice which gained a wavering effect as the flashlight moved in an unsteady hand.

Margo would have cried out if she could. Only to call a warning might attract the attention of eyes that had not yet seen the weave of that shape below the cornice. So far no one in the courtyard seemed to have noticed it; therefore silence was the better course.

Except that there were other eyes that no one took into accounting, not even The Shadow.

From that window of Del Weird's blacked out dressing room, a big gun throated a powerful message. The shot could only have come from Del Weird's oversized pistol for it sounded like a cannon and its flame glared from the wall like a lightning flash in miniature.

That message was meant for The Shadow, and its potency was proved by the result. Blackness was suddenly banished by a topple of something white; then, cleaving the blurred gloom below it, a chunk of cornice came crashing down and smashed the paving of the courtyard with a pulverizing force.

The window was a stern oblong once again. All traces of the spreading blot were gone!

IX.

Inspector Cardona was after the answers to certain questions and wasn't getting them. Maybe it was because the people he was quizzing knew too little; perhaps it was because they knew too much.

At least it was a new experience for Cardona, dealing with a batch of magicians. Every man in the group seemed to be a past master at the art of equivoke, turning questions to suit their own purposes.

Two murders by magic in as many days convinced Cardona that the cases were connected; therefore he had narrowed down his quest to persons concerned in both. Cardona was conducting his quiz in Winstrom's penthouse and the principal guests were three in number: Varno, Frost and Zito.

There were a few others including Margo Lane who had been invited too. One of these was Miss Libra, who in private life answered to the name of Claire Meriden. However Cardona was bearing down upon the men who might have had some individual reasons for murdering Professor Del Weird, only the problem was to find such reasons.

Like Winstrom himself, the three performers from tonight's show all expressed the greatest admiration for Del Weird as they had known him in life and had the greatest regret for his unfortunate death.

"Del Weird was poisoned," announced Cardona, bluntly, as though everybody didn't know it. "What I'm after is who did it. Who fixed that wine and water trick with the kind of chemicals that would kill him?"

Eyes running along a row, Cardona took in Zed Zito and Glanville Frost, seated stiffly a short way apart. He looked at Wade Winstrom standing by the fireplace and studied Claire Meriden seated near, but Cardona gave them not much more than a passing glance.

The inspector's gaze settled stolidly on Val Varno who was almost in a corner by himself. Val had put away his coins and was practicing a triple one-hand cut with a pack of cards. Cardona didn't like the half-smirk that Varno gave him above the flipping pasteboards.

"Maybe you can tell me, Varno."

"Tell you what?" returned Val. "Who killed Del Weird?"

"That's right."

"You really want to know?"

"All right, I'll tell you." Varno drew himself up in his chair, squared the pack with an emphatic clamp of his hand, and with all the manner of a man prepared to make a full confession, delivered his answer: "Del Weird!"

"That's enough smart guy," retorted Cardona. "If you're trying to tell me it was suicide—"

"Only I'm not," interrupted Varno. "The old prof just got absent-minded, that's all. Probably brought along a lot of old-style chemicals forgetting he was going to do the new improved drinkable wine and water."

"Except that somebody could have switched in the poison stuff," reminded Cardona. "Or could they?"

He was leaving the question to Varno as an authority rather than
a suspect, but Val was too smart to be taken in by that.
"I wouldn't know," was Varno's reply. "Wine and water isn't in
my line. I stick to sleights"—he began manipulating the cards as if to
prove it—"except for a few spook effects like the spirit slates. Better
ask somebody who knows magic in general."

Cardona turned to Winstrom as the final authority but the big
man shook his head.

"I am a collector," affirmed Winstrom. "Among my apparatus I
have some involving liquids. For instance"—he turned to a large old-
fashioned conjuring table that fairly teemed with antique apparatus
—"here are two cylinders, two glasses and a decanter that belong
to the 'Wonderful Separation of Liquids' in its improved form of
sixty years ago.

"You mix wine and water in the decanter"—Winstrom gestured
as though performing the trick—"and put the cylinders over the
glasses. You run ribbons—ah, here they are—to each cylinder, white
for water, red for wine. At command the liquid leaves the decanter;
the wine arrives in one glass, the water in the other."

"Now we're getting somewhere," decided Cardona. "This is like
Del Weird's wine and water trick."

"Nothing like it." Winstrom shook his head. "It works on an entirely different principle."

Speculatively Cardona's gaze roved the rest of Winstrom's large
array of antique magic. Joe finally settled on a nickel-plated globe
mounted upon a fluted pedestal. The globe had a dividing band
around the center and it was topped with an ornamental knob.

"What kind of a trick is that?" Cardona asked. "Anything to do
with wine and water?"

That brought a smile from Winstrom.

"It's a cannon ball globe," he said. "I'll show you."

Stepping over, Winstrom lifted the top half of the globe and revealed a fair-sized cannon ball which he lifted, tossed in air, and replaced in the globe. Putting the top half on again, Winstrom twisted
it, lifted it again and showed them the cannon ball was gone, the
globe now being filled with candy.

Even Cardona laughed at that.

"I had one of those in a trick box when I was a kid," said Joe, "only
mine was a pocket model made of wood. They still sell them for

two bits in the Broadway trick stores. Watch me bring back the cannon ball."

Cardona tried and did pretty well. When he put the top half of the
globe in place, twisted it and lifted it, the cannon ball came back,
but it was somewhat awry. It was made in two hollow hemispheres
that fitted the respective halves of the globe, but Cardona was too
hasty and failed to drop the top section of the cannon ball on
straight.

"Anyway, that's the idea," apologized Joe. Then, getting back to
the slight subject of murder, "But how about the wine and water?"

"My books explain numerous methods," stated Winstrom, waving
in the direction of his library, "but I have never bothered with the
trick because it is too messy. In fact I seldom do tricks at all. Not even
these."

Winstrom's weary gesture to his general array of apparatus was
self-expressive. Owning so much of it, Winstrom would hardly know
where to begin and besides, the tricks themselves were mostly out
of date. Cardona decided to concentrate upon something more modern. He turned to Frost.

"You make magic apparatus they tell me," asserted Cardona. "That
wouldn't include a wine and water outfit, would it?"

"It would," returned Frost, coolly, "and it does. As many as five
hundred customers have bought my instructions which include facts
about chemicals, the poison kind that killed Del Weird. That gives
you a lot of suspects, inspector."

His smile as sleek as his smooth, glossy hair, Frost seemed to be
mocking Cardona openly. Rather than show he sensed it, Cardona
turned abruptly to Zito and asked:

"You wouldn't be one of Frost's customers, would you?"

Zito's sneer was prompt.

"Do I look like a sucker?" he demanded. Then, bluntly: "But it
isn't a question of who knows all about the wine and water. It's who
fixed Del Weird's set-up down there in the dressing room."

Cardona decided to question a new and possibly impartial witness on that point. He turned to Claire Meriden.

"Who went into Del Weird's dressing room, Miss Meriden?"

"If you mean before his act," the blonde replied, "I wouldn't know.
We were all back stage"—she was looking from Zito to Frost; then
remembering she'd been in both their acts, she switched her gaze

to Varno who was too busy with his cards to notice—"so any of us might have dropped in to talk with the professor. But after his act was on, I saw a muffled man go into the dressing room."

"The man who was there later?" queried Joe.

"I suppose so," nodded Claire. "I really didn't see his face. He blundered into my dressing room first but I was so busy hunting for something to wear that I hardly looked his way."

"I'd like to know who that chap was," grumbled Cardona, "except that he got to Del Weird's dressing room too late to be responsible for murder."

"I wouldn't say that exactly," put in Winstrom, drily. "From later reports, the fellow was pretty handy with that old gun he found in Del Weird's suit-case."

"It was somebody else who used the gun," corrected Cardona, throwing a significant look about the room. "The man we were after went out through the window. Later somebody threw the light switch and blacked out everything. If you want my opinion it was the man who threw the switch who did the shooting later."

Cold silence followed and Margo particularly felt its chill. Cardona was right; a trip from the back stage light switch to the dressing room would have been simple and the gun was lying where anyone would have stumbled over it. But Margo was thinking not in terms of the marksman but the target.

Half a ton of cornice cracked all over a smashed stone courtyard was a rather harrowing recollection except that no human fragments had been found amid the ruin. That at least gave Margo hope that The Shadow had maneuvered one of his remarkable escapes from an almost certain death. Thinking in just such terms, Margo looked up to see a newcomer who was entering Winstrom's living room. She gave a glad cry:

"Lamont!"

Casual as ever, Cranston curbed Margo's over-enthusiasm with a slight but significant gesture. Then, in calm style he said to Cardona:

"I hear there's been another murder, inspector."

Cardona acknowledged the fact.

"When murder strikes twice," Joe asserted, "it's bad enough. But when the same three people are there both times, it gets worse. However I'm holding nobody. I'll know where to reach them when it's necessary."

Including Zito, Frost and Varno with his round-up gaze, Cardona gave a gesture of dismissal. As the three were filing out, Frost paused to inquire about another matter.

"That pagoda of mine," he reminded. "All right if I truck it out here?"

Cardona nodded.

"Does the same go for my scales?" asked Zito. "I have the pulley rig too."

"Take them," growled Cardona. "There's nothing on the stage that counts, considering that somebody busted Del Weird's pitcher and glasses as soon as the light went out. Only it didn't help because there was enough trace of the liquids to prove that somebody switched in poison chemicals."

Either Cardona's glare was impartial or it was meant for all three of the departing men. Varno, the last to leave, gave a sharp, snappy riffle to the corner of his pack of cards.

"I carry my baggage with me," boasted Varno, fanning the pack as he went through the door. "Fifty-two pieces in all. No, wait! Fifty-three, but I don't need the extra piece. You can have the truck pick it up too."

As he turned the corner, Val Varno deftly plucked the joker from the remaining fifty-two cards. Just when Val was out of sight the card came skimming around the corner and whizzed past Cardona's chin to lodge under the front collar of his vest.

Cardona started toward the door only to stop as Claire Meriden blocked his path by bowing out. Turning to Winstrom, Cardona indignantly exhibited the joker. Winstrom took the card and nodded.

"Wonderful how that chap Varno does it," was Winstrom's comment. He gave the joker a clumsy toss and instead of skimming the card merely fluttered to the floor. "I wish I could be clever like that!"

What Cardona replied failed to reach Margo's ears for she was drawing Cranston into the room where Winstrom kept the playbills. Cranston motioned that he didn't want a report on what had happened in his absence; he'd hear it all from Cardona later. But Margo had something in her mind that she simply had to get off.

"Out in the courtyard!" Margo exclaimed. "Someone was climbing past a window and reaching for a cornice when a shot was fired from Del Weird's window—"

"And the cornice came down," added Cranston. "Only there wasn't anybody with it."

Margo nodded.

"It might have been that he found the cornice was already loose," suggested Cranston. "In that case he'd have swung down into the window instead of continuing up to the roof. Cornices don't make good parachutes, you know."

So that was it! The cornice had already begun its drop before the shot was fired. Its bulk had proven a falling shield against the spraying slugs from the blunderbuss pistol!

Leaving Margo to speculate on whether luck or rapid judgment had served The Shadow more, Lamont Cranston strolled out to the living room to hear Inspector Cardona summarize this night of crime.

X.

Late afternoon.

Nearly six o'clock again, the hour when Demo Sharpe went on duty with his telephone trick or at least pretended to do so.

Only tonight, the night following the murder of Professor Del Weird, Demo was really planning to take over. He was worried though, as he looked up from the undersized portable typewriter where he was working at his manuscript. Pete Noland caught Demo's worried look.

"Take it easy, Demo," urged Pete. "If I believe your story, so will other people. Only you won't have to tell it, because you have a perfect alibi."

Demo shook his head.

"It isn't even a story," he argued, "I didn't get a chance to even see Del Weird. I was away from the place before the shooting started."

"And no one really saw you?"

"The girl did. The one they called Miss Libra, who Frost borrowed for the pagoda production. She might recognize me if she saw me again."

"Then don't let her."

Pete's advice was helpful but it didn't quiet Demo much.

"I want to know what's going on," insisted Demo. "Cigam is in the clear and he probably has heard a lot. If I went over to his shop he might tell me a lot."

"Only his shop closes at six," reminded Pete. "Remember?"

Either Demo didn't remember or he didn't care. Other things were really more important.

"Cigam sent those old tricks to Winstrom yesterday," Demo declared, "and it's a cinch that Del Weird's shipment came in today. When I phoned Del Weird before the show he said he'd crated the stuff and expressed it to the Hotel Chianti. If I'd had a chance to see him he might have agreed to let me have first look at it."

"Instead the first look will be Winstrom's," declared Pete, "if he even bothers to go through the stuff. He must be a couple of months behind, going through that assorted junk of his."

"I wouldn't be too sure." Demo shook his head. "Winstrom has a lot of servants around and any time they're idle, he has them arrange his magic apparatus. Let's hope they don't fool much with the stuff, unless what we want is still on the loose."

"You mean more of Savanti's original apparatus?"

"Yes. There's no way of accounting for all of it. Something else might bob up somewhere and be the very piece that had those Malkara jewels in it. Only the one man who might know is dead."

"Del Weird?"

Nodding, Demo amplified his reply by producing an old frayed playbill. It was of a later date than the Malkara sample, but it advertised the Great Savanti. It was an American playbill announcing Savanti's tour across the country.

Among the big-print items the playbill stated:

THE PAGODA ILLUSION
OR
THE INVISIBLE FLIGHT

Invented by the Great Savanti during his tour of the Orient, this creation proves that a living person can be in two places at once!

Pete was particularly interested in the reference to the pagoda because it was the illusion that Frost had performed the night before, but Demo brushed that factor aside.

"If Frost had found those gems," declared Demo, "he wouldn't be bothering with making magical apparatus. Of course there's just a chance—"

Pausing, Demo snapped his fingers.

"I have it!" he exclaimed. "Frost stays open late. Get over to his workshop, Pete, and ask about the pagoda."

"You mean buy it?"

"Why not?" inquired Demo. "Have it shipped over here. Say you're getting up a big act, that's why you haven't been around much lately. Tell them I'm helping you rehearse."

As Pete started out the door, Demo remembered something.

"Better be back by seven though," said Demo. "I might want an hour for myself. The usual business. By the way, have them send up something to eat from downstairs."

Stopping in the little cafe off the lobby of the Albuquerque Arms, Pete relayed Demo's order. Nodding to clerk and doorman he went outside and was lucky enough to get a cab immediately. What Pete didn't see in the dusk was the cloaked figure close to the wall that signalled the cabby to pick up this passenger and then moved toward the cab to hear the address that the driver repeated a trifle loudly.

The Shadow was picking up Pete's trail on the chance that it would serve as a temporary substitute for Demo's.

Reaching Frost's basement workshop in about twenty minutes, Pete found the place lighted. Inside was Zito, looking over a new guillotine illusion that Frost had just built. Nodding to Pete, Zito gestured to the guillotine which stood waist high. It contained a sort of stock where a girl could insert her head and hands, while above was a large cleaver set in slots.

"A nice chopper," commented Zito. "More gruesome than most. This one slices through the girl's arms as well as her neck, except of course it doesn't hurt her."

"I don't like it," returned Pete. "Any trick is likely to go wrong."

"Not this one," put in Frost, a trifle annoyed at Pete's criticism of his product. "It's fool proof."

"That's what Del Weird said about his wine and water," chimed a voice from a corner. "Maybe he was just a bigger fool than he thought."

The speaker was Val Varno. Why he was here, except to check on two suspects named Glanville Frost and Zed Zito, Pete couldn't guess, unless Val had begun to think in terms of an alibi, like Demo.

Or maybe it was because Val was practicing new manipulations with rhinestone-studded thimbles and wanted to get the opinion of such connoisseurs as Frost and Zito. He was a smoothie, Val Varno, in a way much more convincing than Frost's, if being smooth could be styled a convincing matter.

Pete concentrated on Zito.

"You're buying the guillotine?"

"That's right," replied Zito. "Seems out of my line, but it isn't. I'm going to present it as a feat of hypnotism, saying it can't hurt Claire while she's under the spell."

"You're dropping the light and heavy act?"

"No, no. This will just be an added feature. Useful too in case I'm held over and have to do the usual hyp routine. By the way, how did you like the weight act last night?"

"Didn't catch it," replied Pete. "In fact I've never seen it. By the way, who's Claire?"

"Claire Meriden. She works as Miss Libra. So you missed the Golden Pagoda, too. Claire doubled in that act."

"I've heard it was good," said Pete. He turned to Frost. "Want to sell the pagoda illusion, Glanville?"

Frost showed bland interest which was his equivalent of a nod.

"How much?" asked Pete.

"I couldn't say," returned Frost. "Not until you've seen it."

"And until I've tried it," added Pete. "How about shipping it over to Demo's? I'm staying there, working up my new show."

Frost picked up the telephone.

"The truck is due at the hotel shortly," said Frost. "It would be just as easy to drop the pagoda at the Albuquerque Arms as to bring it back here."

"Provided it isn't off the route to the Club Marimba," put in Zito. "My stuff is going there. And what about the chopper? The truck was to pick it up here."

"Take the guillotine in a cab," suggested Frost. "It's not too big and you won't have to wait around."

Accepting the suggestion, Zito hoisted the portable guillotine and started out with it. He expected Varno to open the door for him but Val was no longer around. Pete made a mental note of that, calculating that Val must have left within the last few minutes. The ways and means of Val Varno seemed devious and doubtful to Pete Noland, which was all the more reason for checking on the card man.

Completing the call to the hotel, Frost made the arrangements for the shipment of the pagoda. Pete thanked him and left, taking a cab back to Demo's apartment. Though he'd met three Class-A suspects, Pete couldn't say that he had learned a thing. However, one item of Savanti's old apparatus would reach Demo, namely the Golden Pagoda.

It was probably the worst bet of all Savanti's equipment from the standpoint of a jewel cache, but Pete was sure that Demo would be pleased.

Demo might have been pleased if he'd been there.

Instead of Demo, Pete found the telephone ringing and answered it to handle one of the telephone trick customers. There was a note under the telephone, reminding Pete that he should have been back by seven.

It was now eight minutes after, so Pete calculated that Demo had been gone about five minutes. Whatever his new mission it must be important or Demo wouldn't have abandoned the telephone. Despite himself, Pete began to wonder about Demo. Maybe the sangfroid shown by the various suspects in magic's double murder had forced Pete to another choice. It took him a little while to shake off his doubts.

The Shadow, too, was wondering about Demo Sharpe. He'd figured that Demo wouldn't leave while Pete was absent, hence he hadn't watched the Albuquerque Arms. Now that Pete was back, The Shadow, returned to the front street, was expecting to spot a figure at a certain window and see it start a sneaky trip along the high ledge.

Only Demo didn't appear; not for five minutes, ten, nor even fifteen. By then The Shadow, in his turn, was thinking he could do better elsewhere.

There was a whispered laugh in the lower darkness as a cloaked figure glided to a waiting cab, but the tone carried no note of prophetic confidence.

Seldom did The Shadow give such a laugh too soon.

XI.

The Shadow hadn't missed much at Frost's. He'd been there in the darkness of the steps leading down into the basement workshop, during the period of Pete's visit. With the door ajar he'd heard enough of what was said.

Blended with darkness The Shadow had stepped aside to let Varno pass when the slinky sleight man had made his surreptitious departure. He'd also seen Zito go the opposite direction, as he had that night at Cigam's.

With Frost closing the shop when Pete left, all three of the promising candidates for double murderer now were at large. That was a definite reason why The Shadow should pick up Demo's trail as soon as possible. Lacking a present trace of Demo, the only compromise was a trip to the Hotel Chianti.

Nearing the hotel The Shadow saw a truck with the name UNICORN STORAGE marked conspicuously on its side with a picture of the fabled beast for which the name stood. Some men on the sidewalk were gesturing to the truck driver and it wasn't good policy for Shrevvy's cab to help block traffic. So The Shadow ordered Shrevvy around the block and there the cloaked investigator dropped off.

When The Shadow came back around the corner, the truck had moved. It was nearer the corner and the truckers were just loading on Frost's pagoda and Zito's scales which they must have found ready for them. Seeing an open doorway, The Shadow glided into it and promptly found another thing that suited him.

This was an empty service elevator. So The Shadow took it and rode straight to Winstrom's penthouse. There was just a chance that Demo might have gone there, for having evidenced a sudden interest in old-time magic apparatus, he would have a reason to look over some of Winstrom's.

Like wispy black smoke, The Shadow glided through a service door and along a hallway that led him into the big living room. Hearing voices, he could tell that Winstrom was in the dining room, having dinner with some guests. Hence living room, library and poster room were all empty. The Shadow made the rounds.

Among the playbills framed on the wall of the little room were some pertaining to Savanti. The Shadow noticed them because of their reference to the Pagoda Illusion and among them was one that closely resembled the bill Demo had shown to Pete. In scanning it, The Shadow noticed the names of the assistants in fine print at the bottom.

One name was significant. It was D. Elward. What the initial "D" stood for didn't matter; The Shadow was more interested in the entire name. It didn't take much imagination to transfer D. Elward into Del Weird. This fitted with two features that were fairly common in magic.

The first was that magicians' assistants quite often became performers themselves; the second that a stage name was often adapted from an actual one. The Shadow was quite sure that some research into Del Weird's early history would prove that he had gained his training under the Great Savanti.

That produced thoughts of Del Weird's apparatus. Going back to a store room off the rear hall, The Shadow found it bulging with crates including some stacked empties. These were stencilled with the name Del Weird and they looked as though they had originally held the pile of smaller boxes which were in another corner. The boxes were heavy, when The Shadow tested them, but none had been opened. How soon Winstrom would be getting around to them would depend upon how much time he could spare from his serious business enterprises.

Here would have been The Shadow's opportunity to go through Del Weird's shipment, though he could more easily have examined the apparatus from Cigam's which was packed loosely in half open boxes in this same store room. But what meant opportunity to Demo Sharpe was of little importance where The Shadow was concerned.

This was just a lot more obsolete magical equipment which had reached its eventual level, Winstrom's collection of forgotten mysteries. Since Winstrom had bought it in bulk and simply stored it, there was no indication that the stuff might have some secret value.

Except that murder by magic was still to be considered; double murder that certainly must have some motive greater than mere jealousy over who invented the paper hat trick or took priority in performing the linking rings. Still seeking Demo's relationship to that odd triangle of Varno, Frost and Zito, The Shadow felt that there might be an answer here.

A logical assumption considering that Cigam's apparatus, part of the setting of a murder scene, had been transferred here; and that Del Weird's apparatus, also on hand, belonged to a murder victim!

So The Shadow stooped to sort through some of the loose gadgets and immediately things happened. A tiny spirit bell began to chime when The Shadow lifted it; the bottom fell from an ornamental box delivering half a dozen billiard balls that clattered and rolled across the floor.

Something metallic whammed as a deluge of silk handkerchiefs shot in fountain style and cascaded all over The Shadow's hat and shoulders. Apparently Cigam believed in keeping hair-trigger gimmicks well-oiled, but The Shadow didn't stay to investigate further. Instead, he swooped for the half-open door, pulled it wide, then went back with it into darkness as one of Winstrom's servants arrived to seek the cause of all the clatter.

The servant was of squatty build and he intended to find the cord of an overhanging light, so being short he was stretching as he pawed the air. Deftly The Shadow's foot eased something the servant's way; hearing a rolling sound on the floor, the fellow turned and took a few short steps. They were enough.

The Shadow's gift consisted of a few odd billiard balls and the stocky man skidded when he stepped on them. Then his feet were sliding on others and he hit the floor in floundering style as The Shadow whisked past him and out through the hallway to the service elevator.

Like the rising crescendo of an orchestra came the increasing crashes from the store room. The floored servant had rolled against a stack of badly balanced boxes and overturned them, bringing a further clatter of glassware, tinware, and general hardware that belonged to Cigam's loosely packed shipment.

Another servant arrived from the dining room and behind him came Winstrom, calling loudly to learn what the trouble was about. They received an answer from the store room and when they reached there and turned on the light, they found the first servant crawling from a mass of nickel-plated debris.

It annoyed Winstrom to find some special glassware broken, for Cigam's shipment included items that would be difficult to duplicate. But Winstrom was even more incensed to find that all this had happened over nothing; that the servant had only thought he heard a prowler in the store room. It would seem that some gadget of Cigam's had popped, starting the rest, except for one factor.

Black against the elevator door, The Shadow was easing its sections open and stepping into the darkness beyond, as he heard the servant's plea.

"I'm sorry, Mr. Winstrom," the stocky man said. "Only I was sort of certain somebody was in here. You see when Frederick found the service elevator up on this floor and nobody in it, he said I'd better look around while he went down—"

The Shadow caught the warning in those words just a trifle too late. Already through the elevator door and easing it shut behind him, he realized that there wasn't any car. His feet meeting the vacancy of the shaft, The Shadow performed a flip in mid-air grabbing for whatever ledge might be within the door.

There was no ledge. The Shadow's only salvation was his cloak, which had caught in the closing door. Ordinarily he could have pulled it free; now he was hoping desperately that it would stay jammed, which it did. But those folds weren't strong enough to hold The Shadow's weight.

With a slow, dooming rip, the black cloth yielded—

XII.

If Wade Winstrom had turned a moment sooner, he might have seen the final closing of the elevator door. As it was, all Winstrom could now have seen was something he didn't notice, a small chunk of black cloth, jammed between the halves of the door.

Nevertheless, the mention of the elevator interested Winstrom. His broad forehead grooved with puzzled lines, he approached with heavy stride. It was only a dozen paces to the elevator and as Winstrom completed them, a sudden clang came from within the shaft.

Winstrom stepped back startled, then relaxed. The elevator door slithered open and out stepped Frederick, a dry-faced servant of the same stocky build that characterized the rest of Winstrom's hired help.

With Frederick was one of the hotel workers, a man named Kirk, who frequently ran the service car. Kirk was lifting a long jaw as he stared upward with deep-set eyes.

"Guess this car needs fixing," Kirk opined. "Getting sort of jolty."

Winstrom responded drily.

"Jolty enough to come up here by itself?" he queried. "Or wouldn't you know?"

"I wouldn't know," admitted Kirk. "Last time we used the car was to bring those crates up here, Mr. Winstrom. That was this afternoon."

Winstrom looked at Frederick who spread his arms in a perplexed gesture.

"I took the car down and found Kirk," reported Frederick. "There wasn't anybody else around, Mr. Winstrom."

"Whoever brought the car up could have gone down the other way," decided Winstrom, slowly. "We'll ask the regular elevator operators if they've seen any strangers. You can go, Kirk."

Kirk went down in the service car; Frederick and the other servants returned to their respective tasks. That left only Winstrom, standing at the closed door of the elevator. When Winstrom looked at the floor, he saw something. It was a jagged triangle of black cloth.

Picking up this memento, Winstrom studied it and tugged it between his heavy hands. Then, rolling it between his fists, he drew it away, made an absent-minded wave and spread his hand. The black cloth had vanished, but it reappeared a moment later when Winstrom clutched the air and literally plucked it into sight.

In his off-moments, Winstrom was a magician of sorts though he preferred not to display his comparatively meager talents in the presence of professionals.

Pocketing the piece of cloth, Winstrom went to the living room and hunted up a flashlight. It needed a new battery so he spent some time in finding one. Again, Winstrom was dropping behind schedule.

Down on the ground floor, Kirk had left the service elevator. Now something was stirring atop the empty car, a shape of living blackness. It rose, reached for a door above and found it. Hands that fumbled at first finally found a catch. The shaft door of the second floor slithered open.

Laboriously The Shadow worked himself through and elbowed the doors shut behind him. He rested there, his cloak oily and bedraggled, his whispered laugh a bit groggy as it emerged from beneath the tilted brim of his slouch hat.

The Shadow was the jolt that Kirk had attributed to some fault of the elevator mechanism.

Frederick's return had been timely for The Shadow. Kirk had been bringing the servant up in the service car all the while The Shadow's cloak had been tearing itself away in a fashion that would have also torn apart a heart less stout than The Shadow's.

The cloak had given just before the elevator arrived. Even a short fall could have proven fatal to The Shadow for the upward speed of the elevator would have added to the impact. But Kirk was braking the car as it scooped The Shadow a moment after his dangle was converted to an actual fall. Elevators frequently jolted when stopped suddenly, so Frederick had accepted Kirk's theory.

Only Winstrom wasn't quite convinced.

Through the cracks of the second floor door, The Shadow saw the broad beam of a strong flashlight glare downward. It stayed there fully half a minute, ample time for anyone above to study the whole top of the elevator as it rested at ground floor level.

And now the top of that car no longer had a huddled passenger.

The ex-passenger, The Shadow, rose to his feet and found a stairway leading down to the ground floor. Becoming steadier as he progressed, The Shadow reached the grand ball room. Going back stage, he paused. By the dim light from a fire exit, The Shadow saw some baggage that the truckers had left.

Among other things they'd forgotten Zito's ropes and pulleys. Also the apparatus of other performers was still there. In fact all they'd taken was Frost's pagoda and Zito's scales.

The Shadow moved toward the thick darkness of the alley exit as he heard the sound of footsteps with accompanying voices, coming from the foyer. Into sight came Zed Zito with a pair of men in the uniform of hotel porters. When they reached the stage, Zito gave a disgusted snarl.

"I knew Frost would bungle it!" exclaimed Zito. "Look, they've left my pulleys! They should have taken them along with the scales."

One of the porters shrugged.

"Better ask the truckers," he said. "It was their job, not ours. Maybe they're still out back."

The Shadow decided to go out back first. He was through the door and had closed it before Zito even started in that direction.

Outside, a truck was just pulling away from the alley. His time sense considerably jarred, The Shadow did not regard it as irregular. All he wanted was Shrevvy's cab and he found it with a probing flashlight as soon as he reached the street.

Or rather, the cab found The Shadow.

That flashlight had a colored lens that could deliver red or green flashes as occasion called. This occasion called for green, and Shrevvy spied the blinks from the corner where he was parked. Whipping up, the cab gathered The Shadow automatically, though Shrevvy was a

bit surprised at the slight delay The Shadow required. Usually
Shrevvy's chief was inside before the brakes really gripped.

This time the cab came almost to a stop. There was a lapse too,
before Shrevvy heard the command:

"Tag that truck."

Shrevvy could have argued the point, but didn't, because he pre-
sumed The Shadow knew what he was about. Nevertheless, as the
trail veered off in a totally wrong direction, Shrevvy pressed closer
to the truck hoping that his chief would see for himself.

And The Shadow did see.

A corner light etched the side of the truck as it swung the corner.
It wasn't the Unicorn truck. Its size was wrong and besides it bore
this name:

VANGUARD VANS INCORPORATED

As Shrevvy expected, The Shadow promptly pulled him off the
trail. Then Shrevvy was explaining through the connecting window:

"The Unicorn job pulled out a while ago, boss. This one must have
come along to pick up another load for somebody else. Or maybe it
was delivering a shipment at the hotel. I didn't see—"

The Shadow's sibilant laugh interrupted Shrevvy's report. Then
came the order:

"Go to the Albuquerque Arms." Curious that The Shadow should
be saying just that and saying it just then. For at practically that
same moment, Inspector Joe Cardona was listening to an anony-
mous voice across his telephone at headquarters. The voice was
saying:

"Go to the Albuquerque Arms."

Long practice had taught Cardona how to handle calls of this type.
Indifferently he queried:

"Yeah? What apartment?"

"Apartment 12-J," said the voice, in a forced monotone that gave
no clue as to its owner. "The apartment occupied by Demo Sharpe."

The name seemed somewhat familiar to Cardona.

"All right, Mr. Bones," said Joe, treating the call as a gag, "and
why should I go to Apartment 12-J at the Albuquerque Arms to find
somebody named Demo Sharpe?"

There was a pause during which Cardona expected to hear a re-

ceiver click. Instead, the voice spoke again, in that same prosaic monotone, but its words were fraught with something akin to menace.

The voice said:

"Because there you will find a murderer."

XIII.

For a place where a murderer was supposed to be, the Albuquerque
Arms was exceedingly quiet, but perhaps that was just the calm that
stood as prelude to tumult.

There was nothing sinister however about the truck that pulled up
at the side entrance. It bore the name "Unicorn Storage" and it had
the type of load that the people at the Arms recognized, for they had
seen things like it before.

Usually though, Demo Sharpe and his friend Pete Noland brought
home smaller apparatus than the gilded pagoda which required a
truck to haul it. The pagoda also looked antique when compared with
other magical equipment that had been seen around the Arms.

The truckers had to weigh the pagoda in order to fix the charges.
They'd been told to do this, one said, by Mr. Frost, the man who had
phoned them to leave the pagoda here.

Weighing the pagoda was simple because in the truck was a pair of
sizable scales, a flat type on rollers. The truckers planted it on the
sidewalk, laid a board up to it and pushed the pagoda up the runway.
The scales registered exactly one hundred and eighty-three pounds.

The clerk used the house phone to call Apartment 12-J. The voice
that answered was Pete's perfect imitation of Demo's because Demo
invariably answered the house phone when at home.

The voice convinced the clerk. Hanging up, he stated:

"Mr. Sharpe says send it up. He'll have Mr. Noland pay the
charges. The pagoda belongs to Mr. Noland."

The door man helped the truckers roll the pagoda into the service
elevator and took them up, since the regular operator was busy. On
the way, the truck man speculated on their gilded shipment.

"Kind of heavy," declared one, "to be lugged all in one piece."

"It's bulky," said the other. "That makes it seem heavier than it is.
Funny how things fool you when they're tough to handle."

"This thing cracks apart, though," said the first man, pointing to a joint between the pagoda and its platform. "It would be easier in two pieces."

That didn't appeal to the second trucker.

"Not for us," he claimed. "They'd expect us to take it apart and put it together. That's more work than hefting it, and anyway it rolls easy."

At the twelfth floor the Unicorn men rolled the platform and pagoda to 12-J where the door man knocked. There was a delay because Demo's voice was coming through the transom. He was talking to somebody over the telephone, telling them they'd taken the three of diamonds, which caused the truckers to look askance as though they doubted Demo's sanity.

The door finally opened and Pete appeared in shirt sleeves. He nodded when he saw the pagoda.

"I'm Mr. Noland," he announced and the truckers didn't doubt it since his voice was entirely different from the one they'd heard. "I'll sign for the shipment. What's the charges?"

The truckers gave the charges and Peter paid them. The apartment door was just broad enough to accommodate the pagoda and its platform when they were tilted slightly. Inside the living room, Pete opened the front of the pagoda and let the truckers see that the interior was in good condition, something on which they insisted rather than have complaints on damage they hadn't checked.

Just as the truckers were leaving, Pete heard the police siren.

It sounded distant, but that was because the apartment windows were tight shut. They were locked too, for Pete thought that was good policy rather than have chance visitors suspect that they were used for more than ventilation. The telephone was ringing so Pete bowed the truck men out, the door man with them, and closed the door.

Just for effect, Pete called:

"Demo! It's probably for you!"

Door man and truckers heard Demo's voice take over the telephone, just as they were getting in the service elevator. By then, the police siren had ceased.

The next interval was something for later speculation.

It couldn't have been very long, for the passenger elevator had gone up when the service car reached the ground floor. Seeing some police in the lobby the door man went to find out why they were there while the truckers, not wanting to get mixed in something that didn't concern them, hurried out to their truck, loaded on the scales and started.

Nobody stopped them because Inspector Cardona had given orders not to disturb anybody downstairs. Still thinking that the mysterious phone call might be a hoax, Cardona wanted to start with a visit to Apartment 12-J. By this time, Joe had recalled what Demo's name meant. It stood for telephone tricks and the fellow might just have the temerity to be staging some sort of publicity stunt to annoy the police, something that would help him peddle his instruction sheets.

Just as the passenger elevator arrived on the twelfth floor, the telephone jangled from Demo's apartment. Nobody answered it, which struck Cardona as odd. Motioning to the elevator man Cardona gestured for the fellow's pass key. The man supplied it and to the tune of the ringing telephone, Cardona unlocked the apartment door with one hand, while gripping a revolver with the other.

Whether or not Joe expected murder, he found it. Stretched on the floor in front of the Golden Pagoda was a body, twisted in death. One look at the chunky frozen face was all the elevator man needed. He gulped:

"Demo Sharpe!"

Wheeling around with leveled gun, Cardona saw that the living room was empty. Keeping his eye on a far door, Cardona picked up the phone receiver and said: "Yeah."

"I have a question, Mr. Sharpe," said a voice. "A friend of mine named Clinton says that you can answer it. I've written the answer here."

"Let's hear the question," Cardona answered gruffly. "Only who are you?"

"Clint says I don't have to tell you."

"He does? Well why not?"

"Because you're supposed to tell me. What I want to know is the name of the card I took."

Savagely, Cardona clamped down the receiver and stalked to the far door. Flinging it open, he saw a lighted bedroom, as empty as the living room. As Cardona came back, the telephone started a new jangle. Unhooking the receiver, Joe left it that way.

"Call the lobby," Joe told the elevator man. "Use the house phone.

Say that I want one of my men to come up in the service elevator. The other is to use the stairs. They're to be on the lookout for a murderer."

"You—you mean Mr. Noland?" stammered the elevator man. "He lives with Mr. Sharpe. Only he isn't a murderer, I wouldn't think."

"I'll do the thinking. Make that call."

Cardona flung open the doors of the pagoda, saw that it was empty. Going to the windows, he checked them, found every window clamped. Continuing through the little apartment, Joe searched it rapidly but thoroughly. There wasn't a place where anybody could hide.

One cop arrived in the service elevator and Cardona sent him down the stairs to meet the other. Meanwhile the door man was staring at Demo's body and protesting that Pete must still be around. He'd come up with the officer, the door man had.

"They were both here!" the door man testified. "Demo was on the phone when we went down. The murder would have taken Pete so long that he couldn't have gotten away before you arrived!"

Cardona wasn't inclined to accept the door man's calculation.

"He's gone now, Noland is," Cardona said. "You two can take those elevators down. I'll stay here and phone the lobby for whatever I need."

Door man and elevator man left. Out in the hallway Cardona watched them close the elevator doors. Along with those heavy clangs, Joe thought he heard something else, but wasn't quite sure what it was.

The sound might have come from Demo's apartment. Going back there, Cardona swung his gun around the place, but in that broad glance he failed to see anything that was disturbed. That fact brought a sharp grunt from the ace inspector.

Joe Cardona had encountered the thing he didn't believe could exist, the perfect sealed room mystery wherein a murderer had vanished, leaving nothing but a victim. Yet in this investigation it was quite logical that such should happen.

This case was one where murder by magic was the rule!

XIV.

There were no police outside the Albuquerque Arms when The Shadow's cab arrived there, but the headquarters car, parked in front, advertised the fact that something had gone wrong. Telling Shrevvy to drive around the block The Shadow looked for traces of the Unicorn truck but it had gone.

That left Demo's window as the next objective, so The Shadow, back in form, dropped from the cab at the right vantage spot. This was where he could reach the next apartment building and use its automatic elevator to the roof, but first The Shadow wanted to see if Demo's window was lighted. There was a convenient spot near the next building which permitted this.

From that spot The Shadow saw Demo's window and more.

Someone was easing along the twelfth floor ledge, someone who wasn't as familiar with that cat-walk as was Demo. This man was practically feeling his way on hands and knees as though he dreaded the transit. It wouldn't take much more than a slip of his own nerves to shake him from that ledge.

From somewhere in the lower darkness a rifle crackled. The Shadow could almost see the ping of the bullet above the crawling man. The fellow hesitated, wavered, and the sniper's long range weapon spoke again.

If smart, the hidden sniper would not try to actually hit his target. The man on the ledge, unquestionably Pete Noland, would soon yield to the threat of those whimpering bullets and their leaden bashes. If his knees gave way to his nerves, he would plunge from the ledge and his death would be attributed to a fall.

They seemed distant, those rifle shots, but they couldn't be too far away. The marksman's gun was probably muffled in lieu of a silencer that would have either limited its accuracy or restricted the number of its rounds. In fact The Shadow was lucky to have heard its reports at all, as he realized when he started in their general direction.

Lost among the restricting walls of buildings, the rifle fire could only be heard from a few special spots. One such place had fortunately been The Shadow's location. In turn, that gave him a clue to where the rifle man might be.

Coming to a long narrow passage between two buildings a block from the Arms, The Shadow saw the rifle deliver an upward spurt and plainly heard its thudding report from straight ahead. Whether the shots had so far taken toll, The Shadow didn't look back to see. The first step was to end the menace; if that failed the next step was to take quick vengeance.

The Shadow simply let blast with his .45 automatic in the direction of the rifle spurt.

There was a sudden clatter, the muffled sound of an overturning ash-can. Automatic still blazing, The Shadow drove ahead and brought up suddenly and hard against a solid brick wall. This alley had a dead-end right in the middle; the rifle had been shooting over the top of it. Therefore The Shadow's return fire had merely warned the sniper to get going from his ash-can pedestal on the other side.

The wall wasn't too high to scale, even though The Shadow lacked an ash-can as a springboard. Unfortunately, the top of the wall was lined with sharp-pointed pickets which had somehow been overlooked in the scrap-metal drives. It took time for The Shadow to maneuver past those and before he could emerge from the alley on the other side, the sound of a motor from the street announced the departure of the rifle expert.

Shrevvy's cab arrived about a minute later. It had a habit of appearing places almost as unexpectedly as The Shadow. But Shrevvy had come from the wrong direction; he hadn't seen the departing car and by now it had gained too good a start to be overtaken.

There were some police whistles sounding, for The Shadow's shots, louder than the muffled rifle, had disturbed the neighborhood. So The Shadow used the cab for a quick departure, watching from the window for traces of Pete Noland. There was no sign of anyone on that high ledge; so if Pete hadn't fallen, he, by this time, had used Demo's favorite route of the elevator in the next building.

The Shadow at least had done his part to make the latter sequel possible.

As Cranston, The Shadow arrived at the Albuquerque Arms and went right up to Demo's apartment. His appearance there was more than a surprise to Cardona; the inspector was almost inclined to regard it with suspicion, now that Cranston had joined a magicians' club and magic was so definitely linked to murder.

But Cranston had an explanation, as good as it was unusual. Nodding to Cardona, he thumbed first at the unhooked telephone receiver, next at Demo's body.

"I thought so," said Cranston.

"Thought what?" demanded Cardona.

"That something had happened to Demo," explained Cranston.

"I was working the telephone trick and the person who called got the connection but nobody answered."

Cranston had pictured it just right, so the explanation went with Cardona. Then:

"If you're so smart at solving riddles," declared Joe, "riddle me this one. What's happened to the murderer?"

"You mean Demo was murdered here?"

"Where else?" retorted Cardona. "There's his body, isn't it? He was talking on the telephone when the pagoda was brought up."

"Did anybody see him?"

"No. The pagoda was for a fellow named Noland. He signed for it and here's the receipt."

"Then where is Noland now?"

"That's what I'm asking," Cardona said glumly. "He didn't have time to lam and we've searched the dump with a fine-tooth-comb. When it comes to murder by magic, this stops any yet."

Mention of magic caused Cranston to repress a smile.

"It's one of those sealed room cases," argued Cardona. "Doors closed, windows clamped; the killer is here, only he isn't anywhere."

Cranston's eye roved expertly.

"Tell me one thing," he said. "Why did you step out of the room after you'd searched the apartment?"

Cardona became sharp.

"How did you know that?"

"Step out again and then come back. I won't leave the living room. But if you want me"—Cranston's tone sounded a bit whimsical—"just call."

It sounded silly to Cardona but he'd seen one gag realize itself tonight, so he was willing to take the bait again, hoping that the result would be more pleasant.

The result was.

Also it proved spectacular.

Going out to the hall, Cardona stamped around and returned. Cranston wasn't anywhere in sight. Remembering that Cranston had said he'd stay in the living room, Cardona gave up. He was staring toward the open pagoda when he called:

"All right, where are you?"

In the blink of an eye, Cardona was seeing things. Cranston didn't have to shut cabinet doors when he did magic. Out of nowhere it seemed, he appeared right inside the golden pagoda. Rising he stepped from it the way Claire had, the night Frost worked the illusion.

"Say—"

From the way Cardona toned the word, he was thinking of something else. Then, glancing at the receipt the truckers had left, he shook his head.

"I was thinking Demo might have come in that pagoda," declared Cardona. "I'd forgotten that they'd heard him talking on the phone. Besides"—he showed Cranston the receipt—"the pagoda only weighs a hundred and eighty-three pounds. Demo himself must weigh a hundred and fifty and thirty-three wouldn't be enough over."

Giving a hoist at the pagoda platform Cardona estimated that it did weigh about a hundred and eighty-three pounds. Then, staring at Cranston, he demanded:

"But what's this got to do with Noland's disappearance?"

"A lot," replied Cranston. "You can vanish from that pagoda as well as appear in it."

"You can?"

"Of course. Want me to show you?"

"I'll take your word for it. So that's why I couldn't find Noland! He worked the illusion backward when he heard me outside the door!"

Cranston nodded his confirmation. He knew what was coming next.

"But where is Noland now?" demanded Cardona. "Let's say he reappeared when I was out in the hall. What happened to him then? That pagoda can't disappear a lot of people, can it?"

There was a head-shake from Cranston.

"You checked the window too early," he told Cardona. "You should have looked at it after you came back."

Cardona looked and saw what Cranston meant. The window was unclamped at present. Hopping over, Cardona hauled it up and saw the ledge outside.

"So that's where the guy went!" exclaimed Joe. "Well, if he's hiding anywhere in the neighborhood we'll find him!"

Cranston doubted that Pete would be, but he didn't say so. Furthermore, Cranston was coming to the conclusion that it would be better to question persons like Varno, Frost and Zito regarding their evening's whereabouts, than to ask Pete Noland.

Still there were things that Pete could tell, if he could be found, so that task would become The Shadow's. This third murder, unfortunate though it was, had at least clinched Demo's innocence of earlier crime.

This was one of those cases where the gradual elimination of suspects would eventually narrow the trail to just one man.

But The Shadow intended to see to it that further eliminations were not the result of more murder by magic!

XV.

Music was mellow at the Club Marimba and Claire Meriden wished that she didn't have to be Miss Libra. It wasn't fun being pawed by customers who tried to lift her when Zito commanded "Light" or "Heavy." Nevertheless it was show business, so Claire was putting up with it.

It was time to be getting ready for the act right now, so Claire went to her dressing room and got out her costume which was necessarily scanty to prove that it didn't have a lot of hidden weights concealed in it. The closet door was open and Claire wondered why she'd left it that way. She didn't realize that she hadn't, until she closed it.

Then from the space that the door had hidden stepped a very grim young man whose picture had been in all the newspapers. Claire recognized Pete Noland, wanted for the murders of Louie the Grift, Professor Del Weird, Demo Sharpe, and perhaps a lot of others whose bodies hadn't yet shown up.

Pete had a gun, a logical accessory for a murderer's kit-bag. Only for some reason Claire wasn't scared. It struck her that Pete was driven by despair more than desperation.

For one thing, his pistol was a long-barreled affair that looked as unprofessional as Del Weird's old blunderbuss model. Obviously something that he had picked up at random, such a gun lessened the menace behind it.

Again, when Pete spoke, his voice carried a plea, rather than a threat.

"You've got to help me," he insisted. "You're the only person who knows that Demo Sharpe was out and around when he was supposed to be handling the telephone stunt. In giving him an alibi, I lost my own!"

This was news to Claire, but of a sort she didn't quite fathom.

"If Demo was murdering people," the blonde said coolly, "how does it happen he became a victim?"

"You don't understand." Finding that Claire at least would listen, Pete parked the pistol on the dressing table. "Demo was after something else, a fortune if he found it. He wasn't out to kill anybody."

"So somebody killed him."

"Yes, but I wasn't the murderer. Look—you worked in the Golden Pagoda illusion the other night, didn't you?"

Claire responded with a nod.

"And nobody knew where you came from, did they?"

Beginning a head-shake, Claire amended it.

"They might have," she said, "if they knew how the illusion worked."

"I know the secret," declared Pete, "because I bought the pagoda. The first thing I did was see if it was in working order."

"Naturally."

"It worked all right." Pete spoke bitterly. "Only nobody popped out alive. Instead, Demo rolled out dead."

Claire's face showed genuine horror. What Pete said was not only graphic but plausible. Claire was thinking how startled she would have been in a similar situation.

"By then the police were coming," continued Pete. "I know I was framed, so I used the pagoda for a vanish—of myself. That's why I'm still on the romp."

Although Pete didn't go into the further details of his sneak trip along the ledge, Claire was quite convinced that his story was true. Before the girl could voice an objection, Pete added:

"What ruins my story is the fact that the pagoda was weighed before it was brought up to the apartment. It only hit a hundred and eighty-three."

"Of course," said Claire brightly. "That's just about what it would weigh."

"Not with Demo in it. The scales should have registered nearly double."

Staring steadily, Claire ended with a sudden exclamation:

"Zito's scales!"

"I figured that," declared Pete triumphantly. "I've heard about the weight changing act and that business with the scales would only work if they were faked."

"Of course they're faked," rejoined Claire. "How could my weight be different if they weren't? I'm just doing the old resistance act as they used to call it."

Pete nodded his understanding.

"And now I'm ahead of you," continued Claire. "You want to know if Zito's scales were on the truck with Frost's pagoda. They were and what's more they could have been set to show the usual weight while Demo's body was in the pagoda."

"That clinches it," affirmed Pete. "Your friend Zed Zito is the murderer."

Claire suddenly became loyal to Zito.

"I don't think so," she argued. "Zito's an all right person. He gave me a job when he first met me at Frost's and he says now I can quit the Libra grind if I don't like it and still be in line for the lead in his bigger show."

"Then maybe Frost was the murderer."

"Now you're talking," Claire told Pete. "Frost is so sleek he's slimy, if you want my unbiased opinion."

"How did you first meet Frost?"

"When he wrote about buying the pagoda illusion. It belonged to my great-uncle."

"Great uncle!" exclaimed Pete. "You don't mean the Great Savanti!"

"Of course. He left me everything; that is, what was left of it. A nice gilded pagoda and a pair of scales to match. Frost bought the works and sold the scales to Zito."

Pete was pondering deeply.

"Did you ever hear talk about some jewels?" he queried, in that frank tone of his. "Gems from the Orient that belonged to your Great-uncle Savanti?"

Eyes wider, Claire shook her head.

"They're what Demo was after," asserted Pete, "but from what you say they're really yours. Maybe we'll find them at Frost's place. Let's go."

"But I have to do a show—"

Interrupting herself, Claire raised a hand for silence. She was sure she heard footsteps stopping just outside the dressing room. Eyes half closed, Pete was pondering and didn't notice Claire's gesture.

"We could get over to Frost's in fifteen minutes," Pete calculated. "Of course we might have a long time hunting there. Fifteen minutes more to get back—"

Claire gripped Pete's shoulder and jogged it, motioning for silence with her other hand. She was sure now that somebody was listening outside that door. Stepping to the door Claire wrenched it inward and a girl came launching through.

The eavesdropper was Margo Lane. She came up with a pocket-sized automatic from her hand-bag. All in one gesture, though a long one, Margo covered Claire and told her to stay where she was. Then Margo turned to look at Pete.

The wanted man was on his feet, coolly aiming the long-barreled pistol at Margo. He gestured for her to hand over her automatic to Claire. Pete told Claire to keep Margo covered, which she did with the brunette's own gun.

And then Pete clicked his own trigger.

Blonde and brunette both gave startled cries that ended as the pistol went off with a noiseless bang. Its barrel clicked apart and the "Bang!" appeared in big letters on a fancy silk handkerchief that unfolded from the trick barrel.

"It was the best thing I could find," apologized Pete. "Besides, I would not want to carry a real gun."

Claire needed no apologies, but Margo did. She was much annoyed at having been tricked so easily. Only it happened that Margo's troubles had just begun.

"Since you broke in here, Miss Smarty," decided Claire, "I think I'll break you into the Miss Libra act." To Pete, Claire added: "Wait for me outside, I'll be right along." Then, tossing the Libra costume to Margo, Claire backed her next order with the captured gun. "Climb out of your own clothes and into these," she told Margo. "Make it snappy, because if this trigger slips, a handkerchief won't drop. You will."

Closing the door, Pete tiptoed out the back way. He heard Claire saying that she'd explain the Miss Libra act while Margo was making the change; then, a few paces along the hall, he could hear no more.

In what amounted to a stage alley outside the Club Marimba, Pete had finished a couple of cigarettes when Claire arrived.

"What about the girl?" he undertoned. "Did she agree?"

"So far, yes," returned Claire with a smile. "It will be up to Zito to convince her further and I think he can. So let's get on to Frost's place."

Just why Claire was so convinced about Margo's willingness to play Miss Libra remained a mystery, but only briefly. In about five minutes, blackness appeared suddenly from a door that led back stage at the Marimba, and The Shadow materialized from his self-made gloom.

Finding Claire's door, The Shadow knocked there; getting no response he turned and knob and peered into the dressing room. Pausing, The Shadow hung his hat and cloak in a dark corner of the corridor and entered the room as Cranston.

In a corner was Margo, attired in the chic costume of Miss Libra. She was seated at the end of the dressing table, her head and hands through the pillories of Zito's new guillotine which Claire had kindly placed at that convenient elevation. Margo was gagged with Claire's scarf and in front of her, where she could read and digest it, was a note.

Strolling over, Cranston picked up the note and looked at it while he was untying Margo's gag. Addressed to Zito, the note was signed by Claire. It said:

"Here is my new understudy. She says she will work as Libra but I'm not sure. If she agrees to keep her promise let her out. Otherwise she can stay until I get back. Good luck."

Unclamping the hand and neck stocks, Cranston released Margo from the guillotine. Drawing her head from beneath the threatening chopper, Margo came to her feet volubly.

"They've gone to Frost's," she began. "Claire and Noland. Wait for me"—Margo gestured to the door—"and I'll be right along. I'll only be a few minutes getting dressed."

Cranston waved Margo back to her chair.

"Did you promise to play Miss Libra, Margo?"

"Yes, but who wouldn't with a gun backing the argument?"

"Claire told you how to work the act?"

"Certainly." Rising, Margo folded her bare arms and thrust them up toward Cranston's chin. "When Zito says 'Heavy!' I do this and it throws anybody off balance who tries to lift me. When he says 'Light!' I relax"—Margo let her arms ease down—"and then I can be lifted."

"You caught on quickly," commended Cranston. "You won't have to show Zito the note. Just tell him you're a friend who promised to take Claire's place."

"Why of all the nerve!" exclaimed Margo indignantly. "Unless you're just kidding me, you're worse than Claire. And anyway, you're wasting precious time!"

"Not at all," returned Cranston. "I'm saving it, because I'm not waiting for you to come along. But whatever you do"—his tone was very serious—"don't tell Zito where Claire went."

When Lamont spoke that way, Margo listened. She realized now that something important must be at stake, that The Shadow's battle to thwart murder by magic was nearing a climax. Arms akimbo, Margo watched Cranston leave; then, when the door closed, she turned and studied herself in the dressing table mirror.

After all, Margo made a trim Miss Libra, better perhaps than Claire. Maybe that was just a matter of opinion, but Margo was willing to let the public judge. Claire wouldn't be too happy if her new understudy stole the show.

Margo Lane was smiling at that thought as she went out to introduce herself to Zed Zito.

XVI.

Frost's cellar was very dark except where Pete Noland pierced it with a flashlight. Finding this cellar beneath the basement workshop had been a real discovery in Pete's opinion. Claire Meriden felt the same, except that none of its discarded junk looked old enough to be magic of the Savanti vintage.

"Anyway, this shows Frost up," claimed Claire. "He says that he only builds streamlined illusions. He bought the pagoda just because it had a modern slant. But look at all this old stuff!"

"Where else would Frost get new ideas?" queried Pete. "It's easier to revive things that have been forgotten than to invent something better. Take Zito and the Libra act for instance."

"Zito can have it," laughed Claire. Then, becoming serious: "Only I hope he did convince that girl."

Pete didn't inquire why. He was busy poking through some old escape tricks, padlocks, handcuffs, and other appliances.

"Mr. Winstrom will be at the club tonight," recalled Claire, "and Zito is trying to get him to back the big show. So if the act flops—"

Claire broke off. She was beginning to feel sorry for letting Zito down. Pete turned the flashlight into an old-fashioned trunk that was packed mostly with broken fish bowls.

"Nothing here," said Pete. "Let's look over in the other corner."

"But that's all new apparatus," objected Claire. "We looked there first."

"Frost may have buried something underneath it," declared Pete, "except that if he did, he knew its real value. No, our best bet with Frost is that he doesn't know anything about those gems."

Rather than waste the dimming battery, Pete turned off the flashlight as they moved to the deep corner. Claire gripped his arm very tightly.

"There's something fearful about this place," she breathed. "I felt it when we first came down those creaky old stairs. Only it's more repressive now. Somehow we don't seem to be alone here!"

The flashlight, twinkling again, cast great sweeping silhouettes across the wall and Claire swallowed hard. Maybe those were just shadows from stacks of old props but one in particular seemed very lifelike as it faded from the dull glare.

Then came the creaks.

Not from the stairs at first, but from the floor of the workshop, direction above. It was Pete now who gave the grip, but only to quiet Claire. The footsteps, which the creaks unquestionably represented, had now reached the top of the cellar steps.

"If only we'd closed that door!" groaned Pete. "Still, it wouldn't help. The door was bolted on the other side, so we couldn't have made it look right."

A horrified thought swept Claire.

"Suppose somebody bolts it now!"

The very suggestion roused Pete to action. Bringing Claire with him, he started for the stairs, making far too much clatter on the stone floor. Creaks paused in answer, a few steps from the stair top, which was around the rear corner of the cellar.

"Wait!"

The tone was whispered, between the strained ears of Pete and Claire. The girl was right, someone else was with them, here in this very cellar!

"Keep talking," ordered the mysterious tone. "Whoever it is, keep him interested. Make him think you've found something."

Pete knew the speaker couldn't be Claire and Claire knew it couldn't be Pete. But they both realized that a friend had found them. They were lucky in that The Shadow had trailed them so promptly from the Club Marimba.

"How about those fish bowls?" queried Pete in a loud tone. "Have you looked through them yet?"

Somebody rattled the trunk with the bowls and the glass responded. Pretending that she'd produced the clatter, Claire spoke as though calling back to Pete.

"I think I have," she said. "Better come over and help me look."

Fish bowls weren't interesting enough to the intruder on the stairs. His creaks moved upward, signifying that he probably intended the inevitable, the bolting of the upper door to lock the prisoners below. It was a strong door too, a fire door, sheathed with metal.

The Shadow's whisper was back again.

"Say you're going up." The whisper was for Pete. "Say that you have a phone call to make."

"I'm going upstairs," announced Pete loudly. "I'm going to use Frost's telephone."

By then, Claire was getting instructions from The Shadow. She replied to Pete in the words The Shadow gave her.

"But you can't do that!" the girl exclaimed. "What would anybody think, getting a call from Pete Noland?"

The Shadow was meanwhile prompting Pete, who carried the conversation according to the whisper.

"It won't matter," declared Pete. "Nobody could trace the call. Are you getting scared, Claire?"

Claire's turn now, instructed by The Shadow.

"But if anything happened"—Claire faltered neatly—"to me, for instance—well, they'd blame you."

"And what if anything happened to me?"

"Well, they'd blame me—or would they?"

All this was as The Shadow prompted it with whispers and there was more to come.

"I guess they would," said Pete with a half-sneer, "if they found us dead with an empty gun. They'd think we'd cancelled each other off."

"Don't talk that way, Pete!" Claire's voice showed horror that she didn't have to fake. "It sounds as though it could happen."

"Except that I haven't any gun," retorted Pete. "Anyway, I'm going up to the workshop. Coming along?"

"Yes, but since we haven't any flashlight," Claire lied glibly, "you'd better use that bulb with the long extension cord."

"A good idea. It ought to reach upstairs. Let's find it."

Scuffling sounds denoted a hunt for the extension light that wasn't there. Why The Shadow had imagined that one was a puzzle to both Pete and Claire as he moved them deeper into the cellar. Anyway, whoever was at the top of the stairs had decided to listen further.

Perhaps he had decided more!

Of a sudden a glowing bulb appeared in the corner where Frost kept his extra supply of modern apparatus. It moved through the air so amazingly that Pete and Claire suddenly realized it was actually drifting there.

The floating light trick!

A favorite with magicians, this feat consisted in making an illuminated bulb literally float in mid-air, clear across the stage, even when the performer remained at the other side. Now The Shadow was performing the floating light effect in the direction of that stairway up to the workshop!

Riveted, Pete and Claire watched the bulb's peculiar action and realized, each in turn, that it could be mistaken for a light on an extension cord, carried in a human hand. In darkness, it didn't look like the floating lamp bulb at all.

This was why The Shadow had spoken in terms of an extension cord along with what the world would think if death occurred involving Pete Noland!

The drifting lamp was around the corner now, and moving toward the stair top. Though they couldn't see it, Pete and Claire knew its location from the way its glow diminished. They realized too that their unseen friend The Shadow was not directly behind it, but actually somewhere in the depth of the cellar proper, safely away from what was soon to come.

The murderer at the top of the stairs had good reason to believe that Claire and Pete were accompanying that ascending light bulb. Now was his time to act.

A gun blasted down the stairway. Its first shot blotted the bulb without a tinkle, for other shots stifled all lesser sounds. There were five of them, all that the killer's gun contained and for the finish, the revolver itself came clattering down the steps.

Those shots would have riddled both Pete and Claire had they been on the stairs!

Another gun was talking now—The Shadow's.

The murderer had no time to waste and knew it. The stabs were coming closer up the stairway, telling that The Shadow was surging on. The killer couldn't hope to bolt the door soon enough, even if he closed it.

Instead, he fled through the workshop. Close on the man's heels, The Shadow knew that Pete and Claire could now look out for themselves. Catching the killer was the task and no easy one.

Into a waiting car, and the murderer was away. Shrevvy's cab took The Shadow on board and the chase continued through a maze of streets, with Shrevvy hanging on like a bulldog.

This time The Shadow was really trailing a murderer to his lair!

XVII.

Shrieking around a corner, the fugitive car disgorged its passenger as a roulette wheel would throw a spinning ball. Huddled over, the killer raced through a back alley to the side door of an old house. Spinning from Shrevvy's arriving cab, The Shadow copied the action and with more speed.

Through a little hallway, into a tiny back room; there, the murderer slammed the door. Out from a front parlor sprang a stocky figure that turned as The Shadow flung inward through the darkness. There was a wild, furious grapple that occupied The Shadow for one full and precious minute; then he and his new adversary hit the door so hard they crashed it, landing in a dimly lighted room.

Coming up with his gun, The Shadow looked for the killer. He was gone! Studying the groggy man who had blocked him and given that stout tussle, The Shadow wearily removed his hat and cloak, tossed them in a darkened corner of the hallway, and helped his late opponent to his feet.

The opposition consisted of Inspector Joe Cardona.

It was several minutes before Cardona regained anything resembling equilibrium. From a chair, he blinked and finally focussed his gaze on Cranston.

"Nice work, inspector," approved Cranston, calmly. "I mean by both of us."

Cardona managed to find the obvious words.

"How did you come to get here?"

"Going past Frost's," related Cranston, "I saw somebody come running out. So I went after him and he crashed in here. How did you happen to be here?"

"Another tip-off," growled Joe. "Like the one telling me about Demo's place. Another phoney."

Cranston raised his eye-brows.

"That's how I figure it," nodded Cardona. "I have a hunch I'd like to talk to young Noland. He wouldn't have murdered Demo."

"Why not?"

"Too silly. None of these magic guys are really cracked; they're just half way. Border line cases, the psycho-what-do-you-call-them. I've been reading that manuscript of Demo's."

Cranston couldn't help but smile, even after the real murderer's getaway.

"It's got a good stunt in it," continued Cardona. "A trick where two guys each learn to talk in the same voice. One turns off the lights while he's talking; the other picks up the spiel and the first guy does a sneak. When the lights come on, everybody wonders how the first fellow vanished."

"Very nice," commented Cranston.

"More than nice," approved Cardona. "Demo said in the manuscript that he'd tested the voice stuff with a friend. Who else could the friend be but Noland and what else could the test be but the telephone stunt?"

Cranston nodded. This was putting Pete well into the clear. So Cranston reverted to something else.

"The vanish idea was nice," he declared, "but it wasn't the way the real murderer worked it just now."

On his feet, Cardona stared all around, then began stamping the floor.

"No trap door there," said Cranston. "It's in the ceiling. Look."

It was in the ceiling all right and it had been clamped tight. Cardona looked at the square opening with its barrier of good stout boards. Then:

"What was the killer's idea of hoaxing me here?"

"To keep you watching a forgotten hideaway," analyzed Cranston. "Then, in a pinch, he found it was the only place that he could use. Of course it may not be a hideaway exactly. We're dealing with somebody very clever—"

Pausing, Cranston proved the point by yanking open a table drawer where he had seen a patch of projecting silk. He pulled out some colorful handkerchiefs of the sort magicians use, a few gimmicks of a common type, and finally what looked to be an ordinary slate.

"Maybe we can trace the killer from these," decided Cardona. "Unless every magician owns this sort of stuff."

"Every magician does," assured Cranston, "and so does every five dollar member of the Universal Wizards Association. Likewise every school-boy who has the price after he has learned of things called magic shops."

Showing the slate back and front, Cranston placed it in Cardona's hands and waved his fingers above it. Taking the slate again, Cranston turned it over.

On the other side the slate said:

"Nine of spades."

Sight of the chalk written message stupefied Cardona. Clapping the inspector on the back, Cranston turned to the door.

"See you later, inspector," said Cranston. "If I run into young Noland I'll have him look you up."

When Cranston arrived at the Club Marimba some time later, he was just in time to hear a loud burst of applause as Margo Lane bowed off quite gracefully in the panty-waist costume that she was wearing as Miss Libra. Intercepting Margo on her way back stage, Cranston queried:

"And how did the act go?"

"Better, this time," replied Margo. "This was the second show."

"When was the first?"

"Soon after you left. I was a good girl and told Zito that Claire was my dearest friend. I just simply had to come here and take her place after I heard she'd fallen down the subway steps and broken a leg."

"Why did you tell Zito that?"

"Because I wished Claire had. Poor Zito! He's been calling every hospital in town and I'm afraid to tell him the truth. I wish I could do something nice for him."

"You have," assured Cranston. "You've given him the alibi he needed. Since Zito has been here all evening, that eliminates him as the murderer."

Over at a table, Winstrom was gesturing for Cranston to join him. Cranston did, hauling Margo along, despite her protests that her Libra costume wasn't quite in keeping with the fashionable gowns worn by the ladies in Winstrom's party.

"You're coming anyway," Cranston told her, "because Zito is over at the table and it's time you admitted the truth about Claire."

It wasn't her costume or lack of it that flustered Margo when she reached the table. It was the pathetic glance that Zito gave her and the kindly way in which he spoke.

"Miss Lane has been so nice," declared Zito. "When she heard that Claire was hurt—"

"Miss Lane!"

It was Winstrom who interrupted, his face quite amazed. Then, with a dawn of recognition, he bowed to Margo and said:

"Do you know, I never recognized you. Why, at the first show, I was wondering why you weren't a blonde. Of course I was called to the telephone and I had to go and meet these friends of mine, so I didn't see much of you."

Margo smiled.

"What about the second show?"

Indulgently, Winstrom gestured to his empty glass.

"I had a few before it began," he admitted. "But I can still do magic. Want to see some?"

Margo nodded and Winstrom brought out a pack of cards. He always needed a few drinks to start doing any tricks and even then Winstrom invariably depended upon mechanical appliances. Margo had heard all that, but there didn't seem to be anything mechanical about a pack of cards.

Holding the pack, Winstrom riffled the end and told Margo to take a card. She inserted her finger and stopped the riffle, then drew out the card she'd found there.

"Name it," said Winstrom. He was turning over the menu card as he spoke.

"The jack of diamonds," stated Margo. "Why!"

There was a reason for the exclamation. In bold letters, Winstrom's menu card bore the written words: "Jack of diamonds."

"It's uncanny," expressed Margo. "How did you do it?"

Winstrom smiled and put the pack away. Across the table, Cranston was finishing an earnest chat with Zito, who nodded very happily. Evidently Cranston had explained that Claire was all right, for rather than have Margo spoil his story, Cranston gave a waving gesture.

Glad of the opportunity, Margo went to the dressing room and discarded the Miss Libra trappings. Just when she had finished dressing, the door opened and Claire appeared, to stop short in surprise.

"It's all right," said Margo, very nicely, "and thanks. Only I have a friend who wants to tell you something before you talk to Zito."

On the way down the corridor, Margo met Cranston. He nodded and went to tell Claire. Only Margo didn't know that the conversation concerned Pete Noland more than it did Zed Zito.

Riding back to her apartment in Shrevvy's cab, Margo was very silent until she arrived there. Then, in a meek tone she said:

"It was very wonderful, Lamont."

"You mean Winstrom's card trick?" inquired Cranston, as though he didn't know that Margo was referring to a great deal else. "Yes, it was good, but everybody does it."

Margo stared.

"It's in every magic catalog, you know," continued Cranston, "and you can buy it in any magic shop. The pack that makes you take the same card every time. All magicians have them, but they don't always write the name on a menu. Sometimes it appears mysteriously on a slate. Always the same card."

"Always the jack of diamonds?"

"With Winstrom's pack, yes," replied Cranston. "But I'm looking for the magician who makes you take the nine of spades."

And with that cryptic statement, Cranston waved good-night.

XVIII.

Pete Noland was still in hiding but he didn't have to be. The police were looking for him only to make other people think they weren't being hunted.

Of the others, one was unofficially eliminated. He was Zed Zito. Inspector Cardona made this official in a sense, but did it privately. He issued the statement in Winstrom's living room in the presence of Wade Winstrom and Lamont Cranston, where the conference was held at Cranston's suggestion.

"There was a lot of shooting at Frost's place last night," explained Cardona, "and that's the sort of stuff you can take or leave. For instance, Louie the Grift was killed in Cigam's shop but we aren't blaming Cigam."

Pausing to let that point sink, Cardona took up the other side of the story.

"Still, Frost could have decoyed somebody there," said Joe. "It would have been a smart move on his part. The very fact that Cigam wound up with a clean slate might have given Frost the idea he could do the same."

Something that Cardona himself had said caused him to become meditative, which wasn't a common thing with Joe, at least not publicly. His voice was almost mechanical when he added:

"What we've still got to establish is a motive. That's what I've got to look into now."

Going down in the elevator, Cardona was thinking of anything but a motive. What was running through Joe's mind was his own statement about Cigam having a clean slate.

That was just what Cardona wanted, a clean slate like the one he'd found in the murderer's hideout, the kind that produced a message when you called for it. Working backwards, Cardona hadn't reached the point of thinking in terms of a playing card rather than a slate.

Reaching Cigam's, Cardona told the drab man the kind of slate he wanted. Cigam asked:

"You mean you want to buy one?"

Cardona nodded.

"Don't be a sucker," confided Cigam. "That single slate job costs too much. They call it the perfect slate, so what? With a pair of ordinary spirit slates you can get the same effect. They cost a buck fifty, the perfect one-slate version is twelve and a half."

Cardona still wanted the single slate version, no matter what the price. So Cigam fished under the counter and found the only one he had. Dusting it off, he wrapped it along with the instruction sheet.

"It works easy," assured Cigam, "only there's not much call for them. By the way, you'll want a Svengali to go along with it."

"A Svengali?"

"Yes. That's what they call this pack." Cigam brought one from the shelf. "Try to make it give you any other card. It won't."

Going out the door, Cardona bumped into Val Varno, who was now doing his coin roll in clusters. Varno gave a wise grin.

"Getting magic-minded, inspector? Better drop around and see me work tonight at the S.O.S."

"Huh?" asked Cardona. "What does that mean?"

"Society of Sorcery," replied Varno. "Cigam is selling tickets. Ask him."

Cardona bought a ticket and went back to his office. There he unwrapped the one-slate miracle and started to read its very explicit instructions. Oddly, Cardona didn't have to learn how the trick was done to do it.

The instructions said to lay the slate flat, turn it sideways to show the other side, then tilt it upward against some object, call for the message and turn the slate around.

Cardona did just that and during the process he saw for himself that the slate was entirely blank. At least it was quite blank until the final turn around. Then, to Cardona's amazement, the slate revealed a chalk-written message.

It wasn't just the magical result that dumbfounded the ace inspector. After all, Cardona had seen Cranston produce a slate message with the same minimum of effort. The thing that would have knocked Joe out of his chair if the chair hadn't had arms, was what the message said.

In capital letters, it read:

LAY OFF COPPER!

That was enough to send a squad car to bring in Cigam and start quizzing him all over again. Only Cardona managed to swallow the insult in favor of gathering more evidence. Remembering the Svengali pack that Cigam had sold him, Cardona decided to play with it.

Quite convinced that no pack in the world could always make you take the same card, Cardona saw a chance to arrest Cigam for taking money under false pretenses. But that failed too, after Joe began trying the wonderful pack. Soon he was working it on all the detectives around the place.

When Joe riffled the pack and a detective took a card it always turned out to be the deuce of diamonds.

Cardona was really getting magic-minded. He was thinking of going back to Cigam's and buying more of those wonderful packs. He'd let anybody say what card they wanted and he'd let them have it—from the correct pack. Out of that mental whirl, Cardona suddenly grabbed the telephone and called the Cobalt Club, where he asked for Lamont Cranston.

Getting the man he wanted, Cardona wasted no more time in ceremony.

"Remember that slate that said the nine of spades?" Joe inquired. "All right, I just bought a pack that makes you take the same card all the time. I got a slate to go with it, or maybe it was the other way around."

Cranston complimented Cardona and suggested that he join the Universal Wizards Association.

"Not much," retorted Joe. "I've heard of a better outfit, the Society of Sorcery. I'm going to their show tonight and I'm going to keep on going to magic shows. Do you know why? Because I'm going to find some magician who always does tricks with the nine of spades.

"The fellow who used that hideaway forgot his slate and probably thought it didn't matter. What he really forgot—and what does matter—was the writing on that slate. It said nine of spades and it's a safe bet that our man has a pack that hands out that card and nothing else."

When the curtain rose on the S.O.S. show, Cranston was there with Cardona. None of the first three acts performed either the paper hat trick or the linking rings. They didn't even do card fans, because of the horrible example set by the U.W.A., where everybody had done card fans.

The S.O.S. was different. Everybody on its bill was so anxious to avoid the hats and the rings that they all did either the milk pitcher or the Hindu sticks.

The milk trick consisted in pouring a pitcher load of milk into a paper cone from which it vanished. The sticks were a pair of wands that had a cord running through holes in one end; whenever the cord was cut it would restore itself when the performer—or more correctly performers—drew it through again.

The spectators had a good nickname for the Society of Sorcery. They simply termed it "Same Old Stuff!" and the soubriquet fitted. The show was even given in the same place as the Wizards' show, the Chianti ball room, and the audience contained its usual quota of regulars.

One act was somewhat different: Val Varno. He did his cigarette routine and for a finish, he performed a singular stunt known as the "Card and Ribbon." An empty envelope was affixed to a ribbon with sealing wax. The other end of the ribbon was hung from a stand so that the envelope dangled below.

Riffling a pack, Val had a spectator take a card and write his name across it. Replaced in the pack, the marked card vanished, Val riffling the pack to show that it wasn't among the rest. The envelope was opened and the card with the writing found inside it. Val took the card to the person who had chosen it and had him identify his signature.

It was all very wonderful and the whole audience appreciated it, particularly Joe Cardona.

For the chosen card that underwent those peregrinations was none other than the nine of spades!

Lamont Cranston could have written a prediction right there and then. As the show neared its conclusion, Cardona left the audience, as Cranston expected. To Margo, Cranston suggested that they walk out too, particularly as the last performer was doing the Hindu wands again.

In the foyer they found Wade Winstrom listening to Glanville Frost trying to sell him what Frost termed an "exclusive." That was one of Frost's rackets, to hook a customer for a fancy price on a single trick. Then after the purchaser popularized it, the trick would suddenly hit the market in quantity.

Knowing this, Winstrom was wary. He was glad when Cranston and Margo appeared for it gave him a chance to shake off Frost. Not a member of the S.O.S. which didn't get along too well with the

U.W.A., Winstrom was a magical second fiddler tonight and was trying to live it down.

"Open house this evening," Winstrom reminded. "Some of the people have gone up to the penthouse already. I guess they couldn't stand this show"—he was shaking his head sadly—"and I must confess it's really terrible. Well, I'll be seeing you all later."

Later wasn't the correct term.

At that moment Cardona appeared from the door that led back stage, bringing Val Varno clipped in a pair of handcuffs. Before anybody could ask why, Varno raised his manacles and shook them at Glanville Frost.

"It's on account of the card and ribbon!" Varno practically shrieked. "Only you're the guy who sold it to me, as one of your exclusives. You can't deny it, Frost!"

For once Frost was too flustered to try. In a nice impartial style, Cardona clamped a pair of handcuffs on Frost's wrists too. With Solomonic wisdom Cardona announced:

"We're going down to headquarters. You fellows can saw each other in half down there."

Cranston stepped forward with a better suggestion.

"What about Winstrom's penthouse?" he inquired. "You held the last quiz up there. I guess Winstrom can call off his little party."

Under the circumstances, Winstrom could. He nodded and the group went to the elevator. On the way up to the penthouse, Margo gave a slight shudder, as she found herself standing between Varno and Frost.

It wasn't pleasant to be in the same elevator with a murderer, particularly the kind whose crimes were worked by magic!

As to which person was the actual killer, Margo was wondering if even The Shadow knew!

XIX.

Several guests were already in the penthouse looking around at Winstrom's apparatus. The library was locked along with the room that held the playbills because Winstrom always locked those rooms when he went out.

Cranston had been up here with other guests earlier. He had seen Winstrom lock up before they all went downstairs to the magic show.

Now Winstrom was politely dismissing the guests, telling them to come some other time. When the unwanted guests were gone, Cardona came right down to business. He spoke his piece to Frost and Varno mutually.

"All right, whichever of you knows," asserted Cardona. "The motive—and out with it."

Both suspects stared blankly.

"I can tell you the motive, inspector," put in Cranston, calmly. "The killer is after some gems once valued at a hundred thousand dollars and probably worth more than that today. They once belonged to the Sultan of Malkara and later became the property of the Great Savanti."

Cardona's mouth went wide; then clamped.

"Who cooked up that story?"

"Demo Sharpe unearthed it," corrected Cranston. "He told it to Pete Noland who passed it along to me."

Cardona was really astonished.

"You've seen Pete Noland?"

"I have," replied Cranston. "I reached him through Claire Meriden, who believed his story just as I do. You were right, inspector, in drawing your conclusions from Demo's manuscript. Pete was doubling for Demo with the telephone test."

Looking triumphant, Cardona suddenly went dumb.

"But how did Noland explain about Sharpe's body?"

"It was shipped up in the pagoda," explained Cranston. "The weight was faked with Zito's scales. We can check all that quite easily, inspector. Now let's get to murder's motive."

Everybody looked interested including Varno and Frost, though their expressions never could be accepted at face value.

Wade Winstrom made one of his big gestures that included all the antique apparatus in the living room.

"Some of this equipment belonged to the Great Savanti!" exclaimed Winstrom. "Could that have anything to do with murder?"

"It had everything to do with it," assured Cranston. "Assuming that Savanti hid the missing gems in some piece of apparatus, they could still be there."

"Let's look!" suggested Winstrom. Then, relaxing: "No, it would take too long right now. Go on with your story, Cranston."

"Since you were buying up all antique apparatus," Cranston told

Winstrom, "Demo Sharpe was trying to examine all such items before they ever reached you." Then, turning to Frost and Varno as though one of them at least deserved more information, Cranston added: "And somebody was trying to get at that apparatus before Demo could go through it."

Cardona snapped up that point.

"That explains what happened at Cigam's!" expressed Joe. "Somebody planted the firing wand to get Demo. Only Louie the Grift walked into it instead."

The theory was approved by Cranston's nod.

"But what about Del Weird?" queried Cardona. "He'd already shipped his apparatus here. Why was Del Weird murdered?"

"Because he knew too much about Savanti," Cranston explained. "Demo Sharpe was trying to reach Professor Del Weird. Probably Del Weird knew nothing about the jewels, but he could have given important clues to them."

Cardona nodded. Then:

"And Demo was bumped because he got too hot on the trail." Joe looked from Varno to Frost. "Say, that business of Zito's scales ought to lead back to one of you fellows. Didn't you own those scales once, Frost?"

"They came with the pagoda," admitted Frost, "but Varno knew how they worked. Talk to him, inspector."

Before Cardona could quiz Varno, Cranston interrupted. He said the room was getting stuffy and asked Winstrom to unlock the other doors. As soon as Winstrom obliged, Cranston called:

"All right! We are ready?"

Out from the library stepped Pete Noland and Claire Meriden, their arms loaded with framed playbills and finely bound books, all from Winstrom's collection!

"Sorry, Winstrom," apologized Cranston. "I brought these people up here earlier and slipped them into the library while you were talking to the other guests. I wanted them to do a little research on the Great Savanti."

The research had been done. Pete and Claire spread the books and playbills on a couch and began to talk about them. It was Pete who stated:

"About the pagoda illusion—"

"Never mind the pagoda illusion," interrupted Winstrom. "We're trying to uncover some mysterious gems. Have you found any traces of them?"

Pete shook his head, but Claire opened one of the books which proved to be a bound set of a long-forgotten magical magazine.

"Here's a report on Savanti's show," Claire said. "It mentions candy and that's something like jewels. In size and shape I mean. It mentions the wonderful vase in which candy appears and a cannon ball vanishes."

Winstrom gave a deprecating gesture toward the cannon ball globe which was standing proudly amid the lesser props.

"Just a hollow cannon ball," said Winstrom. "It's filled with candy which appears when the cannon ball splits apart. I've worked it often."

Cranston smiled as he stepped over to the big globe.

"Not often enough, perhaps," he remarked. "From everything I've heard about the Great Savanti, his work was always somewhat different. This magazine review indicates that."

Staring blankly, Winstrom asked:

"How?"

"Because it says that the candy appeared," recited Cranston, "and that the cannon ball vanished. In the usual version, it's the other way about."

"Maybe the reviewer just happened to write it up wrong."

"Possibly he wrote it right," declared Cranston. "We'll see."

Taking the cannon ball from the globe, Cranston replaced the top half of the latter. Never before had anyone attempted to work the trick in that condition; except of course Savanti. It didn't take Cranston long to find the gadget he wanted.

There was the sound of a plunger, noisy because it needed oil, shooting upward in the pedestal. From within the globe came the rattle of what seemed a miniature hail-storm. Cranston opened the globe and poured its contents into a glass jar that was standing near.

They formed a cascade of living brilliance, the crown jewels of Malkara, as Cranston drained the globe to the final gem. Wonderful candy, this, worth a thousand dollars a bite and guaranteed to retain its taste during all the years it had remained in Savanti's clever cache!

Extremely clever, too, because the trick wouldn't work while the cannon ball was in the globe and anyone who operated this apparatus

—as Winstrom often had—would only have tried it while the cannon ball was inside.

Now Winstrom was coming forward, his hands eager as though he wanted to rinse them in that glittering bath of solidified color. Stepping aside, Cranston swung the jewel-filled jar past Winstrom's grasp and tendered it to Claire Meriden.

"Your legacy," Cranston told Claire with a smile. "From your great-uncle, the Great Savanti!"

XX.

If chagrin had ever overwhelmed any man, that man was Wade Winstrom. Others, their eyes on the splendor of the gems, failed to notice Winstrom's changed expression, but Cranston was watching for it.

This was a pay-off so unexpected that no man could have veiled his true emotions. Certainly Winstrom didn't, though he recovered rapidly. By then, however, his cause had suffered irrevocable damage. The congratulations that Winstrom offered Claire over her new-found wealth sounded as hollow as the cannon ball that lay beside the nickeled globe.

Letting the farce continue, Cranston turned to Pete and reminded:

"You were saying something about the golden pagoda?"

"About the pagoda illusion," corrected Pete. "You ought to know, because you gave me the suggestion."

Cranston nodded slowly as though it was all just coming back to him.

"That's right," he said. "Savanti billed the pagoda illusion as the invisible flight. It wasn't just a production, the way Frost worked it. Evidently it was something in the nature of a transposition."

Winstrom tilted his head as he heard that.

"The scales belonged with the pagoda," continued Cranston, reflectively. "Now suppose somebody vanished from the pagoda. It would have been a great effect, wouldn't it, if the weight had suddenly dropped at the moment of that disappearance!"

Before Pete could say something, Cranston interrupted him.

"But there would have to be something equally sensational to complete the illusion. Suppose there was a second pagoda on the other side of the stage, resting on another set of scales. If the weight over there suddenly raised and the girl appeared from that empty pagoda, it would be very wonderful indeed."

Pausing, Cranston turned to the others and spoke straight to Winstrom.

"It would be so wonderful," added Cranston, "that the Great Savanti would logically have termed the pagoda illusion an invisible flight!"

"And that's what it was," asserted Pete. "There were two pagodas, just as you've said. None of Savanti's playbills dispute it. They just say 'the pagoda illusion' which could mean any number of pagodas. Only there happened to be just two."

Pete was flourishing an old book to prove it, one of Winstrom's very rare volumes that he seldom let people see. For what Winstrom hadn't known about the cannon ball globe, he did know about the pagoda illusion. Angrily, Winstrom made a grab for the book, only to have Cranston block him off.

"You own all sorts of odd apparatus," remarked Cranston. "Tell me, Winstrom, did you ever have a firing wand?"

Winstrom's only answer was a snarl.

"Of course you did," stated Cranston. "You planted it at Cigam's to kill Demo. You were the somebody who wanted to go through Savanti's apparatus first. Until it reached here, you had to block Demo's hunt."

Coldly logical all this, so logical that Cordona wondered why he hadn't figured it. The fact that the apparatus always reached Winstrom eventually was the throw-off, plus the fact that Winstrom played dumb, or at least indifferent.

Only now as Cardona saw it, Winstrom as the prospective owner would have been the first man to protect his coming interest, even with murder as the means.

Evidently Cranston had seen it that way quite a while ago.

"Fixing Del Weird's wine and water set-up was as simple up here as downstairs," analyzed Cranston. "I think Margo will remember that Del Weird was carrying his suitcase flat when he came down, which meant he had everything arranged inside it. So you can't alibi yourself where that murder is concerned, Winstrom."

Winstrom's glower proved he did not intend to try.

"Odd about Demo," continued Cranston, turning to Pete. "He

must have been doing a lot of searching, those long evenings when you handled the telephone mystery for him. Where else could Demo have spent more time than here?"

It was Cranston now, who furnished the broad, sweeping gesture that not only included the masses of antique magic in this room, but carried toward the hall. Stepping in that direction, Cranston indicated the store room.

"You laid a nice trap there, Winstrom," Cranston stated. "Gadgets set so that they'd start working as soon as anybody handled them. That's how you and your servants finally caught Demo. You'd been waiting for Del Weird's shipment to come in with the other pagoda and the scales belonging with it."

So that was the answer!

Duplicate pagoda and scales had been put on the Unicorn truck by Winstrom's servants, after they had murdered Demo Sharpe and stowed him in the pagoda. The Vanguard truck had been summoned separately to take away Frost's pagoda and Zito's scales to some warehouse.

"Of course if you hadn't quite caught Demo," Cranston told Winstrom from the outer door, "he would have fallen down the service elevator shaft. You ought to have that door fixed, Winstrom. Or I might say you already fixed it—in your own way."

It was Margo now who was remembering something. She told it right to Winstrom.

"No wonder you walked out on Zito's act at the Club Marimba!" accused Margo. "When you saw that I was Miss Libra instead of Claire, you figured something odd was brewing, and maybe at Frost's! Cute of you, to pretend you didn't recognize me later, while I was still in that Libra harness!"

"You were cute," corrected Cardona. "Winstrom here was just smart. Playing two bets as usual. When things fluked at Frost's, he headed for that phoney hideaway he'd fixed to look as though it belonged to Varno. He had to plant the goods on somebody.

"I was dumb enough to think that Varno planted that slate at Cigam's. But from the way Cigam dusted it off, I should have known it was there from away back; probably you put it there when you fixed the firing wand, just as a handy thing for the future.

"Nice stuff too, that nine of spades." Cardona turned to Varno and Frost. "Am I guessing right, Frost, in thinking you tried to sell

that card and ribbon stunt to Winstrom, before letting Varno take
it, pack and all?"

Frost nodded.

"That explains how you framed Varno then," Cardona told Winstrom. "So come along and we'll clean up any odd details down at
headquarters. It's the right place for a quiz anyway."

Winstrom didn't think so. He gave a huge bellow that brought
Frederick and the other servants, all of whom had been snooping
close enough to know that their interests were at stake along with
Winstrom's. Horrified, Margo saw that Cranston was gone from the
hallway; then, a sudden stir of blackness proved that The Shadow
had replaced him.

Only The Shadow wasn't needed, not just yet.

In springing for Cardona and Pete, Winstrom's servants ignored
Frost and Varno because the two were handcuffed. The ex-
prisoners took advantage of that oversight. In from the flanks they
came and each brought a pair of handcuffed wrists hard against the
head of a charging servant.

They were escape artists among other things, Frost and Varno.
They knew the system for springing handcuffs, namely, by striking
them sharply against some hard object at just the right angle. The
hard objects in this instance were the skulls of Winstrom's servants.

Handcuffs flew wide and Frost and Varno, with two knock-outs to
their credit were free to help suppress the rest of Winstrom's tribe,
which they did.

Only Winstrom himself managed to start a getaway which carried
him as far as the store room. Passing The Shadow behind a screen of
tumbling servants, Winstrom yanked open the store room door and
wheeled out with a rifle. Backing toward the service elevator, he
aimed the weapon down the hall.

"I nearly finished you with this!" Winstrom was storming at Pete,
who was framed in the living room door. "I was the sniper who
wanted to shake you off that ledge and close the Demo case for good!
Now I'm really going to get you!"

Frantically Claire tried to haul Pete to cover and put herself in
the rifle's path instead, just as Winstrom fired. Only Claire didn't
fall; instead, she picked up the ends of a ribbon that apparently was
running right through her. Surprised, Claire drew the ribbon back
and forth.

The Shadow's laugh explained the mystery.

This wasn't Winstrom's regular rifle. The Shadow had switched it in the store room, leaving a different type in its place. Winstrom had fired a special rifle from his collection of magical apparatus, the one used in a harmless trick called "Shooting Through a Woman."

This time magic hadn't produced murder. Quite the opposite.

Along the hallway, Winstrom heard the whisper of doom. He saw blackness moving toward him, living blackness, a big gun looming from its advancing fist.

The Shadow was approaching, ready to deliver final vengeance should Wade Winstrom ask for it.

Madly, Winstrom flung the useless rifle at the black-cloaked figure and yanked open the door of the service elevator. Frantically he jumped inside, clanging the doors behind him.

Time seemed to hang during those next few seconds until there came a dull, mangling crash from far below, echoing muffled from the elevator shaft.

Winstrom should have remembered that in times of emergency, his servants saw to it that the service elevator was never there.

Another sound stirred from the hallway. It faded with the closing of the outer door that in turn obliterated a departing figure cloaked in black.

The sound was a strange-toned laugh, the weird evanescent mirth of The Shadow, marking the end of the menace called murder by magic!

THE END.